Colin Dexter graduated from Cambridge in 1953. He spent his years wholly in education until his retirement in 1988, first teaching Greek and Latin, then moving to Oxford in 1966 to work for the University Examination Board, where he fought in vain against the cradle-to-coffin philosophy of the GCSE.

He began writing detective fiction comparatively late in life – the first Inspector Morse book appeared in 1975 – and two of his novels have been awarded Daggers by the Crime Writers' Association. The Inspector Morse novels have been successfully translated for the small screen in Central Television's series starring John Thaw.

His interests range from listening to *The Archers* to compiling crosswords. His unfulfilled ambitions are opening the batting for England, and crossing swords with Mrs Thatcher in parliamentary debate.

Also by Colin Dexter in
Pan Books

Colin Dexter

# The Silent World
# of Nicholas Quinn

**Pan Books** in association with
**Macmillan London**

First published 1977 by Macmillan London Ltd
This edition published 1978 by Pan Books Ltd,
Cavaye Place, London SW10 9PG
19 18 17 16 15 14 13 12 11
in association with Macmillan London Ltd
© Colin Dexter 1977
ISBN 0 330 25424 3
Printed in England by Clays Ltd, St Ives plc

*for Jack Ashley*

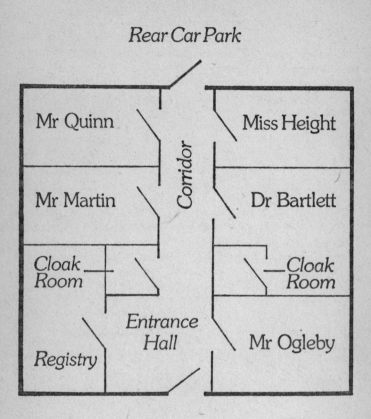

Rear Car Park

Mr Quinn

Miss Height

Mr Martin

Dr Bartlett

Corridor

Cloak Room

Cloak Room

Registry

Entrance Hall

Mr Ogleby

Front Car Park

# prologue

'Well? What do you think?' The Dean of the Foreign Examinations Syndicate addressed his question directly to Cedric Voss, the Chairman of the History Committee.

'No, no, Dean. I think the Secretary should be the first to have his say. After all, it's the permanent staff who'll have to work with whoever we appoint.' In slightly less distinguished company, Voss would have added that he didn't give two monkeys which of them got the job. As it was, he reassumed a characteristically somnolent posture in his comfortable blue leather chair, and prayed they'd all get their fingers out. The meeting had already lasted almost three hours.

The Dean turned to the person sitting on his immediate left, a small twinkling man in his middle or late fifties, who blinked boyishly behind his rimless spectacles. 'Well, Dr Bartlett, let's hear what you've got to say.'

Bartlett, permanent Secretary of the Foreign Examinations Syndicate, glanced good-naturedly round the tables before looking down briefly at his neatly written notes. He was used to this sort of thing. 'It seems to me, Dean, that generally speaking, by and large' (the Dean and several senior members of the Syndicate visibly winced) 'and on the whole, we would all agree that the short list has been a very good one. All the applicants seemed pretty competent, and most of them sufficiently experienced to take on the work. But—' He looked down again at his notes. 'Well, to be truthful, I would not myself wish to appoint either of the two women. The one from Cambridge was, I thought, a little er a little *strident*, shall we say?' He beamed expectantly round the Appointments Committee and a few heads nodded fairly vigorous assent. 'The other woman I thought just a *little* inexperienced, and I er didn't feel much inner surge of conviction about some of her answers.' Again there was no visible sign of dissent from the silent tables, and Bartlett stroked his ample belly with mild satisfaction. 'So. Let's come to the three men. Duckham? Just a little vague, I thought. Nice chap and all that, but I wonder if he's got quite the snap and zip that I'd welcome in the Humanities Department here. He's third, in my book. Then there's Quinn. I liked him: honest, intelligent fellow; firm views; clear brain. Not quite the ideal experience, perhaps, and then— Well, let me be quite honest about it. I think that er I think his er – *handicap* may be a bit too much of a liability here. You know what I mean: phone calls, meetings, that sort of thing. It's a pity, but there it is. Anyway, I'd put him second. That leaves Fielding, and he's the man I'd go for every time: damn good schoolmaster; excellent results from his pupils; just the right age; modest; likeable; and a First in History from Balliol. References quite outstanding. I don't honestly think we could have hoped for a better applicant, and he's my first choice, Dean, without the slightest doubt.'

Not unostentatiously the Dean closed his appointments folder and gently nodded his agreement, noting with gratification that several other heads were nodding too. Including the Dean himself, the full complement of Syndics was present. Twelve of them, each a prominent fellow of his or her college within the University of Oxford, and each called upon to attend the meetings held twice a term at the Syndicate building for the purpose of formulating official examination policy. None of them was on the permanent staff of the Syndicate, and none was paid a penny (apart from travelling expenses) for attendance at these meetings. Yet most of them took an active part on the various Subject Committees, were happy to adopt a policy of enlightened self-interest towards the profitable procedures of public examinations, and during the months of June and July, after their own undergraduates had departed for the long vac, acted as chief examiners and moderators in the GCE Ordinary- and Advanced-level examinations. Of the permanent officers of the Syndicate only Bartlett was automatically invited to participate in the counsels of this governing body (though even he was not entitled to cast a vote), and it was Bartlett who brought the number in the room up to thirteen. Thirteen ... Yet the Dean was not a superstitious man, and he looked round the committee with a degree of mild affection. Tried and trusted colleagues almost all of them, although one or two of the younger dons he'd not yet got to know particularly well: hair rather too

long, and one of them had a beard. Quinn had a beard, too ...
Come on! The appointment would be settled very quickly now,
and with a bit of luck he could be back in Lonsdale College
before six. Tonight was a 'gaudy' and ... Get it over with!
'Well, if I'm right in assuming that the committee agrees to the
appointment of Fielding, there's only the matter of his starting
salary to settle. Let's see, he's thirty-four. I should think the
bottom of the B Lecturers' Scale might—'

'Could I just make one point before you go on, Dean?' It
was one of the younger dons. One of the long-haired ones. The
one with the beard. A chemist from Christ Church.

'Yes, of course, Mr Roope. I didn't mean to give the
impression—'

'If I may say so, I think you're presuming that we all agree
with the Secretary's views; and, of course, it may be that everyone else does. But *I* don't, and I thought the whole purpose of
this meeting—'

'Quite so, quite so, Mr Roope. As I say, I'm sorry if I gave
you the impression that er – you know ... I certainly didn't
mean to do that. It was just that I thought I sensed a feeling of
general agreement. But we're in your hands. If you feel—'

'Thank you, Dean. I do feel strongly about this, and I just
can't agree with the order of merit the Secretary has given. If
I'm going to be frank about it, I thought that Fielding was too
much of a yes-man, too much of a smoothie for me. In fact if he
got the job, it wouldn't be so much a matter of taking the rough
with the smooth as taking the smooth with the smooth.' A
gentle murmur of amusement rippled round the tables, and the
slight tension, perceptible only a minute before, was visibly
relaxed. And as Roope continued, some of his senior colleagues
listened to him with slightly more interest and attention. 'I agree
with the Secretary about the rest, though I can't say I completely agree with his reasons.'

'You mean you'd put Quinn first, is that it?'

'I would, indeed. He's got sound views on examinations, and
he's got a good mind. But what's more important, I reckon he's
got a genuine streak of integrity, and these days—'

'You didn't feel the same about Fielding?'

'No.'

The Dean ignored the Secretary's audible mumble of 'Nonsense!' and thanked Roope for his views. His eyes swept vaguely over the committee, inviting comments. But none was immediately forthcoming. 'Anyone else wish to er—?'

'I think it quite unfair for us to make too many cosmic character-judgements on the strength of a few brief interviews, Dean.' The speaker was the Chairman of the English Committee. 'We must all make our own assessments of these people; of course we must. That's the only reason we're here. But I agree with the Secretary. My order of merit was the same as his: exactly so.'

Roope leaned back and stared at the white ceiling, a yellow pencil balanced between his teeth.

'Anyone else?'

The Vice-Dean sat shuffling uneasily in his chair, profoundly bored, and anxious to be on his way. His notes consisted of an extraordinarily intricate doodle of whorls and scrolls; and he added a further florid curve to the flowing tracery as he made his first and final contribution to the day's deliberations: 'They're both good men, that's obvious. Doesn't seem to me to matter much which we go for. If the Secretary wants Fielding, I want Fielding. A quick vote, perhaps, Dean?'

'If that's er, that's er . . .'

A few members of the committee interjected their muted bleats of approval, and in a vaguely disconsolate voice the Dean called the division lobbies. 'All right. A show of hands, then. All those in favour of appointing Fielding, please?'

Seven or eight hands were being raised when Roope suddenly spoke again, and the hands were slowly lowered.

'Just before we vote, Dean, I would like to ask the Secretary for some information. I'm quite sure he'll have it at his fingertips.'

From behind his spectacles the Secretary eyed Roope with chill distaste, and several committee members could scarcely conceal their impatience and irritation. Why had they co-opted Roope? He was certainly a brilliant chemist and his two years with the Anglo-Arabian Oil Co. had seemed a decided asset in view of the Syndicate's commitments. But he was too young, too cocky; too loud and splashy, like a vulgar speedboat churning through the placid waters of the Syndicate regatta. This wasn't the first time he'd clashed with the Secretary, either. And he didn't even serve on the Chemistry Committee; didn't do a scrap of examining. Always said he was too busy.

'I'm sure the Secretary will be glad to er— What were you thinking of, Mr Roope?'

'Well, as you know, Dean, I've not been with you very long yet, but I've been looking at the Syndicate's Constitution, and as it happens I've got a copy with me here.'

'Oh God!' mumbled the Vice-Dean.

'In paragraph 23, Dean – would you like me to read it?' Since half the committee had never even seen a copy of the Constitution, let alone read it, it seemed wholly inappropriate to dissemble any phoney familiarity, and the Dean nodded reluctant assent.

'Not er too long, I hope, Mr Roope?'

'No, it's very brief. Here's what it says, and I quote: "The Syndicate will endeavour at all times to remember that, wholly dependent as it is for its income on public monies, it owes and must seek to discharge a corresponding responsibility both to society at large and to its own permanent employees. Specifically, it will undertake to employ in its services a small percentage of persons who are variously handicapped, should the disabilities of such persons prove not substantially to interfere with the proper discharge of the duties entrusted to them."' Roope closed the slim document and put it aside. 'Now, my question is this: can the Secretary please tell us how many handicapped people are at present employed by the Syndicate?'

The Dean turned once more to the Secretary, whose customary *bonhomie* had now apparently returned.

'We used to have a one-eyed fellow in the packing department—' In the ensuing laughter the Vice-Dean, whose own particular handicap was a weak bladder, shuffled out of the room, where Roope was pursuing his point with humourless pedantry.

'But presumably he's no longer employed here?'

The Secretary shook his head. 'No. Unfortunately he turned out to have an uncontrollable weakness for stealing toilet rolls, and we—' The rest of the sentence was drowned in a ribald cackle of lavatory laughter, and it was some little while before the Dean could bring the meeting to order again. He reminded the committee that paragraph 23 was not, of course, a statutory injunction – merely a marginal recommendation in the interests of normal civilized er living. But somehow it was the wrong thing to say. Far wiser to have allowed the Secretary a few more anecdotes about his less-than-fortunate experiences with the unfortunately afflicted few. As it was, the subtle shift had been made. The man with the handicap was coming into the betting once more, his odds shortening further as Roope pressed his point neatly and tellingly home.

'You see, Dean, all I really want to know is this: do we feel that Mr Quinn's deafness is going to be a significant liability in the job? That's all.'

'Well, as I said,' replied Bartlett, 'there's the telephone for a start, isn't there? Mr Roope perhaps isn't fully aware of the vast number of incoming and outgoing telephone calls here, and he must excuse me if I suggest that I know slightly more about this than he does. It's a very tricky problem when you're deaf—'

'Surely not. There are all sorts of gadgets these days. You can wear one of those behind-the-ear things, where the microphone is—'

'Does Mr Roope actually know someone who's deaf and who—?'

'As a matter of fact, I don't but—'

'Then I suggest he is in real danger of underestimating the sort of problems—'

'Gentlemen, gentlemen!' The exchanges were becoming increasingly tetchy, and the Dean intervened. 'I think we all agree that it would be *something* of a problem. The real question is – how much of one?'

'But it's not just the telephone, is it, Dean? There are meetings – dozens and dozens of 'em a year. A meeting like this one, for instance. You get stuck in a meeting with somebody on the same side of the table, sitting three or four places away ...' Bartlett warmed to the point, and made his case without interruption. He was on safer ground, he knew that. He was getting just a little deaf himself.

'But it's not beyond the wit of man to arrange the seating of a meeting—'

'No, it isn't,' snapped Bartlett. 'And it's not beyond the wit of man either to rig up a convenient little system of headphones and microphones and God knows what else; and we could all learn the deaf-and-dumb alphabet, if it came to that!'

It was becoming increasingly obvious that there was a festering, strangely personal antipathy between the two men, and few of the older Syndics could understand it. Bartlett was usually a man of wonderfully equable temperament. And he hadn't finished yet: 'You all saw the report from the hospital. You all saw the audiographs. The fact of the matter is that Quinn is very deaf. *Very* deaf.'

'He seemed to be able to hear us all perfectly well, didn't he?' Roope spoke the words quietly, and if Quinn himself had been there he would almost certainly have missed them. But the committee didn't, and it became perfectly clear that Roope had a point. A strong point.

The Dean turned again to the Secretary. 'Mm. You know it's amazing that he *did* seem to hear us so well, isn't it?'

A desultory discussion broke out, gradually drifting further and further away from the immediate decision that still remained to be taken. Mrs Seth, the Chairman of the Science Committee, thought about her father ... He had gone deaf very quickly when he was in his late forties and when she was only a schoolgirl; and he had been dismissed from his job. Redundancy money, and a meagre disability pension from his firm – oh yes, they'd tried to be sympathetic and fair. But he'd had such a clear brain, and he'd never worked again. Confidence irreparably shattered. He could still have done a whole host of jobs infinitely more efficiently than half the layabouts sitting idling on their backsides on office stools. It made her so very sad and so very cross to think of him ...

Suddenly she was aware that they were voting. Five hands went up almost immediately for Fielding, and she thought, as the Secretary did, that he was probably the best of the bunch. She would vote for him too. But for some curious reason her hand remained on the blotting paper in front of her.

'And those for Quinn, please?'

Three hands, including Roope's, were raised; and then a fourth. The Dean began counting from the left: 'One, two, three … four …' Another hand, and the Dean started again: 'One, two, three, four, five. It looks—' And then, slowly and dramatically, Mrs Seth raised her own hand.

'Six.'

'Well, you've made your decision, ladies and gentlemen. Quinn has been appointed. Close vote: six–five. But there it is.' He turned rather awkwardly to his left. 'Are you happy, Mr Secretary?'

'Let's just say we all have our own views, Dean, and the view of the Appointments Committee is not mine. But, as you say, the committee has made its decision and it's my job to accept that decision.'

Roope sat back once more staring vaguely at the ceiling, the yellow pencil once more between his teeth. He may have been inwardly gloating over his minor triumph, but his face remained impassive – detached almost.

Ten minutes later the Dean and the Secretary walked side by side down the flight of stairs that led to the ground floor and to Bartlett's office. 'You really think we've made a bad mistake, Tom?'

Bartlett stopped and looked up at the tall, grey-haired theologian. 'Oh, yes, Felix. Make no mistake about that. We have!'

Roope pushed his way past them on the stairs and volunteered a vague 'Cheerio'.

'Er – goodnight,' said the Dean; but Bartlett remained darkly silent, and watched Roope go before slowly walking down the few remaining stairs and entering his office.

Above his door was a twin-coloured light, similar to the sort found in hospitals, which was operated from two switches on the desk inside. The first switch turned on a red light, signifying that Bartlett was in session with someone, and did not wish to be (and would not be) disturbed; a second switch turned on a green light, indicating that one was free to knock and enter. When neither switch was depressed, no light showed, and the conclusion thence to be drawn was that the room was empty. Since his appointment to the Secretaryship, Bartlett had firmly maintained that if anyone wished to discuss a matter of importance with him, he himself should have the courtesy to ensure an uninterrupted, confidential chat; and his staff fully appreciated and almost invariably observed the arrangement. On the very few occasions that the rule had been infringed, Bartlett had displayed quite uncharacteristic anger.

Once inside the Secretary snapped down the red switch before opening a small cabinet and pouring himself a glass of gin and dry vermouth. Then he sat down behind his desk, opened a drawer and took out a packet of cigarettes. He never smoked at meetings, but he lit one now, inhaled deeply, and sipped his drink. He would send a telegram to Quinn in the morning: it was too late to send one now. He opened his appointments' folder once more and reread the information on Quinn. Huh! They'd picked the wrong fellow – of course they had! All because of Roope, the bloody idiot!

He put the papers away neatly, cleared his desk and sat back in his chair – a curious half-smile forming on his lips.

# WHY ?

# one

Whilst the other four took their seats in the upstairs lounge of the Cherwell Motel, he walked over to the bar and ordered the drinks: two gins and tonics, two medium sherries, one dry sherry – the latter for himself. He was very fond of dry sherry.

'Put them all down to the Foreign Examinations Syndicate, will you? And we shall be having lunch. If you can tell the waiter we're here? Sitting over there.' His north-country accent was still noticeable, though less so than it had been.

'Have you booked a table, sir?'

He enjoyed the 'sir'. 'Yes. The name's Quinn.' He grabbed a handful of peanuts, took the drinks over on a tray, and sat down with the other members of the History Committee.

It was his third Revision meeting since joining the Syndicate, and there were several others fixed for later in the term. He sat back in the low leather chair, drained half his sherry at a gulp, and looked out at the busy lunchtime traffic along the A40. This was the life! A jolly good meal to come, wine, coffee – and then back for the afternoon session. Finish with a bit of luck about five or even earlier. The morning session had been a concentrated, unremitting slog; but they'd done well. Question papers covering the periods from the Continental Crusades to the English Civil War had now assumed the final and definitive form in which they would appear before the following summer's Advanced-level History candidates. Just the five papers left, from the Hanoverians to the Treaty of Versailles; and he felt much more at home with the recent periods. At school History had been his favourite subject, and it was in History that he had won his exhibition to Cambridge. But after Prelims he'd changed over to English, and it had been as an English teacher that he had been subsequently appointed to the staff of Priestly Grammar School, Bradford, only twenty-odd miles from the Yorkshire village in which he was born. Looking back on it, he realized how lucky the switch to English had been: the advertisement for the post with the Syndicate had stressed the need for some qualification in both History and English, and he'd realized that he might stand a pretty good chance, although even now he couldn't quite believe that he had landed the job. Not that his deafness ...

'Your menu, sir.'

Quinn had not heard the man approach, and only when the inordinately large menu obtruded itself into his field of vision was he aware of the head waiter. Yes, perhaps his deafness would be slightly more of a handicap than he'd sometimes assumed; but he was managing wonderfully well so far.

For the moment he sat back, like the others, and studied the bewildering complexity of permutations on the menu: expensive – almost all the dishes; but as he knew from his two previous visits, carefully cooked and appetizingly garnished. He just hoped that the others wouldn't plump for anything *too* exotic, since Bartlett had quietly mentioned to him after the last jollification that perhaps the bill was a *little* on the steep side. For himself, he decided that soup of the day, followed by gammon and pineapple would not be beyond the Syndicate's means – even in these hard days. A drop of red wine, too. He knew it would be red wine whatever happened. Many of them drank red wine all the time in Oxford – even with Dover sole.

'We've got time for another drink, haven't we?' Cedric Voss, Chairman of the History Committee, passed his empty glass across the table. 'Drink up, men. We shall need something to keep us going this afternoon.'

Quinn dutifully collected the glasses and walked over to the bar once more, where a group of affluent-looking executives had just arrived and where a five-minute wait did nothing to quell the vague feeling of irritation which had begun to fester quietly in a corner of his mind.

When he returned to the table, the waiter was taking their orders. Voss, after discovering that the cherries were canned, the peas frozen, and the steak delivered the previous weekend, decided that he would revise his original ideas and go for the escargots and the lobster, and Quinn winced inwardly as he noted the prices. Three times his own modest order! He had pointedly *not* bought a second drink for himself (although he could have tossed another three or four back with the greatest relish) and sat back rather miserably, staring at the vast aerial photograph of central Oxford on the wall beside him. Very impressive, really: the quads of Brasenose and Queen's and—

'Aren't you drinking, Nicholas, my boy?' Nicholas! It was the first time that Voss had called him by his Christian name, and the irritation disappeared like a lizard's eyelid.

'No. I er—'

'Look, if old Tom Bartlett's been griping about the expense, forget it! What do you think it cost the Syndicate to send him to the oil states last year, eh? A month! Huh! Just think of all those belly-dancers—'

'You wanted wine with your meal, sir?'

Quinn passed the wine list over to Voss, who studied it with professional avidity. 'All red?' But it was more a statement than a question. 'That's a nice little wine, my boy.' He pointed a stubby finger at one of the Burgundies. 'Good year, too.'

Quinn noted (he'd known it anyway) that it was the most expensive wine on the list, and he ordered a bottle.

'I don't think one's going to be much good, is it? With five of us—'

'We ought to have a bottle and a half, you think?'

'I think we ought to have two. Don't you, gentlemen?' Voss turned to the others and his proposal was happily approved.

'Two bottles of number five,' said Quinn resignedly. The irritation was nagging away again.

'And open them straight away, please,' said Voss.

In the restaurant Quinn seated himself at the left-hand corner of the table, with Voss immediately to his right, two of the others immediately opposite, and the fifth member of the party at the top of the table. It was invariably the best sort of arrangement. Although he could see little of Voss's lips as he was speaking, he was just about near enough to catch his words; and the others he could see clearly. Lip-reading had its limitations, of course: it was of little use if the speaker mumbled through unmoving lips, or held a hand over his mouth; and absolutely useless when the speaker turned his back, or when the lights went out. But in normal circumstances, it was quite wonderful what one *could* do. Quinn had first attended lip-reading classes six years previously, and had been amazed to discover how easy it was.

He knew from the outset that he must have been blessed with a rare gift: he was so much in advance of the first-year class that his teacher had suggested, after only a fortnight, that he should move up to the second-year class; and even there he had been the star pupil. He couldn't really explain his gift, even to himself. He supposed that some people were talented in trapping a football or in playing the piano: and he had a talent for reading the lips of others, that was all. Indeed, he had become so proficient that he could sometimes almost believe that he was in fact 'hearing' again. In any case, he hadn't completely lost his hearing. The expensive aid at his right ear (the left was completely nerveless) amplified sufficient sound at reasonably close quarters, and even now he could hear Voss as he pronounced the benediction over the escargots just placed before him.

'Remember what old Sam Johnson used to say? "The fellow who doesn't mind his belly can't be trusted to mind anything." Well, something like that.' He tucked a napkin into his waistband and stared at his plate with the eyes of a Dracula about to ravish a virgin.

The wine was good and Quinn had noticed how Voss had dealt with it. Quite beautifully. After studying the label with the intensity of a backward child trying to get to grips with the Initial Teaching Alphabet, he had taken the temperature of the wine, lightly and lovingly laying his hands around the bottleneck; and then, when the waiter had poured half an inch of the ruby liquid into his glass, he had tasted not a drop, but four or five times sniffed the bouquet suspiciously, like a trained alsatian sniffing for dynamite. 'Not bad,' he'd said finally. 'Pour it out.' Quinn would remember the episode. He would try it himself next time. 'And turn the bloody music down a bit, will you,' shouted Voss, as the waiter was about to depart. 'We can't hear each other speak.' The music was duly diminished a few decibels, and a solitary diner at the next table came over to express his thanks. Quinn himself had been completely unaware that any background music was being played.

When the coffee finally arrived Quinn himself was feeling more contented, and a little befuzzled. In fact, he couldn't quite remember whether it was Richard III on the First Crusade or Richard I on the Third Crusade. Or, for that matter, whether either Richard had been on either Crusade. Life was suddenly very good again. He thought of Monica. Perhaps he would call in – just for a second – before they started the business of the afternoon. Monica ... It must have been the wine.

They finally arrived back at the Syndicate building at twenty minutes to three; and whilst the others were making their leisurely way back to the Revision Room upstairs, Quinn himself walked quickly along the corridor and gently knocked on the furthest door on the right, whereon the nameplate read MISS M. M. HEIGHT. He tentatively opened the door and looked in. No one. But he saw a note prominently displayed beneath a paperweight on the neatly cleared desk, and he stepped inside to read it. 'Gone to Paolo's. Back at three.' It was typical of their office life together. Bartlett never minded his staff coming and going just when and how they liked, so long as their work was adequately done. What he did insist upon, however (almost pathologically), was that everyone should keep him informed about exactly where they could be found. So. Monica had gone to have her comely hair coiffured. Never mind. He didn't know what he would have said, anyway. Yes, it was just as well: he would see her in the morning.

He walked up to the Revision Room, where Cedric Voss was leaning back in his chair, his eyes half-closed, an inane grin upon his flabby, somnolent features. 'Well, gentlemen. Can we please try to turn our attention to the Hanoverians?'


# two


By the middle of the nineteenth century radical reforms were afoot in Oxford; and by its end a series of Commissions, Statutes, and Parliamentary Bills had inaugurated changes which were to transform the life of both Town and Gown. The University syllabuses were extended to include the study of the emergent sciences, and of modern history; the high academic standards set by Benjamin Jowett's Balliol gradually spread to other colleges; the establishment of professorial chairs increasingly attracted to Oxford scholars of international renown; the secularization of the college fellowships began to undermine the traditionally religious framework of university discipline and administration; and young men of Romanist, Judaic, and other strange persuasions were now admitted as undergraduates, no longer willy-nilly to be weaned on Cicero and Chrysostom. But, above all, university teaching was no longer concentrated in the hands of the celibate and cloistered clergymen, some of whom, as in Gibbon's day, well remembered that they had a salary to receive, and only forgot that they had a duty to perform; and many of the newly appointed fellows, and some of the old, forswore the attractions of bachelor rooms in the college, got themselves married, and bought houses for themselves, their wives, their offspring, and their servants, immediately outside the old spiritual centre of Holywell and the High, the Broad and St Giles'; especially did they venture north of the great width of tree-lined St Giles', where the Woodstock and the Banbury Roads branched off into the fields of North Oxford, towards the village of Summertown.

A traveller who visits Oxford today, and who walks northward from St Giles', is struck immediately by the large, imposing houses, mostly dating from the latter half of the nineteenth century, that line the Woodstock and the Banbury Roads and the streets that cross their ways between them. Apart from the blocks of weathered yellow stone round the white-painted window frames, these three-storeyed houses are built of attractive reddish brick, and are roofed with small rectangular tiles, more of an orange-red, which slope down from the clustered chimney stacks aslant the gabled windows. Today few of the houses are occupied by single families. They are too large, too cold, and too expensive to maintain; the rates are too high and salaries (it is said) are too low, and the fast-disappearing race of domestic servants demands a colour telly in the sitting-room. So it is that most of the houses have been let into flats, converted into hotels, taken over by doctors, by dentists, by English Language schools for foreign students, by

University faculties, by hospital departments – and, in the case of one large and well-appointed property in Chaucer Road, by the Foreign Examinations Syndicate.

The Syndicate building stands some twenty yards back from the comparatively quiet road which links the busy Banbury and Woodstock thoroughfares, and is modestly sheltered from inquisitive eyes behind a row of tall horse-chestnut trees. It is approached from the front (there is no back entrance) by a curving gravelled drive, allowing space sufficient for the parking of a dozen or so cars. But the Syndicate staff has grown so much of late that this space is now inadequate, and the drive has been extended along the left-hand side of the building, leading to a small concreted yard at the rear, where it has become the custom of the graduates themselves to park their cars.

There are five graduates on the permanent staff of the Syndicate, four men and one woman, severally superintending the fields of study corresponding, in the main, to the disciplines which they had pursued for their university degrees, and to the subjects taught in their subsequent careers. For it is an invariable rule that no graduate may apply for a post with the Syndicate unless he (or she) has spent a minimum of five years teaching in the schools. The names of the five graduates are printed in bold blue letters at the top of the Syndicate's official notepaper; and on such notepaper, in a large converted bedroom on the first floor, on Friday, 31st October (the day after Quinn's deliberations with the History Committee), four of the five young shorthand typists are tapping out letters to the headmasters and headmistresses of those overseas schools (a select, but growing band) who are happy to entrust the public examination of their O- and A-level candidates to the Syndicate's benevolence and expertise. The four girls pick at their typewriters with varying degrees of competence; frequently one of them leans forward to delete a misspelling or a careless transposition of letters; occasionally a sheet is torn from a typewriter carriage, the carbon salvaged, but the top sheet and the undercopies savagely consigned to the wastepaper basket. The fifth girl has been reading *Woman's Weekly*, but now puts it aside and opens her dictation book. She'd better get started. Automatically she reaches for her ruler and neatly crosses through the third name on the headed notepaper. Dr Bartlett has insisted that until the new stocks are ready the girls shall manually correct each single sheet – and Margaret Freeman usually does as she is told:

T. G. Bartlett, PhD, MA  Secretary
P. Ogleby, MA  Deputy Secretary
~~G. Bland, MA~~
Miss M. M. Height, MA
D. J. Martin, BA

Beneath the last name she types 'N. Quinn, MA' – her new boss.

After Margaret Freeman had left him, Quinn opened one of his filing cabinets, took out the drafts of the History question papers, deciding that a further couple of hours should see them ready for press. All in all, he felt quite pleased with life. His dictation (for him, a completely new skill) had gone well, and at last he was beginning to get the knack of expressing his thoughts directly into words, instead of first having to write them down on paper. He was his own boss, too; for Bartlett knew how to delegate, and unless something went sadly askew he allowed his staff to work entirely on their own. Yes, Quinn was enjoying his new job. It was only the phones that caused him trouble and (he admitted it) considerable embarrassment. There were two of them in each office: a white one for internal extensions, and a grey one for outside calls. And there they sat, squat and menacing, on the right-hand side of Quinn's desk as he sat writing; and he prayed they wouldn't ring, for he was still unable to quell the panic which welled up within him whenever their muted, distant clacking compelled him to lift up one or other (he never knew which). But neither rang that morning, and with quiet concentration Quinn carried through the agreed string of amendments to the History questions. By a quarter to one he had finished four of the question papers, and was pleasantly surprised to find how quickly the morning had flown by. He locked the papers away (Bartlett was a martinet on all aspects of security) and allowed himself to wonder whether Monica would be going for a drink and a sandwich at the Horse and Trumpet – a pub he had originally misheard as the

'Whoreson Strumpet'. Monica's office was immediately opposite his own, and he knocked lightly and opened the door. She was gone.

In the lounge bar of the Horse and Trumpet a tall, lank-haired man pushed his way gingerly past the crowded tables and made for the furthest corner. He held a plate of sandwiches in his left hand, and a glass of gin and a jug of bitter in his right. He took his seat beside a woman in her mid-thirties who sat smoking a cigarette. She was very attractive and the appraising glances of the men who sat around had already swept her more than once.

'Cheers!' He lifted his glass and buried his nose in the froth.

'Cheers!' She sipped the gin and stubbed out her cigarette.

'Have you been thinking about me?' he asked.

'I've been too busy to think about anybody.' It wasn't very encouraging.

'I've been thinking about *you*.'

'Have you?'

They lapsed into silence.

'It's got to finish – you know that, don't you?' For the first time she looked him directly in the face, and saw the hurt in his eyes.

'You said you enjoyed it yesterday.' His voice was very low.

'Of course I bloody well enjoyed it. That's not the point, is it?' Her voice betrayed exasperation, and she had spoken rather too loudly.

'Shh! We don't want everybody to hear us, do we?'

'Well – you're so silly! We just can't go on like this! If people don't suspect something by now, they must be blind. It's got to stop! You've got a *wife*. It doesn't matter so much about me, but—'

'Couldn't we just—?'

'Look, Donald, the answer's "no". I've thought about it a lot – and, well, we've just got to stop, that's all. I'm sorry, but—' It *was* risky, and above all she worried about Bartlett finding out. With his Victorian attitudes . . .

They walked back to the office without speaking, but Donald Martin was not quite so heart-broken as he appeared to be. The same sort of conversation had taken place several times before, and always, when he picked his moment right, she was only too eager again. So long as she had no other outlet for her sexual frustrations, he was always going to be in with a chance. And once they were in her bungalow together, with the door locked and the curtains drawn – God! What a hot-pants she could be. He knew that Quinn had taken her out for a drink once; but he didn't worry about that. Or did he? As they walked into the Syndicate building at ten minutes to two, he suddenly wondered, for the first time, whether he *ought* perhaps to be a fraction worried about the innocent-looking Quinn, with his hearing aid, and his wide and guileless eyes.

Philip Ogleby heard Monica go into her office and gave her no second thought today. He occupied the first room on the right-hand side of the corridor, with the Secretary's immediately next door, and Monica's next to that – at the far end. He drained his second cup of coffee, screwed up his thermos flask, and closed an old copy of *Pravda*. Ogleby had been with the Syndicate for fourteen years, and remained as much a mystery to his present colleagues as he had done to his former ones. He was fifty-three now, a bachelor, with a lean ascetic face, and a perpetually mournful, weary look upon his features. What was left of his hair was grey, and what was left of his life seemed greyer still. In his younger days his enthusiasms had been as numerous as they were curious: Morris dancing, Victorian lampposts, irises, steam-locomotives and Roman coins; and when he had come down from Cambridge with a brilliant First, and when he had walked directly into a senior mathematics post in a prestigious public school, life had seemed to promise a career of distinguished and enviable achievement. But he had lacked ambition, even then; and at the age of thirty-nine he had drifted into his present position for no other reason than the vague conviction that he had been in one rut for so long that he might as well try to climb out and fall as gently as possible into another. There remained but few joys in his life, and the chief of these was travel. Though his six weeks annual holiday allowed him less time than he would have wished, at least his fairly handsome salary allowed him to venture far afield, and only the previous summer he had managed a fortnight in Moscow. As well as deputizing for Bartlett, he looked after Mathematics, Physics and Chemistry; and since no one else in the office (not even Monica Height, the linguist) was his equal in the unlikelier languages, he did his best to cope with Welsh and Russian as well. Towards his colleagues he appeared supremely indifferent; even towards Monica his attitude seemed that of a mildly tolerant husband towards his mother-in-law. For their part, the rest of the staff accepted him for what he was: intellectually superior to them all; administratively more than competent; socially a nonentity. Only one other person in Oxford was aware of a different side to his nature ...

At twenty past three Bartlett rang extension five.

'Is that you, Quinn?'

'Hullo?'

'Come along to my office a minute, will you?'

'I'm sorry. I can't hear you very well.'

'It's Bartlett here.' He almost shouted it into the phone.

'Oh, sorry. Look, I can't quite hear you, Dr Bartlett. I'll come along to your office right away.'

'That's what I asked you to do!'

'Pardon?'

Bartlett put the phone down and sighed heavily. He'd have to stop ringing the man; and so would everybody else.

Quinn knocked and entered.

'Sit down, Quinn, and let me put you in the picture. When you were at your meeting yesterday, I gave the others some details of our little er jamboree next week.'

Quinn could follow the words fairly easily. 'With the oil sheiks, you mean, sir?'

'Yes. It's going to be an important meeting. I want you to realize that. The Syndicate has only just broken even these last few years, and – well, but for these links of ours with some of the new oil states, we'd soon be bankrupt, like as not, and that's the truth of the matter. Now, we've been in touch with our schools out there, and one of the things they'd like us to think about is a new History syllabus. O-level only for a start. You know the sort of thing: Suez Canal, Lawrence of Arabia, colonialism, er, cultural heritage, development of resources. That sort of thing. Hell of a sight more relevant than Elizabeth the First, eh?'

Quinn nodded vaguely.

'The point is this. I want you to have a think about it before next week. Draft out a few ideas. Nothing too detailed. Just the outlines. And let me have 'em.'

'I'll try, sir. Could you just say one thing again, though? Better than "a list of metaphors", did you say?'

'Elizabeth the First, man! Elizabeth the First!'

'Oh yes. Sorry.' Quinn smiled weakly and left the room deeply embarrassed. He wished Bartlett would occasionally try to move his lips a little more.

When Quinn had gone, the Secretary half-closed his eyes, drew back his mouth as though he had swallowed a cupful of vinegar, and bared his teeth. He thought of Roope once more. Roope! What a bloody fool that man had been!


# three


Throughout the month of October the health of the pound sterling was a topic of universal, if melancholy, interest. Its effective devaluation against the dollar and against other European currencies was solemnly reported (to two points of decimals) in every radio and TV news bulletin: the pound had a poor morning, but recovered slightly in later dealings; the pound had a better morning, but was later shaky against its Continental competitors. The pound, it seemed, occasionally sat up in its sick bed to prove to the world that reports of its death had been somewhat exaggerated; but almost invariably the effort appeared to have been overtaxing and very soon it was once more lying prostrate, relapsing, slipping, falling, collapsing almost – until finally it struggled up on to its elbow once more, blinked modestly around at the anxious foreign financiers, and moved up a point or two in the international money market.

Yet although, during that autumn, the gap in the balance of payments grew ever wider; although the huge oil deficit could be made up only by massive loans from the IMF; although the number of the unemployed rose sickeningly to unpredicted heights; although the bankruptcy courts were enjoying unprecedented business; although foreign investors decided that London was no longer a worthy recipient for their ever-accumulating cash surpluses – still, in spite of it all, there remained among our foreign friends a firm and charming faith in the efficiency and efficacy of the British educational system; and, as a corollary to this, in the integrity and fair-mindedness of the British system of public examinations. Heigh-ho!

On the night of Monday, 3rd November, many were making their ways to hotel rooms in Oxford: commercial travellers and small business men; visitors from abroad and visitors from home – each selecting his hotel with an eye to business expenses, subsistence allowances, travellers' cheques or holiday savings. Cheap hotels and posh hotels; but mostly of the cheaper kind, though they (Lord knew) were dear enough. Rooms where the cisterns groaned and gurgled through the night; rooms where the window sashes sagged and the floorboards creaked beneath the flimsy matting. But the five emissaries from the Sheikdom of Al-jamara were safely settled in the finest rooms that even the Sheridan had to offer. Earlier in the evening they had eaten gloriously, imbibed modestly, tipped liberally; and each in turn had made his way upstairs and slipped between the crisp white sheets. Domestic problems, personal problems, health problems – certainly any or all of these might ruffle the waters of their silent dreams; but money was a problem which worried none of them. In the years immediately after the Second World War, oil, of high quality and in large accessible deposits, had been discovered beneath their seemingly barren sands; and a benevolent and comparatively scrupulous despot, in the person of the uncle of Sheik Ahmed Dubal, had not only secured American capital for the exploitation of the wells, but had immeasurably enriched the lives of most of the inhabitants of Al-jamara. Roads, hospitals, shopping centres, swimming pools and schools had not only been planned – but built; and in such an increasingly Westernized society the great demand of the wealthier citizens was for the better education of their children; and it was now five years since the first links with the Foreign Examinations Syndicate had been forged.

The two-day conference started at 10.30 a.m. on Tuesday, 4th, and at the coffee session beforehand there was much shaking of hands, many introductions, and all was mutual smiles and general bonhomie. The deeply tanned Arabs were dressed almost identically in dark-blue suits, with sparklingly laundered white shirts and sober ties. Quinn had earlier viewed the day with considerable misgivings, but soon he found to his very great relief that the Arabs spoke a beautifully precise and fluent brand of English, marred, it was true, by the occasional lapse from purest idiom, but distinct and (to Quinn) almost childishly comprehensible. In all, the two days passed rapidly and delightfully: plenary sessions, individual sessions, general discussions, private discussions, lively conversations, good food, coffee, sherry, wine. The whole thing had been an enormous success.

On Wednesday evening the Arabs had booked the Disraeli suite at the Sheridan for a farewell party, and all the Syndicate's permanent staff, together with wives and sweethearts, and all the Syndicate's governing council, were invited to the junketing. Sheik Ahmed himself, resplendent in his Middle-Eastern robes, took his seat beside a radiant Monica Height, exquisitely dressed in a pale-lilac trouser suit; and Donald Martin, as he sat next to his plain-looking little wife, her white skirt creased and her black jumper covered with dandruff, was feeling progressively more miserable. The Sheik had clearly commandeered the fair Monica for the evening and was regularly flashing his white and golden smile as he leaned towards her – intimate, confiding. And she was smiling back at him – attentive, flattered, inviting ... Quinn noticed them, of course, and as he finished his shrimp cocktail he watched them more closely. The Sheik was in full flow, but whether his words were meant for Monica alone, Quinn was quite unable to tell.

'As one of your own Englishmen told me one day, Miss Height,

"Oysters is amorous,
Lobsters is lecherous,
But Shrimps – Christ!" '

Monica laughed and said something close beside the Sheik's ear which Quinn could not follow. How foolish he had been to harbour any hope! And then he was able to follow another brief passage of their conversation, and he knew that the words must certainly have been whispered *pianissimo*. He felt his heart beat thicker and faster. He must surely have been mistaken...

Towards midnight the party had dwindled to about a third of its original number. Philip Ogleby, who had drunk more than anyone, seemed the only obviously sober one amongst them; the Martins had left for home some time ago; Monica and Sheik Ahmed suddenly reappeared after an unexplained absence of over half an hour; Bartlett was talking rather too loudly, and his large solicitous wife had already several times reminded him that gin always made him slur his words; one of the Arabs was in earnest negotiation with one of the barmaids; and of the Syndics, only the Dean, Voss, and Roope appeared capable of sustaining the lively pace for very much longer.

At half past midnight Quinn decided that he must go. He felt hot and vaguely sick, and he walked into the Gentlemen's, where he leaned his head against the coolness of the wall mirror. He knew he would feel rough in the morning, and he still had to drive back to his bachelor home in Kidlington. Why hadn't he been sensible and ordered a taxi? He slapped water over his face, turned on the cold tap over his wrists, combed his hair, and felt slightly better. He would say his thank-yous and good-byes, and be off.

Only a few were left now, and he felt almost an interloper as he re-entered the suite. He tried to catch Bartlett's eye, but the Secretary was deep in conversation with Sheik Ahmed, and Quinn stared rather fecklessly around for a few minutes before finally sitting down and looking again towards his hosts. But still they talked. And then Ogleby joined them; and then Roope walked over, and Bartlett and Ogleby moved away; and then the Dean and Voss went across; and finally Monica. Quinn felt almost mesmerized as he watched the changing groupings and tried to catch the drift of what they were talking about. He felt a simultaneous sense of guilt and fascination as he looked at their lips and followed their conversations, as though he were standing almost immediately beside them. He knew instinctively that some of the words must have been whispered very quietly; but to him most of them were as clear as if they were being shouted through a megaphone. He remembered one occasion (his hearing had been fairly good then) when he had picked up a phone and heard, on a crossed line, a man and his mistress arranging a clandestine rendezvous and anticipating their forthcoming fornication with lascivious delight . . .

He felt suddenly frightened as Bartlett caught his eye and walked over, with Sheik Ahmed just behind him.

'Well? You enjoyed yourself, my boy?'

'Yes, indeed. I – I was just waiting to thank you both—'

'That is a great pleasure for us, too, Meester Queen.' Ahmed smiled his white and golden smile and held out his hand. 'We shall be meeting you again, we hope so soon.'

Quinn walked out into St Giles'. He had not noticed how keenly one of the remaining guests had been watching him for the past few minutes; and it was with considerable surprise that he felt a hand on his shoulder and turned to face the man who had followed him to his car.

'I'd like a word with you, Quinn,' said Philip Ogleby.

At 12.30 the following day, Quinn looked up from the work upon which, with almost no success, he had been trying to concentrate all morning. He had heard no knock, but someone was opening the door. It was Monica.

'Would you like to take me out for a drink, Nicholas?'

# four

On Friday, 21st November, a man in his early thirties caught the train from Paddington back to Oxford. He found an empty first-class compartment with little difficulty, leaned back in his seat, and lit a cigarette. From his briefcase he took out a fairly bulky envelope addressed to himself ('If undelivered please return to the Foreign Examinations Syndicate'), and extracted several lengthy reports. He unclipped his ballpoint pen from an inside pocket, and began to make sporadic notes. But he was left-handed, and with an ungenerous margin, and that only on the right of the closely-typed documents, the task was awkward; and progressively so, as the Inter-City train gathered full speed through the northern suburbs. The rain splashed in slanting parallel streaks across the dirty carriage window, and the telegraph poles snatched up the wires ever faster as he found himself staring out abstractedly at the thinning autumn landscape; and even when he managed to drag his attention back to the tedious documents he found it difficult to concentrate. Just before Reading he walked along to the buffet car and bought a Scotch; then another. He felt better.

At four o'clock he put the papers back into their envelope, crossed out his own name, C. A. Roope, and wrote T. G. Bartlett on the cover. Bartlett, as a man, he disliked (he could not disguise that), but he was honest enough to respect the man's experience, and his flair for administration; and he had promised to leave the papers at the Syndicate that afternoon. Bartlett would never allow a single phrase in the minutes of a Syndicate Council meeting to go forward before the relevant draft had been circulated to every member who had attended. And (Roope had to admit) this meticulous minuting had frequently proved extremely wise. Anyway, the wretched papers were done now, and Roope snapped his briefcase to, and looked out at the rain again. The journey had passed more quickly than he could have hoped, and within a few minutes the drenched grey spires of Oxford came into view on his right, and the train drew into the station.

Roope walked through the subway, waited patiently behind the queue at the ticket barrier, and debated for a second or two whether he should bother. But he knew he would. He took the second-class day-return from his wallet and passed it to the ticket collector. 'I'm afraid I owe you some excess fare. I travelled back first.'

'Didn't the ticket inspector come round?'

'No.'

'We-ll. Doesn't really matter then, does it?'

'You sure?'

'Wish everybody was as honest as you, sir.'

'OK then, if you say so.'

Roope took a taxi and after alighting at the Syndicate tipped the driver liberally. Rectangles of pale yellow light shone in the upper storeys of nearby office blocks, and the giant shapes of the trees outside the Syndicate building loomed black against the darkening sky. The rain poured down.

Charles Noakes, present incumbent in the key post of caretaker to the Syndicate, was (for the breed) a comparatively young and helpful man, whose soul was yet to be soured by years of cumulative concern about the shutting of windows, the polishing of floors, the management of the boiler, and the setting of the burglar alarm. He was replacing a fluorescent tube in the downstairs corridor when Roope entered the building.

'Hello, Noakes. The Secretary in?'

'No, sir. He's been out all the afternoon.'

'Oh.' Roope knocked on Bartlett's door and looked in. The light was on; but then Roope knew that the lights would be on in every room. Bartlett always claimed that the mere switching-on of a fluorescent tube used as much electricity as leaving it on for about four hours, and consequently the lights were left on all day throughout the office – 'for reasons of economy'. For a brief second Roope thought he heard a noise inside the room, but there was nothing. Only a note on the desk which read: 'Friday p.m. Off to Banbury. May be back about five.'

'Not there, is he, sir?' Noakes had descended the small ladder and was standing outside.

'No. But never mind. I'll have a word with one of the others.'

'Not many of 'em here, I don't think, sir. Shall I see for you?'

'No. Don't worry. I'll do it myself.'

He knocked and put his head round Ogleby's door. No Ogleby.

He tried Martin's room. No Martin.

He was knocking quietly on Monica Height's door, and lean-

35

ing forward to catch any response from within, when the caretaker reappeared in the well-lit, well-polished corridor. 'Looks as if Mr Quinn's the only graduate here, sir. His car's still out the back, anyway. I think the others must have gone.'

When the cat's away, thought Roope ... He opened Monica's door and looked inside. The room was tidiness itself, the desk clear, the leather chair neatly pushed beneath it.

It was the caretaker who tried Quinn's room, and Roope came up behind him as he looked in. A green anorak was draped over one of the chairs, and the top drawer of the nearest cabinet gaped open to reveal a row of buff-coloured file cases. On the desk, placed under a cheap paperweight, was a note from Quinn for his typist's attention. But Quinn himself was nowhere to be seen.

Roope had often heard tell of Bartlett's meticulous instructions to his staff not only about their paramount duty for ensuring the strictest security on all matters concerning question papers, but also about the importance of leaving some notification of their whereabouts. 'At least he's left a note for us, Noakes. More than some of the others have.'

'I don't think the Secretary would be very happy about this, though.' Noakes gravely closed the top drawer of the cabinet and pushed in the lock.

'Bit of a stickler about that sort of thing, isn't he, old Bartlett?'

'Bit of a stickler about everything, sir.' Yet somehow Noakes managed to convey the impression that if he were on anyone's side, it would be Bartlett's.

'You don't think he's too much of a fusspot?'

'No, sir. I mean, all sorts of people come into the office, don't they? You can't be too careful in a place like this.'

'No. You're absolutely right.'

Noakes felt pleasantly appeased, and having made his point he conceded a little to Roope's suspicions. 'Mind you, sir, I reckon he might have picked a warmer week for practising the fire drill.'

'Gives you those, does he?' Roope grinned. He hadn't been on a fire drill since he was at school.

'We had one today, sir. Twelve o'clock. He had us all there, standing in the cold for something like a quarter of an hour.

Freezing, it was. I know it's a bit too hot in here but ...' Noakes was about to embark on an account of his unequal struggle with the Syndicate's antiquated heating system, but Roope was far more interested in Bartlett, it seemed.

'Quarter of an hour? In *this* weather?'

Noakes nodded. 'Mind you, he'd warned us all about it earlier in the week, so we had our coats and everything, and it wasn't raining then, thank goodness, but—'

'Why as long as that, though?'

'Well, there's quite a lot of permanent staff now and we had to tick our names off a list. Huh! Just like we was at school. And the Secketary gave us a little talk ...'

But Roope was no longer listening; he couldn't stand there talking to the caretaker all night, and he began walking slowly up the corridor. 'Bit odd, isn't it? Everybody here this morning and nobody here this afternoon!'

'You're right, sir. Are you sure I can't help you?'

'No, no. It doesn't matter. I only came to give this envelope to Bartlett. I'll leave it on his desk.'

'I'm going upstairs for a cup o' tea in a minute, sir, when I've fixed this light. Would you like one?'

'No, I've got to be off. Thanks all the same, though.'

Roope took advantage of the Gentlemen's lavatory by the entrance and realized just how hot it was in the building: like walking into a Turkish bath.

Bartlett himself had been addressing a group of Banbury headmasters and headmistresses on the changing pattern of public examinations; and the last question had been authoritatively (and humorously) dispatched at almost exactly the same time that Roope had caught his taxi to the Syndicate. He was soon driving his pride and joy, a dark brown Vanden Plas, at a steady sixty down the twenty-odd-mile stretch to Oxford. He lived out at Botley, on the western side of the city, and as he drove he debated whether to call in at the office or to go straight home. But at Kidlington he found himself beginning to get caught up in the regular evening paralysis, and as he negotiated the roundabouts on Oxford's northern perimeter he decided to turn off right along the ring-road instead of carrying straight over towards the city centre. He would call in the office a bit later, perhaps, when the evening rush-hour had abated.

When he arrived home, at just gone five his wife informed him that there had been several phone calls; and even as she was giving him the details the wretched thing rang again. How she wished they had a number ex-directory!

On Saturday, 22nd November (as on most Saturdays), the burglar alarm system was switched off at 8.30 a.m., one hour later than on weekdays. During the winter months there were only occasional Saturday workings, and on this particular morning the building was, from all appearances, utterly deserted. Ogleby was on foot, and let himself in quietly. The smell of floor polish, like the smell of cinema seats and old library books, took him back tantalizingly to his early schooldays, but his mind was on other things. Successively he looked into each room on the ground floor in order to satisfy himself that no one was around. But he was aware of this instictively: there was an eerie, echoing emptiness about the building which the quiet clickings-to of the doors served merely to re-emphasize. He went into his own room and rang a number.

'Morning, Secretary. Hope I didn't get you out of bed? No? Ah, good. Look. I know it sounds a bit silly, but can you remind me when the alarm's turned off on Saturday mornings? I've got to ... 8.30? Yes, I thought so, but I just wanted to make sure. I didn't want ... No. Funny, really. I'd somehow got it into my head that there'd been some change ... No, I see. Well, sorry to trouble you. By the way, did the Banbury meeting go off all right? ... Good. Well, I'll be off.'

Ogleby walked into Bartlett's room. He looked around quickly and then took out his keys. Botley was at least twenty minutes' drive away: he could probably allow himself at least half an hour. But Ogleby was a cautious soul, and he allowed himself only twenty minutes.

Twenty-five minutes later, as he was sitting at his own desk, he heard someone enter the building, and almost immediately, it seemed, his door was opened.

'You got in all right then, Philip?'

'Yes thanks. No bells ringing in the police station this morning.'

'Good.' Bartlett blinked behind his spectacles. 'I've er got a few things I want to clear up myself.' He closed the door and walked into his own office. He knew what had been happening, of course. For a clever man, Ogleby's excuse about the burglar alarm had been desperately thin. But what had he been looking for? Bartlett opened his cabinets and opened his drawers; but everything was in order. Nothing seemed to have been taken. What *was* there to take? He sat back and frowned deeply: the whole thing was strangely disturbing. He walked up the corridor to Ogleby's room, but Ogleby had gone.

# five

Morse looked directly into the large mirror in front of him, and there surveyed the reflection of the smaller hand mirror held behind him, in which, in turn, he considered the occipital regions of what he liked to think of as a distinguished skull. He nodded impassively as the hand mirror was held behind the left side of his neck, nodded again as it was switched to the right, declined the suggested application of a white, greasy-looking hair oil which stood on the surface before him, arose, like a statue unveiled, from the chair, took the proffered tissue, rubbed his face and ears vigorously, and reached for his wallet. That felt much better! He was never happy when his hair began to grow in untidy, curly profusion just above his collar, and he wondered sadly why it now failed to sustain such luxuriance upon the top of his head. He tipped the barber generously and walked out into Summertown. Although not so cold as in recent days, it was drizzling slightly, and he decided to wait for a bus up to his bachelor flat at the top of North Oxford. It was 10.15 a.m. on Tuesday, 25th November.

It would be unlikely that anything of importance would require his immediate attention at HQ, and he had to call in home anyway. It was a ritual with Morse. As a young recruit in the army he had been driven almost mad by the service issue of prickly vests, prickly shirts, and prickly trousers. His mother had told him that he had an extremely sensitive skin; and he believed her. It was always the same after a haircut. He would take off his shirt and vest, and dip his head into a basin full of hot water. Bliss! He would shampoo his hair twice, and then flannel his face and ears thoroughly. He would then rub his back with a towel, dry his hair, wash down the short, black hairs from the sides of the basin, select a clean vest and shirt, and finally comb his hair with loving care in front of the bathroom mirror.

But this morning it *wasn't* quite the same. He was just about to rinse off the second application of medicated shampoo when the phone rang. He swore savagely. Who the hell?

'Hoped I might find you at home, sir. I couldn't find anyone who'd seen you at the office.'

'So what? I've had a haircut. Not a crime, is it?'

'Can you get here straight away, sir?' Lewis's tone was suddenly grave.

'Give me five minutes. What's up?'

'We've got a body, sir.'

'Whereabouts are you?'

'I'm phoning from the station. Do you know Pinewood Close?'

'No.'

'Well, I think you'd be best to call here first anyway, sir.'

'OK. Wait for me there.'

Chief Superintendent Strange was waiting for him, too. He stood impatiently on the steps outside the Thames Valley Police HQ in Kidlington, as Morse hurriedly parked the Lancia and jumped out.

'Where have you been, Morse?'

'Sorry, sir. I've had a haircut.'

'You *what*?'

Morse said nothing, not the slightest flicker of guilt or annoyance betraying itself in the light grey eyes.

'A fine advertisement, eh? Citizens under police care and

protection getting themselves bumped off, and the only Chief Inspector I've got on duty is having his bloody hair cut!'

Morse said nothing.

'Look, Morse. You're in charge of this case – is that clear? You can have Lewis here if you want him.' Strange turned away, but suddenly remembered something else. 'And you won't get another haircut until you've sorted this little lot out – that's an order!'

'Perhaps I shan't need one, sir.' Morse winked happily at Lewis and led the way into his office. 'What's it look like from behind?'

'Very nice, sir. They've cut it very nicely.'

Morse sat back in his black leather armchair and beamed at Lewis. 'Well? What have you got to tell me?'

'Chap called Quinn, sir. Lives on the ground floor of a semi-detached in Pinewood Close. He's been dead for a good while by the look of him. Poisoned, I shouldn't wonder. He works' ('worked', muttered Morse) 'at the Foreign Examinations Syndicate down the Woodstock Road somewhere; and one of his colleagues got worried about him and came out and found him. I got the call about a quarter to ten, and I went along straightaway with Dickson and had a quick look round. I left him there, and came back to call you.'

'Well, here I am, Lewis. What do you want me to do?'

'Knowing you, sir, I thought you might want me to arrest the chap who found him.'

Morse grinned. 'Is he here?'

'In the Interview Room. I've got a rough statement from him, but it'll need a bit of brushing up before he signs it. You'll want to see him, I suppose?'

'Yes, but that can wait. Got a car ready?'

'Waiting outside, sir.'

'You've not called the path. boys in yet, I hope?'

'No. I thought I ought to wait for you.'

'Good. Go and get your statement tarted up and I'll see you outside in ten minutes or so.'

Morse made two phone calls, combed his hair again, and felt inordinately happy.

❋

Several faces peeped from behind ground-floor lace-curtained windows as the police car drove into Pinewood Close, a small, undistinguished crescent wherein eight semi-detached houses, erected some fifty years previously, stood gently fading into a semi-dignified senescence. Most of the wooden fences that bordered the properties managed to sustain only a precarious pretence to any upright posture, the slats uncreosoted and insecure, the crossrails mildewed, sodden with rain, and rotten. Only at each end of the crescent had the original builder left sufficient sideroom for the erection of any garage, and it was at the house at the extreme left that the bulky figure of Constable Dickson stood, stamping his feet on the damp concrete in front of a prefabricated unpainted garage, and talking to a woman in her early fifties, the owner of the property and rentier of some half a dozen other houses in the neighbourhood. But whatever other benefits her various incomes conferred upon her, her affluence appeared not to be reflected in her wardrobe: she wore no stockings and was pulling a shabby old coat more closely over a grubby white blouse as Morse and Lewis stepped out of the car.

' 'Ere come the brains, missus,' muttered Dickson, and stepped forward to greet the Chief Inspector. 'This is Mrs Jardine, sir. She owns the property and she's the one who let us in.'

Morse nodded a friendly greeting, took the Yale key from Dickson, and instructed him to take Mrs Jardine to the police car and get a statement from her. He himself stood for a while in silence with his back to the house, and looked around him. In a kerbed oval plot, a thick cluster of small trees and variagated bushes sheltered the houses from the main road and gave to the crescent the semblance of partial privacy. But the small curved stretch of road itself was poorly maintained and unevenly surfaced, with a long, irregular black scar, running parallel to the pavement, where the water mains had recently been dug up again. The gutter was full of sopping brown leaves, and the lamppost immediately outside No 1 had been vandalized. The front door of the next house opened a few inches and a middle-aged woman directed inquisitive eyes towards the centre of activity.

'Good morning,' said Morse brightly.

The door was closed in a flash, and Morse turned round to survey the garage. Although the claw of the lock which secured the doors was not pushed home, he touched nothing, contenting himself with a quick glance through the glass panels at the top. Inside he saw a dark-blue Morris 1300 which allowed little more than a foot of space between the wall and the driver's door. He walked over to the front porch and inserted the key. 'Good job he doesn't drive a Cadillac, Lewis.'

'Didn't,' corrected Lewis quietly.

The front door of No 1 Pinewood Close opened on to a narrow hallway, with a row of clothes pegs at the foot of the staircase which climbed the wall to the left. Morse stood inside and pointed to the door immediately to his right. 'This the one?'

'Next one, sir.'

The door was closed and Morse took out his pen and depressed the handle carefully. 'I hope you haven't left your prints all over the place, Lewis?'

'I opened it the same way as you, sir.'

Inside the room the electric light was still turned on; the dull-orange curtains were drawn; the gas fire was burning low; and lying in a foetal posture on the carpet was the body of a young man. The fire was flanked by two old, but comfortable-looking armchairs; and beside the one to the right, on a low french-polished coffee table, stood a bottle of dry sherry, almost full, and a cheap-looking sherry glass, almost empty. Morse bent forward and sniffed the pale, clear liquid. 'Did you know, Lewis, that about eighteen per cent of men and about four per cent of women can't smell cyanide?'

'It *is* poison, then?'

'Smells like it. Peach blossom, bitter almonds – take your pick.'

The dead man's face was turned towards them, away from the fire, and Morse knelt down and looked at it. A small quantity of dry froth crusted the twisted mouth, and the bearded jaw was tightly clenched in death; the pupils of the open eyes appeared widely dilated, and the skin of the face was a morbid, blotchy blue. 'All the classic symptoms, Lewis. We hardly need a post-mortem on this one. Hydrocyanic acid. Anyway the path. boys should be here any minute.' He stood up and walked over to the curtains, which had obviously shrunk in a not particularly recent wash, and which gaped open slightly towards the top. Outside Morse could see the narrow garden, with its patchy, poor-quality grass, a small vegetable plot at the far end, and a section of fencing missing on the left. But the view appeared to convey little of significance to his mind, and he turned his attention back to the room itself. Along the wall opposite the fire were a dozen or so bundles of books, neatly tied with stout cord, and a dark mahogany sideboard, the left-hand door of which gaped open to reveal a small collection of assorted tumblers and glasses, and an unopened bottle of whisky. Everywhere seemed remarkably clean and tidy. A small wastepaper basket stood in the shallow alcove to the left of the fire; and inside the basket was a ball of paper, which Morse picked out and smoothed gently on the top of the sideboard:

Mr Quinn. I can't do all the cleaning this afternoon because Mr Evans is off sick and I've got to get him a prescription from the doctor. So I'll call back and finish just after six if that's convenient for you.
A. Evans (Mrs)

Morse handed the note over to Lewis. 'Interesting.'

'How long do you think he's been dead, sir?'

Morse looked down at Quinn once more and shrugged his shoulders. 'I dunno. Two or three days, I should think.'

'It's a wonder someone didn't find him earlier.'

'Ye-es. You say he just has these downstairs rooms?'

'So Mrs Jardine says. There's a young couple living upstairs usually, but she's in the John Radcliffe having a baby, and he works nights at Cowley and he's been staying with his parents in Oxford somewhere.'

'Mm.' Morse made as if to leave, but suddenly stopped. The bottom of the door had been amateurishly planed to enable it to ride over the carpet and a noticeable draught was coming beneath it, occasionally setting the low, blue gas jets flickering fitfully into brighter yellow flames.

'Funny, isn't it, Lewis? If I lived in this room I wouldn't choose the armchair immediately in line with the draught.'

'Looks as if he did, sir.'

'I wonder, Lewis. I wonder if he did.'

The front-door bell rang and Morse sent Lewis to answer it. 'Tell 'em they can start as soon as they like.' He walked out of the room and through into the kitchen at the back of the house. Again, everywhere was tidy. On a red Formica-topped table stood a stack of recently purchased provisions: half a dozen eggs in their plastic container; ½ lb butter; ½ lb English Cheddar; two generous slices of prime steak under a cellophane wrapper; and a brown paper bag full of mushrooms. Beside the groceries was a curling pay-out slip from the Quality super-market, and a flicker of excitement showed in Morse's grey eyes as he looked it through.

'Lewis!'

Nothing else here looked particularly interesting: a sink unit, a gas cooker, a fridge, two kitchen stools, and by the side of the back door, filling the space under the stairs, a small larder. Lewis, who had been chatting to the police surgeon, appeared at the door. 'Sir?'

'What's going on in there?'

'Doc says he's been poisoned.'

'Amazing thing – medical science, Lewis! But we've got other things to worry about for the minute. I want you to make a complete inventory of the food in the fridge and in this larder here.'

'Oh.' Lewis was almost thinking that a man of his own rank and experience should be above such fourth-grade clerical chores; but he had worked with Morse before, and knew that whatever other faults he had the Chief Inspector seldom wasted his own or other people's time on trivial or unnecessary tasks. He heard himself say he would get on with it – immediately.

'I'm going back to the station, Lewis. You stay here until I get back.'

Outside, Morse found Dickson and Mrs Jardine standing beside the police car. 'I want you to drive me back to HQ, Dickson.' He turned to Mrs Jardine. 'You've been very kind and helpful. Thank you very much. You've got a car?'

The landlady nodded and walked away. In truth, she felt disappointed that her small part in the investigation seemed now to be over, and that she had warranted no more than a cursory question from the rather abrupt man who appeared to be in charge. But as she drove away from the crescent her thoughts soon veered to other, more practical considerations. Would anyone be over-anxious to move into the rooms so lately rented by that nice young Mr Quinn? People didn't like that sort of thing. But as she reached the outskirts of Oxford she comforted herself with the salutary thought that the dead are soon forgotten. Yes, she would soon be able to let the rooms again. Just give it a month or so.

Morse read the statement aloud to the youngish man seated rather nervously at the small table in Interview Room No 1.

I have known Nicholas Quinn for three months. He came to work at the Foreign Examinations Syndicate as an assistant secretary on 1st September this year.

On Monday, 24th November, he did not appear at the office and did not ring in to say that anything was wrong. It is not unusual for the graduates to take a day or two off when they can, but the Secretary, Dr Bartlett, always insists that he should be kept fully informed of any such arrangement. None of my colleagues saw Mr Quinn on Monday, and no one knew where he was. This morning, Tuesday, 25th November, Dr Bartlett came to my office and said that Mr Quinn had still not arrived. He said that he had tried to phone him, but that there was no reply. He then asked me to drive round to Mr Quinn's house and I did so, arriving at about 9.30 a.m. The front door was locked and no one answered the doorbell. I could see that Mr Quinn's car was still in the garage, so I proceeded to the back of the house. The light was on in the ground-floor room and the curtains were drawn; but there was a gap in the curtains and I looked inside. I could see someone lying quite still on the floor in front of the fireplace, and I knew that something was seriously wrong. I therefore rang the police immediately from the public call box in the main street, and was told to wait at the house until the police came. When Sergeant Lewis arrived with a constable, they discovered who owned the house. The landlady turned up with the key about ten minutes later. The police then proceeded into the house for a short while, and when Sergeant Lewis came out he told me that I must prepare myself for a shock. He said that Mr Quinn was dead.

'You happy to sign this?' Morse pushed the statement across the table.

'I didn't use the word "proceeded".'

'Ah, you must forgive us, sir. We never "go" anywhere in the force, you know. We always "proceed".'

Donald Martin accepted the explanation with a weak smile and signed the statement with nervy flourish.

'How well did you know Mr Quinn, sir?'

'Not very well really. He's only been with us—'

'So you say in your statement. But why did the Secretary send you – not one of the others?'

'I don't know. I suppose I knew him as well as any of them.'

'What did you expect to find?'

'Well, I thought he was probably ill or something, and couldn't let us know.'

'There's a phone in the house.'

'Yes, but it could have – well, it could have been a heart attack, or something like that.'

Morse nodded. 'I see. Do you happen to know where his parents live?'

'Somewhere in Yorkshire, I think. But the office could—'

'Of course. Did he have a girlfriend?'

Martin was aware of the Inspector's hard grey eyes upon him and his mouth was suddenly very dry. 'Not that I know of.'

'No pretty fillies he fancied at the office?'

'I don't think so.' The hesitation was minimal but, for Morse, sufficient to set a few fanciful notions aflutter.

'I'm told such things are not unknown, sir. He was a bachelor, I take it?'

'Yes.'

'You a married man, sir?'

'Yes.'

'Mm. Perhaps you've forgotten what it's like to be single.' Morse would have been happier if Martin had told him not to talk such drivel. But Martin didn't.

'I don't quite see what you're getting at, Inspector.'

'Oh, don't worry about that, sir. I often don't know what I'm getting at myself.' He stood up, and Martin did the same, fastening his overcoat. 'You'd better get back to the office, or they'll be getting worried about you. Tell the Secretary I'll be in touch with him as soon as I can – and tell him to lock up Mr Quinn's room.'

'You've no idea—?' said Martin quietly.

'Yes, I'm afraid I have, sir. He was almost certainly murdered.' The sinister word seemed to hang on the air, and the room was suddenly and eerily still.

# six

During the previous decade the Foreign Examinations Syndicate had thrown its net round half the globe; and for its hundred or so oversea centres the morning of Tuesday, 25th November, had been fixed for the 'retake' of the Ordinary-level English Language papers. For the vast majority of the foreign candidates involved, the morning afforded the chance of a second bite at the cherry; and such was the importance of a decent grade in English Language, either for future employment or for admission to higher education, that there were very few of the candidates who were treating the two question papers (Essay and Comprehension) with anything but appropriate respect. Only those few who had been ill during the main summer examination were taking the examination for the first time; the remainder were the 'returned empties' who, either through some congenital incapacity or a prior history of monumental idleness, had yet to succeed in persuading the examiners that they had reached a standard of acceptable competence in the skills of English usage.

At 11.55 a.m. this same morning, in strict accord with the explicit instructions issued by the examining body, invigilators in Geneva, in East and West Africa, in Bombay, and in the Persian Gulf, were reminding their candidates that only five minutes remained before scripts would be collected; that all candidates should ensure that their full names and index numbers appeared on each sheet of their work; and that all sheets must be handed in in the correct order. Some few candidates were now scribbling furiously and for the most part fruitlessly; but the majority were having a final look through their answers, shuffling their sheets into order, and then leaning back in more relaxed postures, shooting the occasional grin at fellow examinees who sat at desks (the regulation five feet apart) in commandeered classrooms or converted gymnasiums.

At twelve noon, in an air-conditioned, European-style class-room in the Sheikdom of Al-jamara, a young Englishman, who was invigilating his first examination, gave the order to stop writing. There were only five pupils in the room, all Arabs, all of whom had finished writing several minutes previously. One of the boys (not a pupil of the school, but the son of one of the sheiks) had in fact finished his work some considerable time earlier, and had been sitting back in his chair, arms folded, an arrogant, self-satisfied smirk upon his dark, semitic features. He was the last of the five candidates, and handed in his script without saying a word.

Left alone, the young Englishman filled in the invigilation form with great care. Fortunately, no candidate had failed to turn up for the examination, and the complexities of the sec-tions dealing with 'absentees' could be ignored. In the appro-priate columns he filled in the names and index numbers of the five candidates, and prepared to place the attendance sheet, together with the scripts, in the official buff-coloured envelope. As he did so his eyes fell momentarily upon the work of Muhammad Dubal, Index Number 5; and he saw immediately that it was very good – infinitely better than that of the other four. But then the sheik's son had doubtless had the privilege of high-class private tuition. Ah well. There would be plenty of opportunity for him to try to jack up the standards of his own pupils a bit before next summer . . .

He left the room, licking the flap of the envelope as he did so, and walked through to the school secretary's office.

It was just after noon, too, that Morse returned to Pinewood Close. He made no effort to move on the curious crowd who thronged the narrow crescent, for he had never understood why the general public should so frequently be castigated for wishing to eye-witness those rare moments of misfortune or tragedy that occurred in their vicinity. (He would have been one of them himself.) He threaded his way past the three police cars, past the ambulance, its blue light flashing, and entered the house once more. There were almost as many people inside as outside.

'Sad thing, death,' said Morse.

'*Mors, mortis*, feminine,' mumbled the ageing police surgeon. Morse nodded morosely. 'Don't remind me.'

'Never mind, Morse. We're all dying slowly.'

'How long's he been dead?'

'Dunno. Could be four, five days – not less than three, I shouldn't think.'

'Not too much help, are you?'

'I shall have to take a closer look at him.'

'Have a guess.'

'Unofficially?'

'Unofficially.'

'Friday night or Saturday morning.'

'Cyanide?'

'Cyanide.'

'You think it took long?'

'No. Pretty quick stuff if you get the right dose down you.'

'Minutes?'

'Much quicker. I'll have to take the bottle and the glass, of course.'

Morse turned to the two other men in the room who had been brushing the likeliest-looking surfaces with powder.

'Anything much?'

'Seems like his prints all over the place, sir.'

'Hardly surprising.'

'Somebody else's, though.'

'The cleaner's, most likely.'

'Just the one set of prints on the bottle, sir – and on the glass.'

'Mm.'

'Can we move the body?'

'Sooner the better. I suppose we'd better go through his

pockets, though.' He turned again to the surgeon. 'You do it, will you, doc?'

'You getting squeamish, Morse? By the way, did you know he wore a hearing aid?'

At one minute to two, Morse got to his feet and looked down at Lewis.

'Time for another if you drink that up smartish.'

'Not for me, sir. I've had enough.'

'The secret of a happy life, Lewis, is to know when to stop and then to go that little bit further.'

'Just a half, then.'

Morse walked to the bar and beamed at the barmaid. But in truth he felt far from happy. He had long since recognized the undoubted fact that his imagination was almost invariably fired by beer, especially by beer in considerable quantities. But today, for some reason, his mind seemed curiously disengaged; sluggish even. After the body had been removed he had spent some time in the downstairs front room, used by Quinn as a bedroom-cum-study; he had opened drawers, looked through papers and folders, and half-stripped the bed. But it had all been an aimless, perfunctory exercise, and he had found nothing more incriminating than the previous month's copy of *Playboy*; and it was whilst sitting on the uncovered mattress scanning a succession of naked breasts and crotches that Lewis, after completing his tedious inventories, had found him.

'Anything interesting, sir?'

'No.' Morse had guiltily returned the magazine to the desk and fastened up his overcoat.

Just as they were about to leave, Morse had noticed the green anorak on one of the clothes pegs in the narrow hallway.

# seven

Bartlett knew that the man had been drinking and found himself feeling surprised and disappointed. He had been expecting the call all the afternoon, but it had not come through until half past three. The four of them had been seated in his office since lunchtime (the red light on outside) talking in hushed voices amongst themselves about the shattering news. Graphically Martin had recounted again and again the details of his morning discovery, and had taken some muted pleasure, even in these grim moments, at finding himself, quite unprecedentedly, at the centre of his colleagues' attention. But invariably the conversation had reverted to the perplexing question of who had been the last to see Quinn alive – and where. They all agreed, it seemed, that it had been on Friday, but exactly when and exactly where no one seemed able to remember. Or cared to tell . . .

Monica Height watched the Inspector carefully as he came in, and told herself, as they were briefly introduced, that his eyes held hers a fraction longer than was strictly necessary. She liked his voice, too; and when he informed them that each would be interviewed separately, either by himself or by Sergeant Lewis (standing silently by the door), she found herself hoping that in her case it would be him. Not that she need have worried on that score: Morse had already mentally allocated her to himself. But first he had to see what Bartlett could tell him.

'You've locked Quinn's door, I hope, sir.'

'Yes. Immediately I got your message.'

'Well, I think you'd better tell me something about this place: what you do, how you do it, anything at all you think may help. Quinn was murdered, sir – little doubt about that; and my job's to find out who murdered him. There's just a possibility, of course, that his murder's got nothing at all to do with this place, or with the people here; but it seems much more probable that I may be able to find something in the office here that will give me some sort of lead. So, I'm afraid I shall be having to badger you all for a few days – you realize that, don't you?'

Bartlett nodded. 'We shall all do our best to help you, Inspector. Please feel completely free to carry out whatever inquiries you think fit.'

'Thank you, sir. Now, what can you tell me?'

During the next half-hour Morse learned a great deal. Bartlett told him about the purpose, commitments, and organization of the Syndicate, about the personnel involved at all stages in the running of public examinations. And Morse found himself surprised and impressed: surprised by the unexpected complexities of the operations involved; and, above all, impressed by the extraordinary efficiency and grasp of the Pickwickian little Secretary sitting behind his desk.

'What about Quinn himself?'

Bartlett opened a drawer and took out a folder. 'I looked this out for you, Inspector. It's Quinn's application for the job here. It'll tell you more than I can.'

Morse opened the folder and his eyes hurriedly scanned the contents: curriculum vitae, testimonials, letters from three referees, and the application form itself, across the top of which Bartlett had written: 'Appointed w.e.f. 1st Sept.' But again Morse's mind remained infuriatingly blank. The cogs in the machine were beginning to turn all right, but somehow they refused to engage. He closed the folder, defensively mumbling something about studying it later, and looked again at Bartlett. He wondered how that clear and supremely efficient mind would be tackling the problem of Quinn's murder, and it appeared that Bartlett could almost read his thoughts.

'You know that he was deaf, don't you, Inspector?'

'Deaf? Oh yes.' The police surgeon had mentioned it, but Morse had taken little notice.

'We were all very impressed by the way he coped with his disability.'

'How deaf was he?'

'He would probably have gone completely deaf in a few years' time. That was the prognosis, anyway.'

For the first time since Bartlett had been talking the merest flicker of interest showed itself in Morse's eyes. 'Little surprising you appointed him, perhaps, sir?'

'I think it's you who would have been surprised, Inspector.

You could hardly tell he was deaf, you see. Apart from dealing with the phone, which *was* a problem, he was quite remarkable. He really was.'

'Did you er did you appoint him, you know, because he *was* deaf?'

'Did we feel sorry for him, you mean? Oh no. It seemed to the er the er committee that he was the best man in the field.'

'Which committee was that?'

Did Morse catch a hint of guardedness in Bartlett's eyes? He wasn't sure. What he did know was that the teeth of the smallest cog had now begun to bite. He sat back more happily in his chair.

'We er had all twelve Syndics on that committee – plus myself, of course.'

'Syndics? They're er—?'

'They're like governors of a school, really.'

'They don't work here?'

'Good gracious, no. They're all university dons. They just meet here twice a term to see if we're doing our job properly.'

'Have you got their names here?'

Morse looked with interest down the typed list that Bartlett handed to him. Printed beside the name of each of the Syndics were full details of university, college, degrees, doctorates and other academic honours, and one name in the list jumped out at him. 'Most of them Oxford men, I see, sir.'

'Natural enough, isn't it?'

'Just one or two from Cambridge.'

'Ye-es.'

'Wasn't Quinn at Magdalene College, Cambridge?' Morse began to reach for the folder, but Bartlett immediately confirmed the fact.

'I see that Mr Roope was at the same college, sir.'

'Was he? I'd never noticed that before.'

'You notice most things, if I may say so.'

'I always associate Roope with Christ Church, I suppose. He's been appointed a fellow there: "student", rather, if we want to be pedantic, Inspector.' His eyes were utterly guileless now, and Morse wondered if he might earlier have been mistaken.

'What's Roope's subject?'

'He's a chemist.'

'Well, well.' Morse tried to suppress the note of excitement in his voice, but realized that he wasn't succeeding. 'How old is he? Do you know?'

'Youngish. Thirty or so.'

'About Quinn's age, then?'

'About that.'

'Now, sir. Just one more thing.' He looked at his watch and found that it was already a quarter to five. 'When did you last see Quinn? Can you remember?'

'Last Friday, sometime. I know that. But it's a funny thing. Before you came in, we were all trying to think when we'd last seen him. Very difficult, you know, to pinpoint it exactly. I certainly saw him late on Friday morning; but I can't be sure about Friday afternoon. I had to go to a meeting in Banbury at three o'clock, and I'm just not sure if I saw him before I went.'

'What time did you leave the office, sir?'

'About a quarter past two.'

'You must drive pretty fast.'

'I've got a fast car.'

'Twenty-two, twenty-three miles?'

Bartlett's eyes twinkled. 'We've all got our little weaknesses, Inspector, but I try to keep within the speed limits.'

Morse heard himself say he hoped so, and decided it was high time he saw Miss Monica Height. But before he did so he had a very much more urgent call to pay. 'Where's the nearest Gents? I'm dying for—'

'There's one right here, Inspector.' He got up and opened the door to the right of his desk. Inside was a tiny lavatory with a small wash basin tucked away behind the door; and as Morse blissfully emptied his aching bladder, Bartlett was reminded of the mighty out-pourings of Niagara.

After only a few minutes with Monica Height, Morse found himself wondering how the rest of the staff could ever manage to keep their hands off her, and cynically suspected that perhaps they didn't. The bright-green, flower-patterned dress she wore was stretched too tightly across her wide thighs, yet somehow managed to mould itself softly and suggestively around her full breasts. Biddable, by the look of it – and eminently beddable.

She wore little make-up, but her habit of passing her tongue round her mouth imparted a moist sheen to her slightly pouting lips; and she exuded a perfume that seemed to invite instant and glorious gratification. Morse felt quite sure that at certain times and in certain moods she must have proved well-nigh irresistible to the young and the susceptible. To Martin, perhaps? To Quinn? Yes, surely the temptation must always have been there. Morse knew that he himself, the middle-aged and the susceptible ... But he pushed the thought to the back of his mind. What about Ogleby? Or even Bartlett, perhaps? Whew! It was a thought! Morse recalled the passage from Gibbon about one of the tests designed for the young novitiate: stick him in a sack all night with a naked nun and see if ... Morse shook his head abruptly and passed his hand over his eyes. It was always the same when he'd had a lot of beer.

'Do you mind if I just ring my daughter, Inspector?' (Daughter?) 'I'm usually on my way home by this time, and she'll probably wonder where I've got to.' Morse listened as she rang a number and explained her whereabouts.

'How old is your daughter, Miss er er Miss Height?'

She smiled understandingly. 'It's all right, Inspector. I'm divorced, and Sally's sixteen.'

'You must have married young.' (Sixteen!)

'I was foolish enough to marry at eighteen, Inspector. I'm sure you had much more sense than that.'

'Me? Oh yes, em no, I mean. I'm not married myself, you see.' Their eyes held again for a brief second and Morse sensed he could be living dangerously. It was time he asked the fair Monica a few important questions.

'When did you last see Mr Quinn?'

'It's funny you should ask that. We were only ...' It was like listening to a familiar record. She'd seen him on Friday morning – quite sure of that. But Friday afternoon? She couldn't quite remember. It was difficult. After all, Friday was – what? – five days ago now. ('Could have been four, five days' hadn't the police surgeon said?)

'Did you like Mr Quinn?' Morse watched her reaction carefully, and suspected that this was one question for which she hadn't quite prepared herself.

'I haven't known him all that long, of course. What is it? Two or three months? But I liked him, yes. Very nice sort of person.'

'Did he like you?'

'What do you mean by that, Inspector?'

What *did* he mean? 'I just thought – well, I just thought—'

'You mean did he find me attractive?'

'I don't suppose he could help that.'

'You're very nice, Inspector.'

'Did he ever ask you out with him?'

'He asked me out to the pub once or twice at lunchtimes.'

'And you went?'

'Why not?'

'What did he drink?'

'Sherry, I think.'

'What about you?'

Her tongue moistened her lips once more. 'I've got slightly more expensive tastes myself.'

'Where did you go?'

'The Horse and Trumpet – just at the end of the road. Nice, cosy little place. You'd love it.'

'Perhaps I'll see you in there one day.'

'Why not?'

'Your tastes are expensive, you say?'

'We could work something out.'

Again their eyes met and the danger bells were ringing in Morse's brain. He stood up: 'I'm sorry to have kept you so long, Miss Height. I hope you'll apologize for me to your daughter.'

'Oh, she'll be all right. She's been home a lot of the time recently. She's retaking a few O-levels, and the school lets her go home when she hasn't got an examination.'

'I see.' Morse stood at the door, and seemed reluctant to leave. 'We shall be seeing each other again, no doubt.'

'I hope so, Inspector.' She spoke pleasantly and quietly and – damn it, yes! – sexily.

Her last words re-echoed in Morse's mind as he walked abstractedly down the corridor.

'At last!' muttered Lewis to himself. He had been sitting in the entrance foyer for the past twenty minutes with Bartlett, Ogleby and Martin. All three had their overcoats and briefcases with them but were obviously reluctant to depart until Morse came and said the word. The death of Quinn had obviously thrown a pall of gloom over everything, and they had little to say to each other. Lewis had liked Ogleby, but had learned little from him: he'd remembered seeing Quinn the previous Friday morning, but not in the early afternoon; and to each of Lewis's other questions he had appeared to answer frankly, if uninformatively. Martin, though, had seemed a completely different proposition: intense and nervous now, as the shock of the whole business seemed to catch up with him, he'd said he couldn't really remember seeing Quinn at all on Friday.

Rather awkwardly, Morse thanked them for their co-operation, and gathered from Bartlett that it would be perfectly in order for himself and Lewis to stay in the building: the caretaker would be on the premises until at least 7.30 p.m., and naturally the building would be kept open for them as long as they wished. But before handing over the keys to Quinn's office and to his filing cabinets, Bartlett gave the policemen a stern-faced little lecture on the strictly confidential nature of most of the material they would find; it was of the greatest importance therefore that they should remember ... Yes, yes, yes, yes. Morse realized how he would have hated working under Bartlett, a man for whom the sin against the Holy Ghost was clearly that of leaving filing cabinets unlocked whilst nipping out to pee.

After they had gone, Morse suggested a quick stroll round the block, and Lewis responded willingly. The building was far too hot, and the cool night air was clean and refreshing. On the corner of the Woodstock Road they passed the Horse and Trumpet and Morse automatically consulted his watch.

'Nice little pub, I should think, Lewis. Ever been in?'

'No, sir, and I've had enough beer, anyway. I'd much rather have a cup o' tea.' Relieved that it still wanted ten minutes to opening time, he told Morse of his interviews, and Morse in turn told Lewis of his. Neither of them, it seemed, felt unequivocally convinced that he had stared into the eyes of a murderer.

'Nice-looker, isn't she, sir?'

'Uh? Who do you mean, Lewis?'

'Come off it, sir!'

'I suppose she is – if you go for that sort.'

'I notice you kept her all to yourself.'

'One o' the perks, isn't it?'

'I'm a bit surprised you didn't get a bit more out of her, though. Of the lot of 'em she seemed to me the one most likely to drop her inhibitions pretty quickly.'

'Drop her knickers pretty smartish, too, I shouldn't wonder.'

Lewis sometimes felt that Morse was quite unnecessarily crude.

# eight

Quinn's office was large and well furnished. Two blue leather chairs, one on each side, were neatly pushed beneath the writing desk, the surface of which was clear, except for the in- and out-trays (the former containing several letters, the latter empty) and a large blotter, with an assortment of odd names and numbers, and meaningless squiggles scribbled round its perimeter in black biro. Lining two complete walls, right up to the ceiling, were row upon row of History texts and editions of the English classics, with the occasional yellow, red, green and white spine adding a further splash of colour to the brightly lit and cheerful room. Three dark green filing cabinets stood along the third wall, whilst the fourth carried a large plywood notice board and, one above the other, reproductions of Atkinson Grimshaw's paintings of the docks at Hull and Liverpool. Only the white carpet which covered most of the floor showed obvious signs of wear, and as Morse seated himself magisterially in Quinn's chair he noticed that immediately beneath the desk the empty waste-paper basket covered a patch that was almost threadbare. To his right, on a small black-topped table stood two telephones, one white, one grey, and beside them a pile of telephone directories.

'You go through the cabinets, Lewis. I'll try the drawers here.'

'Are we looking for anything in particular, sir?'

'Not that I know of.'

Lewis decided to plod along in his own methodical manner: at least it promised to be a bit more interesting that listing tins of rice pudding.

Almost immediately he began to realize what an enormous amount of love and labour went into the final formulation of question papers for public examinations. The top drawer of the first cabinet was stuffed with bulky buff-coloured folders, each containing copies of drafts, first proofs, first revises, second revises – even third revises – of papers to be set for the Ordinary-level English syllabuses. 'I reckon I could get a few quick O-levels this way, sir.'

Morse mumbled something about not being worth the paper they were printed on, and carried on with his own desultory investigation of the top right-hand drawer of Quinn's desk, wherein it soon became abundantly clear that he was unlikely to make any cosmic discoveries: paper-clips, bulldog-clips, elastic bands, four fine-pointed black biros, a ruler, a pair of scissors, two birthday cards ('Love, Monica' written in one of them – well, well!), a packet of yellow pencils, a pencil sharpener, several letters from the University Chest about the transfer of pension rights to the University Superannuation Scheme, and a letter from the Centre for the Deaf informing Quinn that the lip-reading classes had been transferred from Oxpens to Headington Tech. After poking haphazardly around, Morse turned to the books behind him and found himself in the middle of the M's. He selected Marvell's *Collected Poems*, and as if someone else had recently been studying the same page, the book fell open of its own accord at the poem written 'To His Coy Mistress', and Morse read again the lines which had formed part of his own mental baggage for rather more years than he wished to remember:

'The grave's a fine and private place,
But none, I think, do there embrace . . .'

Yes, Quinn was lying in the police mortuary, and Quinn had hoped his hopes and dreamed his dreams as every other mortal soul . . . He slotted the book back into its shelf, and turned with a slightly chastened spirit to the second drawer.

The two men worked for three-quarters of an hour, and Lewis felt himself becoming progressively more dispirited. 'Do you think we're wasting our time, sir?'

'Are you thirsty, or something?'

'I just don't know what I'm looking for, that's all.'

Morse said nothing. He didn't either.

By seven o'clock Lewis had looked through the contents of two of the three cabinets, and now inserted the key into the third, whence he took a further armful of thick folders and once again sat down to his task. The first file contained many carbons of letters, stretching back over two years, all marked GB/MF, and the replies from various members of the Syndicate's English Committee, all beginning 'Dear George'.

'This must be the fellow Quinn took over from, sir.'

Morse nodded cursorily and resumed his study of a black Letts desk diary which was the only object of even minimal interest he had so far unearthed. But Quinn had obviously shown no inclination to emulate an Evelyn or a Pepys, and little more than the dates and times of various meetings had been entered. 'Birthday' (under 23rd October), and 'I owe Donald £1' seemed to form the only concession to an otherwise autobiographical blank. And since he could think of nothing more purposeful to pursue, Morse idly counted the meetings: ten of them, almost all for the revisions of various question papers, within twelve weeks or so. Not bad going. And one or two other meetings: one with the English Committee on 30th September and one, a two-day meeting, with AED – whatever that was – on the 4th and 5th November.

'What's AED stand for, Lewis?'

'Dunno, sir.'

'Have a guess.'

'Association of Eccentric Dentists.'

Morse grinned and shut the diary. 'You nearly finished?'

'Two more drawers.'

'Think it's worth it?'

'Might as well go through with it now, sir.'

'OK.' Morse leaned back in the chair, his hands behind his head, and looked across the room once more. Not a particularly memorable start to a case, perhaps; but it was early days yet.

He decided to put a call through to HQ. The grey telephone seemed the one used for outside calls, and Morse pulled it towards him. But as soon as he had picked up the receiver he put it down again. Underneath the orange code book he saw a letter which had escaped his notice hitherto. It was written on the official notepaper of the Frederic Delius School, Bradford, and was dated Monday, 17th November:

Dear Nick,
Don't forget me when you sort out your examining teams for
next year. I trust you've had the form back by now. Gryce wasn't
all that co-operative about the testimonial at first, but you'll have
noticed that I'm 'a man of sound scholarship, with considerable
experience of O- and A-level work'. What more can you ask for?
Martha sends her love, and we all hope you'll be up here on your
old stamping ground this Christmas. We've decided we can't
please both lots of parents, and so we are going to please neither –
and stay at home. By the way, old sour-guts has applied for the
headship of the new Comprehensive! O tempora! O mores!
As ever,
Brian.

The letter was ticked through in black biro, and Morse considered it carefully for a moment. Had Quinn rung up his friend? A former colleague, possibly? If so, when? It might be worth while finding out.

But it was Lewis who, quite accidentally, was to stumble through the trip-wire and set off the explosive that blew the case wide open, although he himself was quite unaware at the time of his momentous achievement. As he was about to jam the latest batch of files back into its cabinet he caught sight of an envelope, squashed and crumpled, which had become wedged beneath the moveable slide designed to keep the file cases upright. He worked it out and took the single sheet of paper from the envelope. 'I can tell you what AED stands for, sir.' Morse looked up without enthusiasm and took the letter from him. It was an amateurishly-typed note, written on the official, headed notepaper of the Al-jamara Education Department, and dated 3rd March.

Dear George,
Greetings to all at Oxford. Many thanks for your
letter and for the summer examination package.

All Entry Forms and Fees Forms should be ready
for final dispatch to the Syndicate by Friday
20th or at the very latest, I'm told, by the 21st.
Admin has improved here, though there's room
for improvement still; just give us all two or three
more years and we'll really show you! Please
don't let these wretched 16+ proposals destroy
your basic O- and A-pattern. Certainly this
sort of change, if implemented immediately,
would bring chaos.
Sincerely yours,

Apart from the illegibly scrawled signature, that was all.

Morse frowned slightly as he looked at the envelope, which
was addressed to G. Bland, Esq, MA, and marked 'STRICTLY
PRIVATE AND CONFIDENTIAL' in bold red capitals. But
his face quickly cleared, and he handed the letter back to Lewis
without a word. It really was time they went.

Idly he opened the Letts diary again and his eyes fell upon
the calendar inside the front page. And suddenly the blood began
to freeze in his arms, and from the quiet, urgent tone of his voice
Lewis immediately realized that the Inspector was strangely
excited.

'What's the date of the postmark on that envelope, Lewis?'

'Third of March.'

'This year?'

Lewis looked again. 'Yes, sir.'

'Well, well, well!'

'What is it?'

'Funny, wouldn't you say, Lewis? Friday the 20th, it says in
the letter. But *which* Friday the 20th?' He looked down at the
calendar again. 'Not March. Not April. Not May. Not June. Not
July. And it must refer to entry forms for last summer's examinations.'

'Somebody could have made a mistake over the date, sir.
Could have been using last year's—'

But Morse wasn't listening. He picked up the letter again and
studied it for several minutes with a fierce intensity. Then he
nodded slowly to himself and a quiet smile spread over his face.
'Lewis, my boy, you've done it again!'

'I have, sir?'

'I'm not saying we're much nearer to finding out the identity of the person who murdered Nicholas Quinn, mind you. But I'll tell you one thing: I'm beginning to think we've got a pretty good idea *why* he was murdered! Unless it's a cruel coincidence—'

'Hadn't you better explain, sir?'

'Look at the letter again, Lewis, and ask yourself why such a seemingly trivial piece of correspondence was marked "Strictly Private and Confidential". Well?'

Lewis shook his head. 'I agree, sir, that it doesn't seem very important but—'

'But it *is* important, Lewis. That's just the point! *We* start reading from the left and then go across, agreed? But they tell me that some of these cockeyed foreigners start from the right and read down!'

Lewis studied the letter once more and his eyes gradually widened. 'You're a clever old bugger, sir.'

'Sometimes, perhaps,' conceded Morse.

At 7.35 p.m. the caretaker knocked deferentially and put his head round the door. 'I don't want to interrupt, sir, if—'

'Don't, then,' snapped Morse, and the door was quietly reclosed. The two policemen looked across the table at each other – and grinned happily.

# WHEN ?

# nine

Morse had never been in the slightest degree interested in the technicalities of the science of pathology, and on Wednesday morning he read the reports before him with the selectivity of a dedicated pornophilist seeking out the juciest crudities. 'The smallest dose which has proved fatal is a ½ drachm of the pharmacopoeial acid, or 0.6 gram of anhydrous hydrocyanic acid ... rapidly altered in the body after death, uniting with sulphur ...' Ah, here we are: '... and such in this instance were the post-mortem appearances that there is reason to believe that death must have occurred almost immediately ... fruitless, in the absence of scratches or abrasions, to speculate on the possibility of the body having been moved after death ...' Interesting. Morse skipped his way along. '... would suggest a period of between 72–120 hours before the body was discovered. Any greater precision about these time limits is precluded in this case ...' As in *all* cases you ever have, muttered Morse. He had never ceased to wonder why, with the staggering advances in medical science, all pronouncements concerning times of death remained so disconcertingly vague. For that was the real question: *when* had Quinn died? If Aristotle could be believed (why not?) the truth would probably lie somewhere in the middle: 94 hours, say. That meant Friday lunchtime or thereabouts. Was that possible? Morse put the report aside, and reconsidered the little he as yet knew of Quinn's whereabouts on the previous Friday. Yes. Perhaps he should have asked Quinn's colleagues where *they* were on Friday, not when they had last seen Quinn. But there was plenty of time; he would have to see them all again soon, anyway. At least one thing was clear. Whoever had tinkered with Quinn's sherry bottle had known something about poison – known a great deal about poison, in fact. Now who ...? Morse went to his shelves, took down Glaister and Rentoul's bulky and definitive tome on *Medical Jurisprudence and Toxicology*, and looked up 'Hydrocyanic Acid' (page 566); and as he skimmed over the headings he smiled to himself. The compiler of the medical report he had just read had beaten him to it: some of the sentences were lifted almost verbatim. Why not, though? Cyanide wasn't going to change much over the years ... He recalled Hitler and his clique in the Berlin bunker. That was cyanide, wasn't it? Cyanide. Suicide! Huh! The obvious was usually the very last thing that occurred to Morse's mind; but he suddenly realized that the most obvious answer to his problem was this: that Quinn had committed suicide. Yet, come to think of it, that was no real answer either. For if he had, why on earth ... ?

Lewis was surprised when half an hour later Morse took him to his home in North Oxford. It was two years since he had been there, and he was pleasurably surprised to find how comparatively neat and clean it was. Morse disappeared for a while, but put his head round the door and told Lewis to help himself to a drink.

'I'm all right, sir. Shall I pour one for you?'

'Yes. Pour me a sherry. And pour one for yourself.'

'I'd rather—'

'Do as you're told for a change, man!'

It wasn't unusual for Morse suddenly to turn sour, and Lewis resigned himself to the whims of his superior officer. The cabinet was well-stocked with booze, and Lewis took two small glasses and filled them from a bottle of medium sherry, sat back in an armchair, and wondered what was in store for him now.

He was sipping his sherry effeminately when Morse reappeared, picked up his own, lifted it to his lips and then put it down. 'Do you realize, Lewis, that if that sherry had been poisoned, you'd be a goner by now?'

'So would you, sir.'

'Ah, no. I've not touched mine.'

Lewis slowly put down his own glass, half-empty now, and began to understand the purpose of the little charade. 'And there'd be my prints on the bottle and on the glass ...'

'And if I'd carefully wiped them both before we started, I've just got to pour my own sherry down the sink, wash the glass – and Bob's your uncle.'

'Somebody still had to get into Quinn's place to poison the sherry.'

'Not necessarily. Someone could have given Quinn the bottle as a present.'

'But you don't give someone a bottle that's been opened! You'd have a hell of a job trying to reseal a sherry bottle. In fact, you couldn't do it.'

'Perhaps there wasn't any need for that,' said Morse slowly; but he enlightened Lewis no further. For a moment he stood quite still, his eyes staring into the hazy past where a distant memory lingered on the threshold of his consciousness but refused the invitation to come in. It was something to do with a lovely young girl; but she merged into other lovely young girls. There had been so many of them, once . . . Think of something else! It would come. He drained his sherry at a gulp and poured himself another. 'Bit like drinking lemonade, isn't it, Lewis?'

'What's the programme, sir?'

'Well – I think we've got to play things a bit delicately. We might be on to something big, you must realize that; but it's no good rushing things. I want to know what all of 'em in the office were doing on Friday, but I want 'em to *know* what I'm going to ask them.'

'Wouldn't it be better—?'

'No. It wouldn't be fair, anyway.'

Lewis was getting lost. 'You think one of the four of them murdered Quinn?'

'What do you think?'

'I don't know, sir. But if you let them know beforehand—'

'Yes?'

'Well, they'd have something ready. Make something up—'

'That's what I want them to do.'

'But surely if one of them murdered Quinn—?'

'He'd have an alibi all ready, you mean?'

'Yes.'

Morse said nothing for a few seconds and then suddenly changed tack completely. 'Did you see me last Friday, Lewis?' Lewis opened his mouth and shut it again. 'Come on! We work in the same building, don't we?' Lewis tried hard, but he couldn't get hold of the problem at all. Friday. It seemed a long way away. What had he done on Friday? Had he seen Morse?

'You see what I mean, Lewis? Not easy, is it? We ought to give 'em a chance.'

'But as I say, sir, whoever killed Quinn will have something pretty good cooked up for last Friday.'

'Exactly.'

Lewis let it go. Many things puzzled him about the chief, and he felt even more puzzled as Morse pulled the front door to behind him: 'And what makes you so sure that Quinn was murdered on Friday?'

Margaret Freeman was unmarried – a slim, rather plain girl, with droopy eyelashes, who had worked for the Syndicate for just over three years. She had earlier been confidential secretary to Mr Bland, and had automatically been asked to transfer her allegiance to Mr Quinn. She had slept little the previous night, and not until the late grey dawn had she managed to rein in the horses of her terror. But Morse (who thought he understood such things) was still surprised when she broke down and wept after only a few minutes of gentle interrogation. She had certainly seen Quinn on Friday morning. He had dictated a whole sheaf of letters to her at about 10.45, and these had kept her busy until fairly late that same afternoon, when she had taken them into Quinn's office and put them in the in-tray. She hadn't seen him that Friday afternoon; yet she'd had the feeling that he was about somewhere, for she could almost positively recall (after some careful prodding) that Quinn's green anorak had been draped over the back of one of the chairs; and yes! there had been that little note for her, with her initials on it, MF, and then the brief message ('Dr Bartlett liked them to leave messages, sir'); but she couldn't quite remember ... something like ... no. Just something about 'going out', she thought. About being 'back soon', perhaps? But she couldn't really remember – that was obvious.

Morse had interviewed her in Quinn's office, and after she had gone he lit a cigarette and considered things anew. It was certainly interesting. Why wasn't the note still there? Quinn must have come back, crumpled up the note ... But the wastepaper basket was empty. Cleaners! But Quinn had been alive at about 11 or 11.15 that Friday morning. That was something to build on, anyway.

To Lewis was entrusted the task of finding the caretaker and of discovering what happened to the Syndicate's rubbish. And for once the luck was with him. Two large, black plastic sacks of wastepaper were standing in a small loading bay at the side of the building, awaiting collection, and the job of sifting through the papers was at least a good deal more congenial than delving into rubbish bins. Comparatively quick, too. Most of the waste-paper was merely torn across the middle, and not screwed into crumpled balls: outdated forms mostly and a few first drafts of trickier letters. No note from Quinn to his confidential secretary, though, and Lewis felt disappointed, for that was the prime object of the search. But there were several (identical) notes from Bartlett, which Lewis immediately sensed might well be of some interest; and he took them along to Quinn's office, where the receiver that Morse held to his ear was emitting the staccato bleeps of the 'engaged' signal. He further smoothed out one of the notes, and Morse put down the receiver and read it:

Mon, 17th Nov

*Notice to all Staff*

PRACTICE FIRE DRILL

The fire alarm will ring at 12 noon, on Friday, 21st Nov, when all staff must immediately stop working, turn off all fires, lights and other electrical appliances, close all windows and doors, and walk through the front door of the building and out into the front parking area. No one is to remain in the building *for any reason*, and normal work will not be resumed until everyone is accounted for. Since the weather seems likely to be cold and wet, staff are advised to take their coats etc., although it is hoped that the practice will take no longer than ten minutes or so. I ask and expect your full co-operation in this matter.
Signed T. G. Bartlett (Secretary)

'He's a careful soul, isn't he, Lewis?'
'Seems pretty efficient, sir.'
'Not the sort to leave anything to chance.'
'What's that supposed to mean?'
'I was just wondering why he didn't tell me about this fire

drill, that's all.' He smiled to himself, and Lewis knew that that *wasn't* all.

'Perhaps he didn't tell you because you didn't ask him.'

'Perhaps so. Anyway, go along and ask him if there was a roll-call. You never know – we may be able to postpone Quinn's execution from 11.15 to 12.15.'

The red light showed outside Bartlett's office, and as Lewis stood undecided before the door, Donald Martin walked past.

'That light means he's got somebody with him, doesn't it?'

Martin nodded. 'He'd be very annoyed if any of the staff interrupted him, but – I mean . . .' He seemed extremely nervous about something, and Lewis took the opportunity (as Morse had instructed him) of disseminating the news that Quinn's colleagues would all soon be asked to account for their whereabouts the previous Friday.

'But what—? He can't really think—'

'He thinks a lot of things, sir.'

Lewis knocked on Bartlett's door and went in. Monica Height turned round with some annoyance on her face, but the Secretary himself, smiling benignly, made no reference whatsoever to the infraction of the golden rule. In answer to his query, Lewis was informed that he'd better see the chief clerk upstairs, who had been in charge of the whole operation and who almost certainly would have kept the register of all those who had been present for the fire drill.

After Lewis had left the room, Monica turned around and looked hard at Bartlett. 'What's all that about, pray?'

'You know you mustn't blame the police for trying to find out when Mr Quinn was last seen alive. I must admit I'd not mentioned the fire drill—'

'But he was alive last Friday *afternoon* – there's not much doubt about that, is there? His car was here until about twenty to five. So Noakes says.'

'Yes, I know all about that.'

'Don't you think we ought to tell the police straight away?'

'I've got a strong suspicion, my dear, that Chief Inspector Morse is going to find out far more than some of us may wish.'

But whatever might have been the cryptic implication of this remark, Monica appeared not to notice it. 'Don't you agree it may be very important, though?'

'Certainly. Especially if they think that Mr Quinn was murdered last Friday.'

'Do *you* think he was murdered on Friday?'

'Me?' Bartlett looked at her with a gentle smile. 'I don't think it matters very much what I think.'

'You haven't answered my question.'

Bartlett hesitated and stood up. 'Well, for what it's worth the answer's "no".'

'When—?'

But Bartlett held up his finger to his lips and shook his head. 'You're asking as many questions as they are.'

Monica rose to her feet and walked to the door. 'I still think you ought to let them know that Noakes—'

'Look,' he said in a kindly way. 'If it'll make you happier, I'll let them know straight away. All right?'

As Monica Height left the room, Martin came up to her and said something urgently into her ear. Together they disappeared into Monica's office.

The chief clerk remembered the fire drill well, of course. Everything had gone according to plan, and the Secretary had scrutinized the final list himself before allowing his staff to resume their duties. Of the twenty-six permanent staff, only three had not ticked themselves off. But all had been accounted for: Mr Ogleby was down at the Oxford University Press; one of the typists had flu; and one of the junior clerks was on holiday. Against Quinn's name was a bold tick in black biro. And that was that. Lewis walked downstairs and rejoined Morse.

'Have you noticed how everyone in this office uses black biro, Lewis?'

'Bartlett's got 'em all organized, sir – even down to the pens they use.'

Morse seemed to dismiss the matter as of no importance, and picked up the phone once more. 'You'd have thought this bloody school would have more than one line, wouldn't you?' But this time he heard the ringing tone, and the call was answered almost immediately. Morse heard a cheerful north country voice telling him that she was the school secretary and asking if she could help. Morse explained who he was and what information he required.

'Friday, you say? Yes, I remember. From Oxford, that's right ... Oh, must have been about twenty past twelve. I remember I looked on t'timetairble and Mr Richardson was teaching until a quarter to one ... No, no. He said not to bother. Just asked me to give him t'message, laik. He said he would be inviting Mr Richardson to do some marking this summer ... No, I'm sorry. I can't remember t'name for the minute, but Mr Richardson would know, of course ... Yes. Yes, I'm sure that was it. Quinn – that's right. I hope there's nothing ... Oh dear ... Oh dear ... Shall I tell Mr Richardson? ... All right ... All right, sir. Goodbye.'

Morse cradled the phone and looked across at Lewis. 'What do you think?'

'I think we're making progress, sir. Just after eleven he finishes dictating his letters; he's here for the fire drill at twelve; and he rings up the school at twenty past.' Morse nodded and Lewis felt encouraged to go on. 'What I'd really like to know is whether he left the note for Miss Freeman *before* or *after* lunch. So perhaps we'd better try to find out where he had a bite to eat, sir.'

Morse nodded again, and seemed to be staring at nothing. 'I'm beginning to wonder if we're on the right track, though, Lewis. You know what? I wouldn't be at all surprised if—'

The internal phone rang and Morse listened with interest. 'Well, thank you for telling me, Dr Bartlett. Can you ask him to come along straight away?'

When the sycophantic Noakes began his brief tale, Morse wondered why on earth he had not immediately sought the caretaker's confidence; for he knew full well that in institutions of all kinds throughout the land it was the name of the caretaker which should appear at the top of all official notepaper. Wherever his services were called upon (including Police HQ) it seemed to be the caretaker, with his strangely obnoxious combination of officiousness and servility, whose goodwill was prized above all; whose co-operation over rooms, teas, keys and other momentous considerations was absolutely indispensable. On the face of it, however, Noakes seemed one of the pleasanter specimens of the species.

'Yes, sir, his coat *was* there – I remember it distinct like, because his cabinet was open and I closed it. The Secketary wouldn't 'ave wanted that, sir. Very particular he is, about that.'

'What there a note on his desk?'

'Yes, we saw that as well, sir.'

'"We", you say?'

'Mr Roope, sir. He was with me. He'd just—'

'What was he doing here?' said Morse quietly.

'He wanted to see the Secketary. But he was out, I knew that, sir. So Mr Roope asked me if any of the assistant secketaries was in – he had some papers, you see, as he wanted to give to somebody.'

'Who did he give them to?'

'That's just it. As I was going to say, sir, we tried all the other secketaries' offices, but there was nobody in.'

Morse looked at him sharply. 'You're quite sure about that, Mr Noakes?'

'Oh yes, sir. We couldn't find anybody, you see, and Mr Roope left the papers on the Secketary's desk.'

Morse glanced at Lewis and his eyebrows rose perceptibly. 'Well, well. That's very interesting. Very interesting.' But if it was as interesting as Morse would have the caretaker imagine, it prompted no further questions. At least not immediately so. The plain truth was that the information was, for Morse, completely unexpected, and he now regretted his earlier (stupidly theatrical) decision of allowing word to be spread on the office grapevine (it had surely got round by now?) that he would be asking all of them to account for their movements on Friday afternoon. The last thing he had expected was that they'd *all* need an alibi. Bartlett, he knew, had been out at Banbury. But where had the others been that fateful afternoon? Monica, Ogleby, Martin, and Quinn. *All of them out of the office.* Whew!

'What time was all this, Mr Noakes?'

''Bout half-past four, sir.'

'Had any of the others left a note?'

'I don't think so.'

'Could any of them have been upstairs, do you think?'

'Could 'ave been, sir, but – well, I was here quite a long while. I was in the corridor, you see, fixin' this broken light when Mr Roope came in.'

Morse still seemed temporarily blown off course, and Lewis decided to see if he could help. 'Could any of them have been in the lavatory?'

'Must have been in there a long time!' It was quite clear from the slightly contemptuous smirk that crossed Noakes's face that he was not prepared to pay any particular respect to the suggestions of a mere sergeant, and the almost inevitable 'sir' was noticeably absent.

'It was raining on Friday afternoon, wasn't it?' said Morse at last.

'Yes, sir. Rainin', blowin' – miserable afternoon it was.'

'I hope Mr Roope wiped his feet,' said Morse innocently.

For the first time Noakes seemed uneasy. He passed his hands one over the other, and wondered what on earth *that* was supposed to mean.

'Did you see any of them at all – later on, I mean?'

'Not really, sir. I mean, I saw Mr Quinn leave in his car about—'

'You *what?*' Morse sat up and blinked at Noakes in utter bewilderment.

'You saw him *leave*, you say?'

'Yes, sir. About ten to five. His car was—'

'Were there any other cars here?' interrupted Morse.

'No, sir. Just Mr Quinn's.'

'Well, thank you, Mr Noakes. You've been very helpful.' Morse got up and walked to the door. 'And you didn't see anyone else – anyone at all – after that?'

'No, sir. Except the Secketary himself. He came back to the office about half-past five, sir.'

'I see. Well, thank you very much.' Morse had scarcely been able to hide his mounting excitement and he fought back the strong impulse to push Noakes out into the corridor.

'If I can be of any help any time, sir, I hope you . . .' He stood fawning at the door like a liegeman taking leave of his lord. But Morse wasn't listening. A little voice within his brain was saying

75

'Bugger off, you obsequious little creep,' but he merely nodded good-naturedly and the caretaker finally sidled through the door.

'Well, Lewis? What do you make of that little lot?'

'I expect we shall soon find somebody who saw Quinn in a pub on Friday night. About chucking-out time.'

'You think so?' But Morse wasn't really interested in what Lewis was making of it. The previous day the cogs had started turning all right, but turning, it now appeared, in the wrong direction; and whilst Noakes had been speaking they'd temporarily stopped turning altogether. But they were off again now, in forward gear, with two or three of them whirring furiously. He looked at his watch, and saw that the morning was over. 'What swill do they slop out at the Horse and Trumpet, Lewis?'

# ten

Few of the buildings erected in Oxford since the end of the Second World War have met with much approval from either Town or Gown. Perhaps it is to be expected that a public privileged with the daily sight of so many old and noble buildings should feel a natural prejudice against the reinforced concrete of the curious post-war structures; or perhaps all modern architects are mad. But it is generally agreed that the John Radcliffe Hospital on Headington Hill is one of the least offensive examples of the modern design – except, of course, to those living in the immediate vicinity who have found their expensive detached houses dwarfed by the gigantic edifice, and who now view from the bottom of their gardens a broad and busy access road instead of the green and open fields of Manor Park. The seven-storeyed hospital, built in gleaming, off-white brick, its windows painted chocolate brown, is set in spacious, tree-lined grounds, where royal-blue notice boards in bold white lettering direct the strangers towards their destinations. But few are strangers here, for the John Radcliffe Hospital is dedicated to the safe delivery of all the babies to be born beneath the aegis of the Oxfordshire Health Authority, and in it almost all the pregnant mums have suffered their precious embryos to be coddled and cosseted, turned and tested many many times before. Joyce Greenaway has. But with her ('one in a thousand', they'd said) things have not gone quite according to the gynaecological guarantee.

Frank Greenaway had Wednesday afternoon free and he drove into the hospital car park at 1 p.m. He was feeling much happier than he had done, for it now looked as if everything was going to be all right after all. But it still annoyed him that the incompetent nitwit of a foreman at Cowley had not been able to get the message to him the previous Friday evening, and he felt that he had let his wife down. Their first, too! Not that Joyce had been over-worried: when things seemed to her to be getting to the critical stage, she had shown her usual good sense and contacted the hospital direct. But it still niggled a bit; he couldn't pretend it didn't. For when he had finally arrived at the hospital at 9.30 p.m., their underweight offspring – some three weeks premature – was already putting up its brave and successful little fight in the Intensive Care Unit. It wasn't *his* fault, was it? But for Frank (who had little imagination, but a ready sympathy) it was something like arriving ten minutes late for an Oxford United fixture and finding he'd missed the only goal of the match.

He, too, was no stranger now. The doors opened for him automatically, and he walked his way confidently down the wide, blue carpeted entrance hall, past the two enquiry desks, and made straight for the lift, where he pressed the button and, with a freshly laundered nightie, a box of Black Magic, and a copy of *Woman's Weekly*, he ascended to the sixth floor.

Both Joyce and the baby were still isolated – something to do with jaundice ('Nothing to worry about, Mr Greenaway'), and Frank walked once more into Private Room 12. Why he felt a little shy, he could hardly begin to imagine; but he knew full well that he had every cause for continued apprehension. The doctors had been firmly insistent that he should as yet say nothing whatsoever about it. ('Your wife has had a pretty rough time, Mr Greenaway.') She would have to know *soon*, though; couldn't *help* getting to know. But he had willingly agreed to play the game, and the sister had promised to have a word with each of Joyce's visitors. ('The post-natal period can be very difficult, Mr Greenaway.') No *Oxford Mail* either, of course.

'How are we then, love?'

'Fine.'

'And the little one?'

'Fine.'

They kissed, and soon began to feel at ease again.

'Has the telly-man been yet? I meant to ask you yesterday.'

'Not yet, love. But he'll fix it – have no fear.'

'I should hope so. I shan't be in here much longer – you realize that, don't you?'

'Don't you worry about that.'

'Have you put the cot up yet?'

'I keep telling you. Stop *worrying*. You just get on your feet again and look after the little feller – that's all that matters.'

She smiled happily, and when he stood up and put his arm around her she nestled against his shoulder lovingly.

'Funny, isn't it, Frank? We'd got a name all ready, if it was a girl. And we were so sure it would be.'

'Yeah. I been thinking, though. What about "Simon"? Nice name, don't you think. "Simon Greenaway" – what about that? Sounds sort of – distinguished, if you know what I mean.'

'Yeah. Perhaps so. Lots of nice names for boys, though.'

'Such as?'

'Well. You know that chap downstairs – Mr Quinn? His name's "Nicholas". Nice name, don't you think? "Nicholas Greenaway." Yeah. I quite like that, Frank.' Watching his face closely, she could have sworn there was *something* there, and for a second she felt a surge of panic. But he *couldn't* know. It was just her guilty conscience: she was imagining things.

The Horse and Trumpet was quite deserted when they sat down in the furthest corner from the bar, and Lewis had never known Morse so apparently uninterested in his beer, over which he lingered like a maiden aunt sipping homemade wine at a church social. They sat for several minutes without speaking, and it was Lewis who broke the silence. 'Think we're getting anywhere, sir?'

Morse seemed to ponder the question deeply. 'I suppose so. Yes.'

'Any ideas yet?'

'No,' lied Morse. 'We've got to get a few more facts before we start getting any fancy ideas. Yes ... Look, Lewis. I want you to go along and see Mrs What's-her-name, the cleaner woman. You know where she lives?' Lewis nodded. 'And you might as well call on Mrs Jardine – isn't it? – the landlady. You can take my car: I expect I'll be at the Syndicate all afternoon. Pick me up there.'

'Anything particular you want me to—?'

'Christ, man! You don't need a wet nurse, do you? Find out all you bloody well can! You know as much about the case as I do!' Lewis sat back and said nothing. He felt more angry with himself than with the Inspector, and he finished his pint in silence.

'I think I'll be off then, sir. I'd just like to nip in home, if you don't mind.'

Morse nodded vaguely and Lewis stood up to go. 'You'd better let me have the car keys.'

Morse's beer was hardly touched and he appeared to be staring with extraordinary intensity at the carpet.

Mrs Evans had been cleaning the ground floor of No 1 Pinewood Close for several years, and had almost been part of the tenancy for the line of single men who had rented the rooms from Mrs Jardine. Most of them had been on the lookout for something a little better and had seldom stayed long; but they'd all been pleasant enough. It was chiefly the kitchen that would get so dirty, and although she dusted and hoovered the other rooms, her chief task always lay in the kitchen, where she usually spent half an hour cleaning the stove and another half-hour ironing the shirts, underwear and handkerchiefs which found their weekly way into the local launderette. It was just about two hours' work – seldom more, and often a little less. But she always charged for two hours, and none of the tenants had ever demurred. She liked to get things done whilst no one was about; and, with Quinn, 3–5 p.m. on Fridays was the regularly appointed time.

It was about poor Mr Quinn, she knew that, and she invited Lewis in and told him the brief story. She had usually finished and gone before he got back home. But the previous Friday she had to call at the Kidlington Health Centre for Mr Evans, who had bronchitis and was due to see the doctor again at 4.30 that day. But the weather was so dreadful that she thought he ought to stay in. So she went herself to get Mr E another prescription, called in at the dispensing chemist, and then went home and got the tea. She got back to Quinn's house at about a quarter past six and stayed about half an hour to do the ironing.

'You left a note for him, didn't you, Mrs Evans?'

'I thought he'd wonder why I hadn't finished.'

'That was at about four o'clock, you say?'

She nodded, and felt suddenly nervous. Had poor Mr Quinn died on *Friday night*, just after she'd left, perhaps?

'We found the note in the wastepaper basket, Mrs Evans.'

'I suppose you would, sir. If he screwed it up, like.'

'Yes, of course.' Lewis found himself wishing that Morse was there, but he put the thought aside. A few interesting ideas were beginning to develop. 'You left the note in the lounge?'

'Yes. On the sideboard. I always left a note there at the end of the month – when me four weeks' cleaning was up, like.'

'I see. Can you remember if Mr Quinn's car was in the garage when you got back?'

'No, Sergeant. I'm sorry. It was raining, and I was on me bike and I just got in as fast as I could. Anyway, why should I look in the garage? I mean—'

'You didn't see Mr Quinn?'

'No, I didn't.'

'Ah well. Never mind. We're obviously anxious—'

'You think he died on Friday night, then?'

'No, I wouldn't say that. But if we could find what time he got back from the office – well, it would be a great help. For all we know, he didn't get back home at all on Friday night.'

Mrs Evans looked at him with a puzzled frown. 'But *I* can tell you what time he got home.'

The room was suddenly very quiet and Lewis looked up tensely from his notes. 'Will you say that again, Mrs Evans?'

'Oh yes, Sergeant. You see, I left this note for him and he must have seen it.'

'He *must* have done, you say?'

'Must have done. You just said it was in the wastepaper basket.'

Lewis sank back in the sofa, his excitement ebbing away. 'He could have found the note any time, I'm afraid, Mrs Evans.'

'Oh no. You don't understand. He'd seen the note before I got back at quarter past six.' Lewis was sitting very still again and listening intently. 'You see, he left a note for me, so—'

'*He left a note for you?*'

'Yes. Said he'd gone shopping, or something. I forget exactly – but something like that.'

'So you—' Lewis started again. 'You left the note at four o'clock and went back there at quarter past six, you say?'

'That's right.'

'So you think he must have got home – when? About five?'

'Well, yes. He usually got home about then, I think.'

'You're sure the note was for you?'

'Oh yes. It got me name on it.'

'Can you – can you remember exactly what it said?'

'Not really. But I tell you what, Sergeant. I might have still got it. I probably put it in me pinny, or something. I always wear—'

'Can you try to find it for me?'

As Mrs Evans went out into the kitchen, Lewis found himself praying to the gods that for once they would smile upon him, and he felt almost sick with relief when she came with a small folded sheet of paper, and handed it to him. He read it with the awesome reverence of a druid brooding on the holy runes:

Mrs E,
Just off shopping – shan't be long. NQ

It couldn't have been much briefer and it puzzled him a little; but he was fully aware of its huge importance.

' "Shopping", he says. Funny time for shopping, isn't it?'

'Not really, sir. The supermarket's open till nine of a Friday night.'

'The Quality supermarket, is that?'

'Yes, sir. It's only just behind the house, really. There's a pathway by the side of the crescent, and now that the fence is down you can get on to it from the side of the garden.'

Five minutes later Lewis thanked her fulsomely and left. By Jove, old Morse was going to be pleased!


It was just after one when Monica walked into the lounge bar. She spotted Morse immediately (though he appeared not to notice her) and after buying a gin and Campari she walked across and stood beside him.

'Can I get you a drink, Inspector?'

Morse looked up and shook his head. 'I seem to be off the beer today.'

'You weren't yesterday.'

'I wasn't?'

She sat down beside him and brought her lips close to his ear. 'I could smell your breath.'

'You smelled pretty good, too,' said Morse, but he knew that this was not to be a time for high romance. He could read the signs a mile away.

'I thought I might find you here.'

Morse shrugged non-committally. 'What have you got to tell me?'

'You don't beat about the bush, do you?'

'Sometimes I do.'

'Well, it's – it's about Friday afternoon.'

'News gets around.'

'You wanted to know what we were all doing on Friday afternoon, is that right?'

'That's it. Seems none of you were in the office, wherever else you were.'

'Well, I don't know about the others – no, that's not quite true. You see – Oh dear! You don't make it very easy for me. I was out all the afternoon and, well – I was with somebody else; and I suppose sooner or later you'll have to know who I was with, won't you?'

'I think I know,' said Morse quietly.

Monica's face dropped. 'You can't know. Have you already spoken—?'

'Have I spoken to Mr Martin? No, not yet. But I shall be doing so very soon, and I suppose he'll tell me the whole story, with the usual dose of reluctance and embarrassment – perhaps with a bit of anxiety, too. He *is* married, isn't he?'

Monica put her hand to her forehead and shook her head rather sadly. 'Are you a clairvoyant?'

'I'd solve all my cases a bit quicker if I were.'

'Do you want to hear about it?' She looked at him unhappily.

'Not now. I'd rather hear it from your boyfriend. He's not a very good liar.' He stood up and looked down at her empty glass. 'Gin and Campari, was it?'

She nodded, and thanked him; and as Morse walked over to the bar, she lit another cigarette and inhaled deeply, her immaculately plucked eyebrows narrowing into a worried frown. What on earth was she going to do if . . . ?

Morse was soon back again, and placed her drink neatly on to a beer mat. 'I see what you mean about expensive tastes, Miss Height.'

She looked up at him and smiled feebly. 'But – aren't you going to join me?'

'No. Not now, thank you. I'm a bit busier than usual this week, you know. I've got a murder to investigate, and I don't usually mix much with tarts, anyway.'

After he had gone Monica felt utterly miserable, her thoughts a pallid multitude that drifted along the sunless waters. How cruel he had been just now! Only yesterday she had experienced an unwonted warmth of pleasure in his company. But how she hated him now!

Morse, too, was far from happy with himself. He shouldn't really have treated her as callously as that. How stupid it was, anyway – feeling so childishly jealous! Why, he'd only met her once before. He could go back, of course, and buy her another drink . . . and say he was sorry. Yes, he could do that. But he didn't; for interwoven with the jealousy motif was something else: he sensed intuitively that Monica had lied to him.

# eleven

Apart from the fact that Mrs Greenaway, the upstairs tenant, had been delivered of a baby boy the previous Friday evening, Lewis had learned nothing much of interest from Mrs Jardine. She was unable to add anything of substance to the statement made to Constable Dickson the previous day, and Lewis had stayed with her no more than ten minutes. But he'd had his earlier triumph. Oh yes! And as that same afternoon he recounted to Morse his interview with Mrs Evans – and presented his prize – he felt very pleased with himself indeed. Yet Morse's reactions seemed decidedly lukewarm; certainly he'd looked long and hard at Quinn's brief note, but in general he appeared preoccupied with other things.

'You don't seem very happy with life, sir.'

'The majority of men lead lives of quiet desperation.'

'But if this doesn't cheer you up—'

'What? Don't be daft!' Almost physically Morse tried to shake off his mood of temporary gloom, and he looked down at the note once more. 'I couldn't have done much better myself.' He said it flippantly, but Lewis knew him better.

'Let's have it, sir.'

'What do you mean?'

'What would you have asked her?'

'Just what you did – I told you.'

'What else?'

Morse appeared to consider the question carefully. 'Perhaps one or two other things.'

'Such as?'

'Perhaps I'd have asked her if she'd looked in the wastepaper basket.'

'Really?' Lewis sounded unimpressed.

'Perhaps I'd have asked her if Quinn's anorak was there.'

'But—' Lewis let it ride.

'I'd certainly have asked her if the gas fire was on.'

Lewis began to catch the drift of Morse's mind, and he nodded slowly to himself. 'I suppose we'd better see her again, sir.'

'Oh yes,' said Morse quietly. 'We shall have to see her again.

But that's no problem, is it? The main think is that we seem
to have got Quinn alive till about six o'clock. I wonder ... ?' His
thoughts floated away again, but suddenly he sat upright and took
out his Parker pen. 'There's still a good deal to do here, though,
Lewis. Nip and see if he's back from lunch.'

'Who do you mean, sir?'

'I just told you – Martin. You going deaf?'


As Martin painfully corroborated Monica's story, Morse's facial
expression was that of a man with a rotten egg stuck just beneath
his nose. The pair of them had left the office at about 1.10 p.m.
No, not together – in separate cars. Yes, to Monica's bungalow.
Yes, to bed. (Putrescent, fetid egg!) That was all really. (All!
Christ! That was *all*, he'd said.)

'What time did you leave?'

'About a quarter to four.'

'And you didn't come back to the office at all?'

'No. I went straight home.'

'Nice little surprise for your wife.'

Martin was silent.

'Lewis! Go and see Miss Height. You've heard what this man
says. Get her story, and see if it fits.'

After Lewis had gone Morse turned to Martin and looked him
hard in the eyes. 'You're a cock-happy young sod, aren't you?'

The young man shook his head sadly. 'I'm not really, you
know, Inspector. I've only been unfaithful with Monica, never
anyone else.'

'You in love with her?'

'I don't know. This business has – I don't know, Inspector.
She's— Ah, what's it matter now!'

'Why did you leave so early?'

'There's Sally – that's Monica's daughter. She usually gets
home from school about quarter past four.'

'And you didn't want her to find you shagging her mother, is
that it?'

Martin looked up miserably. 'Haven't you ever been unfaithful, Inspector?'

Morse shook his head. 'No, lad. I've never had to be faithful,
you see.'

'There's – there's no need for all this to come out, is there?'

'Not really, no. Unless—'

'Unless what?' A look of alarm sprang into Martin's eyes, and Morse did nothing to dispel it.

'Tell me. This girl Sally: is she at school in Oxford?'

'Oxford High School.'

'Bit awkward with examinations, isn't it? I mean, with her mother—'

'No. You don't quite understand, Inspector. This Board doesn't examine in England at all.'

'Who examines Oxford High?'

'Oxford Locals, I think.'

'I see.'

After Martin had gone, Morse rang HQ and gave Constable Dickson his instructions; and he was smiling contentedly to himself when Lewis returned.

'She confirms what Martin says, sir.'

'Does she now?'

'You sound a bit dubious.'

'Do I?'

'You don't believe 'em?'

'For what it's worth, Lewis, I think they're a pair of bloody liars. But I may be wrong, of course. As you know, I often am.' He had that deprecatingly conceited look on his face which many found the Chief Inspector's least attractive trait, and Lewis was determined not to demean himself by trying to delve further into that cocky logic. For his part, he believed them, and high-and-mighty Morse could mumble away as he pleased.

'Didn't you hear me, Lewis?'

'Pardon sir?'

'What the hell's up with you today, man? I said go and get Ogleby. Can you do that small thing for me?'

Lewis slammed the door behind him and walked out into the corridor.

Morse had spoken no more than half a dozen words to Ogleby when they had been formally introduced the previous day, yet he had felt an instinctive liking for the man; and this impression was confirmed as Ogleby began to chat informatively and authoritatively about the work of the Syndicate.

'What about security?' asked Morse cautiously, like a timid skater testing the ice.

'It's a constant problem, of course. But everyone's conscious of it, and so in an odd sort of way the problem solves itself – if you see what I mean.'

Morse thought he did. 'I gather the Secretary's pretty keen on that side of things.'

'Yes, I suppose you could say that.'

Morse eyed him sharply. Had there been a tinge of irony – or even jealousy, perhaps – in Ogleby's reply? 'Is there *never* any malpractice?'

'Oh, I wouldn't say that. But that's a completely different question.'

'Is it?'

'You see if a candidate decided to cheat in the examination room, either by taking notes in with him or copying from someone else, then we've just got to rely on the invigilators keeping a very careful eye on things, and reporting anything suspicious directly to us.'

'That happens, does it?'

'Two or three times a year.'

'What do you do about it?'

'We disqualify the candidates concerned from every subject in the examinations.'

'I see.' Morse tried another angle. 'You send out the question papers before the examination, don't you?'

'Wouldn't be much good holding the examinations if we didn't, would it?'

Morse realized what a stupid question he'd asked, and continued rather hastily. 'No. I mean – if one of the teachers was dishonest, or something?'

'The question papers are sent out directly to examination departments, and then distributed to heads of centres – not to individual teachers.'

'But let's take a headmaster, then. If he was a crook – let's say he opened a particular package of question papers and showed them to his pupils—'

'It's as good a way as any for the headmaster to slit his throat.'

'You'd know, you mean?'

Ogleby smiled. 'Gracious, yes. We've got examiners and awarders who'd smell anything like that a mile away. You see we've got records going back over the years of percentage passes for all the subjects examined, and so we know the sort of pupils we're examining, the types of schools – all that sort of thing. But that's not really the point. Like all the examining Boards we inspect our centres regularly after they've been accepted, and they have to meet pretty high standards of integrity and administrative competence before they're recognized in the first place.'

'The schools are regularly inspected then?'

'Oh yes.'

'Is that the sort of job Mr Bland does in Al-jamara?'

Morse watched Ogleby carefully, but the deputy sailed serenly on. 'Among other things, yes. He's in charge of the whole administrative setup there.'

Morse decided that he might as well tackle the problem from the other end, and he delicately tiptoed his way over the ice again.

'Would it be possible for an outsider, one of the cleaners, say, to get into the cabinets in this office? And get the papers he wanted?'

'Technically, I suppose, yes. If he had the keys, knew where to look, knew the complicated system of syllabus numbering, had the intelligence to understand the various amendments and printing symbols. Then he'd have to copy what he'd got, of course. Every page of proofs and revises is carefully numbered, and no one could get away with just pinching a page.'

'Mm. What about examiners? Let's say they put a high mark down for a particular candidate who's as thick as a plank.'

'Wouldn't work, I'm afraid. The arithmetic of every single script is checked against the marksheet.'

'Well, let's say an examiner gives high marks for all of the answers on the script – even if they're rubbish.'

'If an examiner did that, he would have been kicked out years ago. You see the examiners are themselves examined by a team of what we call "awarders", who report on all the members of the various panels after each examination.'

'But the awarders could ...' No, Morse, let it go. He began

to see that it was all far more complex that he had imagined.

But Ogleby finished the thought for him. 'Oh, yes, Inspector. If one of the people *at the top* was crooked, it would be very easy. Very easy indeed. But why are you asking me all this?'

Morse pondered a while, and then told him. 'We've got to find a motive for Quinn's murder, sir. There are a hundred and one possibilities, of course, but I was just wondering if – if perhaps he'd found some er some suggestion of jiggery-pokery, that's all. Anyway, you've been very helpful.'

Ogleby stood up to go, and Morse too rose from his chair. 'I've been asking the others what they were doing last Friday afternoon. I suppose I ought to ask you too. If you can remember, that is.'

'Oh, yes. That's easy enough. I went down to the Oxford University Press in the morning, had a pretty late lunch at the Berni place there with the chief printer, and got back here about, oh, about half-past three, I should think.'

'And you spent the rest of the afternoon in the office here?'

'Yes.'

'Are you sure about that, sir?'

Ogleby looked at him with steady eyes. 'Quite sure.'

Morse hesitated, and debated whether to face it now or later. 'What is it, Inspector?'

'It's a bit awkward, sir. I understand from er from other sources that there was no one here in the latter part of Friday afternoon.'

'Well, your sources of information must be wrong.'

'You couldn't have slipped out for a while? Gone up to see the chief clerk or something?'

'I certainly didn't go out of the office. I might have gone upstairs, but I don't think so. And if I had, it would only have been for a minute or two, at the very outside.'

'What would you say, then, sir, if someone said there was no one here on Friday afternoon between a quarter past four and a quarter to five?'

'I'd say this someone was mistaken, Inspector.'

'But what if he insisted—?'

'He'd be a liar, then, wouldn't he?' Ogleby smiled serenely, and gently closed the door behind him.

Or *you* would, thought Morse, as he sat alone. And although you don't know it, my good friend Ogleby, there are two some-ones who say you weren't here. And if you weren't here, where the hell *were* you?

# twelve

The police car, white with a broad, pale blue stripe along its middle, stood parked by the pavement, and Constable Dickson knocked at the spruce detached bungalow in Old Marston. The door was immediately opened by a smartly dressed, attractive woman.

'Miss Height?'

'Yes?'

'Is your daughter in?'

Miss Height's features crumpled into a girlish giggle. 'Don't be silly! I'm only sixteen!'

Dickson himself grinned oafishly, and accepted the young lady's invitation to step inside.

'It's about Mr Quinn, isn't it? Ever so exciting. Coo. Just think. He worked in the same office as Mummy!'

'Did you ever meet him, miss?'

'No, worse luck.'

'He never came here?'

She giggled again. 'Not unless Mummy brought him here while I was slaving away at school!'

'She wouldn't do that, would she?'

She smiled happily. 'You don't know Mummy!'

'Why aren't you at school today, miss?'

'Oh, I'm taking some O-levels again. I took them in the summer but I'm afraid I didn't do too well in some of them.'

'What subjects are they?'

'Human Biology, French and Maths. Not that I've got much chance in Maths. We had Paper Two this morning – a real stinker. Would you like to see it?'

'Not now, miss. I er – I was just wondering why you weren't at school, that's all.' It wasn't very subtle.

'Oh, they let us off when we haven't got an exam. Great really. I've been off since lunchtime.'

'Do you always come home? When you're free, I mean?'

'Nothing else to do, is there?'

'You revise, I suppose?'

'A bit. But I usually watch telly. You know, the kiddies' programmes. Quite good, really. Sometimes I don't think I've grown up at all.'

Dickson felt he shouldn't argue. 'You've been here most days recently, then?'

'Most afternoons.' She looked at him innocently. 'I shall be here again tomorrow afternoon.'

Dickson coughed awkwardly. He'd done the bit of homework that Morse had told him to. 'I watched one of those kiddies' films, miss. About a dog. Last Friday afternoon, I think it was.'

'Oh yes. I watched that. I cried nearly all the way through. Did it make *you* cry?'

'Bit of a tearjerker, I agree, miss. But I mustn't keep you from your revising. As I say, it was your mother I really wanted to see.'

'But you said – you said you wanted to see *me*!'

'I got it a bit muddled, miss, I'm afraid. I sort of thought—' He gave it up and got to his feet. He hadn't done too badly at all really, and he thought the Chief Inspector would be pleased with him.

At 7 p.m. the same evening Morse sat alone in his office. A single tube of white strip-lighting threw a harsh unfriendly glare across the silent room, and a single yellow lamp in the yard outside the uncurtained window did little more than emphasize the blackness of the night. Occasionally, especially at times like this, Morse wished he had a home to welcome him, with a wife to have his slippers warmed and ready. It was at times like this, too, that murder seemed a crude and terrifying thing ... Dickson had reported on his visit to Sally Height, and the silhouettes on the furthest walls of the darkened cave were now assuming a firmer delineation. Monica had lied to him. Martin had lied to him.

It was odds-on that Ogleby had lied to him. Had Bartlett lied as well? Stocky, cautious little Bartlett, meticulous as a metronome. If *he* had murdered Nicholas Quinn ...

For half an hour he let his thoughts run wild and free, like randy rabbits in orgiastic intercourse. And then he put a stop to it. He needed a few more facts; and facts were facing him, here and now, in the dark blue plastic bag containing the items found in Quinn's pockets, in Quinn's green anorak, and in Lewis's inventories. Morse cleared the top of his desk and set to work. Quinn's pockets had thrown up little of surprise or interest: a wallet, a grubby handkerchief, half a packet of Polos, a diary (with not a single entry), 43½p, a pink comb, one half of a cinema ticket, two black biros, a strip of tired-looking Green Shield stamps, and a statement from Lloyds Bank (Summertown branch), showing a current account balance of £114.40. That was the lot, and Morse arranged each item neatly before him and sat surveying them for minutes, before finally taking a sheet of notepaper and listing each item carefully. Ye-es. The thought had flashed across his mind a few minutes earlier. Decidedly odd ... Next he picked up the anorak and took a further selection of objects from each side pocket: another grubby handkerchief, car keys, a black key case, two ancient raffle tickets, a further 23p, and an empty white envelope addressed to Quinn, with the word 'Bollox' written on the flap in pencil. 'Well, well,' mumbled Morse to himself. His randy rabbits could have a field day with *that*, but he decided to give them no chance. Again he listed each item with great precision and again sat back. It was just as he had thought, but it was too late to go back to the lonely rooms in Pinewood Close that night. A bit too creepy, anyway.

Having completed a synoptic review of the evidence before him, Morse systematically tackled each item severally. The wallet first: a driving licence, RAC membership card, Lloyds Bank cheque card, an outdated NHS prescription for Otosporon, the previous month's pay-slip, a blue outpatients' appointment card for the ENT department at the Radcliffe Infirmary, one five-pound note, three one-pound notes, and a Syndicate acknowledgement card on which were written two telephone numbers. Morse picked up the phone and dialled the first, but his ears were greeted only by a continuous high-pitched monotone. He dialled the second.

'Hello? Monica Height here.'

Morse hastily put down the receiver. It was naughty of him, he knew, but he had the feeling that Monica would not be very happy with him for the moment. Or with Constable Dickson. Yet it made him wonder exactly what the pattern of cross-relationships in the Syndicate had been.

It was the buff-coloured right-hand half of the cinema ticket which next attracted Morse's attention. Across the top were the numbers 102, beneath them the words 'Rear Lounge', and along the right edge, running down, the numbers 93550. On the back of the ticket was the design of a pentagram. Somebody must know which cinema it was, he supposed. Job for Lewis, perhaps ... And then it struck him. Fool of a fool! It wasn't 102 across the top at all. There was just the slightest gap between the 0 and the 2 and Morse saw the name of the cinema staring up at him: STUDIO 2. He knew the place – in Walton Street. Morse had bought a copy of the previous day's *Oxford Mail* (wherein the Quinn murder had been briefly reported) and he turned the pages and found that Tuesday was the critics' day for reporting to the citizens of Oxford on the quality of the entertainments currently available. Yes, there it was:

It is all too easy to see why *The Nymphomaniac* has been retained for a further week at Studio 2. The aficionados have been flocking to see the Swedish sexpot, Inga Nielsson, dutifully exposing her 40" bosom at the slightest provocation. Flock on.

Morse read the review with mixed feelings. Clearly, the critics hadn't yet gone metric, and this particular aficionado couldn't even spell the word. Yet big Inga seemed to Morse a most inviting prospect; and doubtless to many another like him. Especially perhaps when the boss was away one Friday afternoon ...? He flicked through the telephone directory, found the number, and asked to speak to the manager who surprisingly turned out to be the manageress.

'Oh yes, sir. All our tickets are traceable. Buff, you say? Rear circle? Oh yes. We should be able to help you. You see all the blocks of tickets are numbered and a record is kept at the start of each matinée, and then at six o'clock, and then at ten o'clock. Have you got the number?'

Morse read out the number and felt curiously excited.

'Just one minute, sir.' It turned into three or four, and Morse fiddled nervously with the directory. 'Are you there, sir? Yes, that's right. Last Friday. It's one of the first tickets issued. The doors opened at 1.15 and the programme started at 1.30. The first rear lounge number is 93543, so it must have been issued in the first five or ten minutes, I should think. There's usually half a dozen or so waiting for the doors to open.'

'You quite sure about this?'

'Quite sure, sir. You could come down and check if you wanted to.' She sounded young and pretty.

'Perhaps I will. What film have you got on?' He thought it sounded innocent enough.

'Not quite your cup of tea, I don't think, Inspector.'

'I wouldn't be too sure about that, miss.'

'*Mrs*. But if you do come, ask for me and I'll see you get a free seat.'

Morse wondered sadly how many more gift horses he'd be looking in the mouth. But it wasn't that at all really. He was just frightened of being seen. Now if she'd said ...

But she said something else, and Morse jolted upright in his chair. 'I think I ought to mention, Inspector, that someone else asked me the very same sort of thing last week and ...'

'*What?*' He almost screamed down the phone, but then his voice became very quiet. 'Say that again, will you, please?'

'I said someone else had—'

'When was this, do you remember?'

'I'm not quite sure; sometime – let's see, now. I ought to remember. It's not very often—'

'Was it Friday?' Morse was excited and impatient.

'I don't know. I'm trying to remember. It was in the afternoon, I remember that, because I was doing a stint in the ticket office when the phone rang, and I answered it myself.'

'Beginning of the afternoon?'

'No, it was much later than that. Just a minute. I think it was ... Just a minute.' Morse heard some chattering in the background, and then the manageress's voice spoke in his ear once more. 'Inspector, I think it was in the late afternoon, sometime. About five, perhaps. I'm sorry I can't—'

'Could have been Friday, you think?'

'Ye-es. Or Saturday, perhaps. I just—'

'A man, was it?'

'Yes. He had a nice sort of voice. Educated – you know what I mean.'

'What did he ask you?'

'Well, it was funny really. He said he was a detective story writer and he wanted to check up on some details.'

'What details?'

'Well, I remember he said he'd got to put some numbers on a ticket his detective had found, and he wanted to know how many figures there were – that sort of thing.'

'And you told him?'

'No, I didn't. I told him he could come round to see me, if he liked: but I felt a bit – well, you know, you can't be too careful these days.'

Morse breathed heavily down the phone. 'I see. Well, thank you very much. You've been extremely kind. I think, as I say, I shall probably have to bother you again—'

'No bother, Inspector.'

Morse put down the phone, and whistled softly to himself. Whew! Had someone else found Quinn's body and the cinema ticket before Tuesday morning? Long before? Saturday; the manageress had said it might have been Saturday. And it couldn't have been Friday, could it? About five, she'd said. Morse looked quickly again at the *Oxford Mail* and saw the times: *The Nymphomaniac*. 1.30 to 3.20 p.m. Until twenty past three on Friday Quinn had been feasting his eyes on Inga Nielsson's mighty bosom and few things, surely, would have dragged him out of Studio 2 before the film had finished. Unless, of course ... At long last it struck him: *the pretty strong probability that Quinn had not been sitting alone in Studio 2 that Friday afternoon.*

# thirteen

As Morse stood with Lewis in Pinewood Close at 2 p.m. on the following afternoon, awaiting the arrival of Mrs Jardine, he tried with little success to draw a veil over the harrowing events of the morning. Mr and Mrs Quinn had trained down from Huddersfield, and somewhere amid the wreckage of their lives, somewhere amid the tears and the heartbreak, they had managed to find reserves of quiet dignity and courage. Morse had accompanied Mr Quinn senior to the mortuary for the formal identification of his son, and then spent over an hour with them both in his office, unable to tell them much, unable to offer anything except the usual futile words of sympathy. And as Morse had watched the tragic couple climb into the police car for Oxford, he felt great admiration – and even greater relief. The whole interview had upset him, and apart from a few brief minutes with a reporter from the *Oxford Mail*, he had not been in the mood to grapple with the perpetually multiplying clues to the last hours lived by Nicholas Quinn.

Two men were repairing the street lamp in front of No 1, and Morse strolled over to them. 'How long before they come and smash it up again?'

'You never know, sir. But, to be truthful, we don't get too much vandalism round 'ere, do we, Jack?'

But Morse had no chance of hearing Jack's views on the local yahoos, for Mrs Jardine drew up in her car and the three of them disappeared into the house, where for half an hour they sat together in the front room. Mrs Jardine told them as much as she knew about her former tenant: about his coming to see her in mid-August; about her chat with Bartlett (Quinn's choice as referee); about his tidy habits and his punctuality in paying his rent; about his usual weekend routine; and about any and every thing Morse could think of asking her that might add to his picture of Mr Quinn alive. But he learned nothing. Quinn had been a model tenant, it seemed. Quiet, orderly, and no gramophone. Girlfriends? Not that she knew of. She couldn't stop that sort of thing, of course, but it was much better if her tenants

– well, you know, *behaved* themselves. The others – upstairs? Oh, they got along well with Mr Quinn, she thought, though she couldn't really *know*, could she? What a good job Mrs Greenaway hadn't been there on Tuesday, though! You could never tell – with the *shock*. Yes, that had been a real blessing.

It was another chilly afternoon, and Morse got up to light the fire, turning the automatic switch on the side as far as he could. But nothing happened.

'You'll have to use a match, Inspector. Those things never seem to work. How the manufacturers get away with it—'

Morse struck a match and the fire exploded into an orange glow.

'Do you make any extra charge for gas and electricity?'

'No. It's included in the rent,' replied Mrs Jardine. But as if to dispel any possible suspicion of excessive generosity, she hastily added that the tenants had to share the telephone bill, of course.

Morse was puzzled. 'I don't quite follow you.'

'Well, there's a shared line between them, you see. There's a phone upstairs in the Greenaways' bedroom and one here in this room.'

'I see,' said Morse quietly.

After the landlady had left them, Morse and Lewis went into the room where Quinn had been found. Although the curtains were now drawn back, it seemed no less sombre than when they were in it last; and certainly colder. Morse bent down and tried turning the switch on the gas fire. He tried again; and again. But nothing.

'Probably no batteries in it, sir.' Lewis unfastened the side panel, and produced two stumpy Ever Ready batteries, now covered with a slimy, mildewed discharge.

The same Thursday morning Joyce Greenaway had been moved from the Intensive Care Unit at the John Radcliffe Hospital; and when one of her old schoolfriends came to see her at 2.30 p.m. she was in a pleasant ward, two storeys below, in the company of three other recently delivered mothers. Conversation was babies, babies, babies, and Joyce felt buoyant. She should be out in a few days, and she felt a strangely satisfying surge of maternal emotions developing deep within herself. How she loved her darling little boy! He was going to be fine – there was no doubt of that now. But the problem of what to call him remained unresolved. Frank had decided that he didn't really like 'Nicholas' all that much, and Joyce wanted *him* to make the choice. She herself wasn't all that smitten with the name, anyway. It had been awfully naughty of her to mention the name in the first place. But she'd just *had* to see if Frank had suspected anything, and despite her earlier fears she now felt convinced that he hadn't. Not that there was *much* to suspect.

It had started just after Nicholas had come, at the beginning of September, when he'd always seemed to be running out of matches, or sugar, or milk tokens; and he'd been so grateful, and so attentive towards her – and she over six months gone! Then that Saturday morning when *she* had been out of milk, with Frank on one of his everlasting shifts, and she had gone down in her nightie and housecoat, and they had sat for a long time drinking coffee together in the kitchen, and she had longed for him to kiss her. And he had, standing beside her with his hands on her shoulders, and then, after delicately unfastening her housecoat, putting his right hand deep inside her nightie and gently fondling her small firm breasts. It had happened three times after that, and she'd felt a deep tenderness towards him, for he made no other demands upon her body than to pass the tips of his fingers silkily over her legs and over her swollen belly. And just that once she had done more than passively lean back and surrender herself to the exquisite thrill that his hands could bring to her. Just the once – when so diffidently and so lightly, her outstretched fingers had caressed him. Oh yes, so very, very lightly! She had felt an enormous inner joy as he had finally buried his head on her shoulder, and the things she'd whispered to him then were now the focus of her conscience-stricken thoughts. But Frank would never know, and she promised herself that never, never again would she ... would she ...

She was awoken by the clatter of cups at four o'clock, and a quarter of an hour later the trolley came round with books and newspapers. She bought the *Oxford Mail*.

Morse was a few minutes early for his appointment, but the Dean of the Syndicate was ready for him in his oak-panelled rooms on the Old Staircase in the inner quad, and the two men were chatting vaguely of this and that when at five past four a scout knocked and came in with a tray.

'I thought we'd have a drop of Darjeeling. All right with you?' The voice, like the man, was syrupy and civilized.

'Lovely,' said Morse, wondering what Darjeeling was.

The white-coated scout poured the dark brown liquid into bone china cups, embossed with the crest of Lonsdale College. 'Milk, sir?'

Morse watched it all with an amused detachment. The Dean, it seemed, always had a slice of lemon, and one half-teaspoonful of sugar, which the scout himself measured out, almost to the grain, and stirred in with high seriousness. The old boy probably got his scout to tie his shoelaces up for him! Cloud-cuckoo-land! Morse took a sip of the tea, sat back, and saw the Dean smiling at him shrewdly.

'You don't really approve, I see. Not that I blame you. He's been with me almost thirty years now, and he's almost—But, I'm sorry, I'm forgetting. You've come to see me about Mr Quinn. What can I tell you?'

The Dean was clearly a sensitive and cultured soul: he was due to retire in one year's time, at sixty-five, and was clearly saddened that the tragedy of Quinn's murder should have clouded a long and distinguished connection with the Syndicate. To Morse, it seemed a curiously self-centred commiseration.

'Would you say the Syndicate is a happy sort of place, sir?'

'Oh yes. I think everybody would tell you that.'

'No hostility? No er personal animosities?'

The Dean looked a little uneasy, and it was clear that he might have one or two reservations – minor ones, of course. 'There are always a few er difficulties. You find them in every er—'

'What difficulties?'

'Well – basically, I think, there'll always be just a little er friction, shall we say, between the older generation – my generation – and some of the younger Syndics. You always get it. It was just the same when I was their age.'

'The younger ones have their own ideas?'

'I'm glad they have.'

'Are you thinking of any particular incident?'

Again the Dean hesitated. 'You know the sort of thing as well as I do, surely? One or two people get a bit hot under the collar now and again.'

'Has this got anything to do with Mr Quinn?'

'Quite honestly, Chief Inspector, I think not. You see, one of the incidents I'm thinking of happened before Quinn was appointed – in fact it happened when we were appointing him.' He gave a brief account of the interviewing committee's disagreement over the choice of candidates, and Morse listened with deep interest.

'You mean Bartlett didn't want to appoint Quinn?'

The Dean shook his head. 'You misunderstand me. The Secretary was quite happy about him. But, as I say, personally he would have given the job to one of the others.'

'What about you, sir? What did you feel?'

'I er I thought the Secretary was right.'

'So Mr Roope was the fly in the ointment?'

'No, no. You still misunderstand me. Quinn was appointed by the *committee* – not by Roope.'

'Look, sir. Please be quite frank with me. Would I be right in saying that there's not much love lost between Bartlett and Roope?'

'Aren't you enjoying your tea, Chief Inspector? You've hardly touched a drop yet.'

'You're not going to answer my question, sir?'

'I really do think it would be fairer if you asked *them*, don't you?'

Morse nodded, and drained the lukewarm liquid. 'What about the permanent staff? Any er friction there?'

'Amongst the graduates, you mean? N-o, I don't think so.'

'You sound a bit dubious.'

The Dean sat back and slowly finished his own tea, and Morse realized he would have to push his luck a bit.

'Miss Height, for instance?'

'A lovely girl.'

'You mean we can't blame the others too much if . . .'

'If there's any of er of that sort of thing going on, I can only say that I know nothing about it.'

'Rumours, though?'

'We've all got more sense than to listen to rumours.'

'Have we?' But it was clear that the Dean was not to be drawn, and Morse switched the line of his questioning once more. 'What about Bartlett? Is he well liked?'

The Dean looked at Morse keenly, and carefully poured out more tea. 'What do you mean?'

'I just wondered if any of the other graduates had any cause to – to, you know—' Morse didn't know what he wondered; but the Dean, it seemed, did.

'I suppose you're thinking of Ogleby?'

Morse nodded sagely, and tried to ooze omniscience. 'Yes, it was Mr Ogleby I was wondering about.'

'That's ancient history, though, isn't it? It's a long time ago, now. Huh! I remember at the time thinking that Ogleby was potentially the better man. In fact, I voted for him. But with hindsight I'm sure that Bartlett was the wiser choice, and we were all very glad that Ogleby was willing to accept the post of Deputy Secretary. Very able man. I'm quite sure that if he'd wanted to, he ...' The Dean talked freely now, and Morse felt his own attention drifting further and further away. So, Bartlett and Ogleby had applied for the Secretaryship together, and Ogleby had been turned down; and perhaps the slight had rankled on and on over the years – might still be rankling on. But what on earth could that have to do with the murder of Quinn? If Bartlett had been murdered – or even Ogleby – yes! But ...

The Dean stood at the window and watched Morse walk briskly around the quad. He knew that for the last ten minutes his words had fallen on deaf ears, and for the life of him he was completely unable to fathom the look of quiet contentment which had so suddenly appeared on the Chief Inspector's face.

Lewis finished his own cup of tea and was leaving the police canteen as Dickson walked in.

'I see you're appealing for help, Sarge. Old Morse stuck, is he?'

He handed Lewis the *Oxford Mail* and pointed to a paragraph at the bottom of the front page:

MURDER INQUIRY
Police investigating the murder of Mr N. Quinn, 1 Pinewood
Close, Kidlington, whose body was found on Tuesday
morning by a colleague from the Foreign Examinations
Syndicate, are appealing to anyone who may have seen the
murdered man on either the evening of Friday, 21st November,
or on Saturday, 22nd November, to come forward. Chief
Inspector Morse, who is heading the inquiry, said today that
any such information could be vital in establishing the time
of Mr Quinn's death. An inquest will be held next Monday.

Lewis looked at the photograph beside the article, and handed the paper back to Dickson. In his inside pocket was the original which Morse had asked the Quinns to bring with them from Huddersfield. Sometimes, he had to agree, Morse *did* take on the dirty work; compared to which his present little assignment was a doddle.

He soon found the young manager and learned that the flimsy short roll of paper he had brought with him was a richly-seamed mine of information: the date at the top; the 'customer-reading' number on the right; the items purchased each classified according to the various departments, and designated by one of the Roman numerals I-IV; the number of the till at the bottom. 'Customer flow' (Lewis learned) was fairly constant on Fridays, with high takings for most of the day, and (though the manager refused to be precise) the items listed had doubtless been purchased in the late afternoon or early evening. If he had to guess? Well, between 5 and 6.30 p.m. Unfortunately, however, the plump waddling little woman who was summoned in her capacity as i/c Till 3 could remember nothing, and failed to register even the vaguest recollection of ever having seen the face on the photograph she was shown. It was the goods she always watched, you see; seldom the faces.

Ah well!

Lewis thanked the manager and left the Kidlington premises of the Quality supermarket. Morse wouldn't be too pleased, perhaps, but all the clues seemed to be fitting into a firm, clear pattern.

'But why why *why* didn't you tell me? You must have realized—'

'Come off it, Joyce! You *know* why. It would have upset you, and we've—'

'It wouldn't have been half such a shock as reading about it in the paper!'

He shook his head sadly. 'I just thought I was doing right, luv. That's all. Sometimes you just can't win, can you?'

'No, I suppose not.' She understood all right, but she knew that *he* didn't. How could he?

'As I say, there's no need to worry about *anything*. When you're better again, we can talk about things. But not now. It'll soon all blow over – you see; and we're all fixed up for the time being.'

No, he couldn't begin to understand. He was trying hard not to put it into so many words, but he'd got it all wrong. The fact was that she hadn't as yet given a single thought as to whether they should go back to live in Pinewood Close or not. No. There was something much more urgent on her mind for the minute, and of that she would tell him nothing. Not yet anyway.


# fourteen


Christopher Roope had willingly agreed to meet Morse, on Friday just after 12 noon, at the Black Dog in St Aldates, just opposite the great portal of Christ Church. Roope had mentioned that he might be a few minutes late – he had a tutorial until twelve – but Morse waited happily with a pint of beer in front of him. He looked forward to meeting the young chemist, for if any outsider was involved in the murder of Quinn, he'd decided that Roope was the likeliest candidate, and already he had gleaned a few significant facts about him. First, he had learned that Roope had spent some time with one of the Gulf Petroleum companies, and might therefore have been in some sort of liaison with the men of power. For a deal there must have been at some stage, doubtless (though later) involving Bland at the Oxford end, in a perverse, though infinitely profitable, betrayal of public trust. It was certainly a possibility. Second, Roope was a chemist : and whoever had murdered Quinn had a great deal of technical knowledge about the fatal dosages of cyanide. Who better than Roope? Third, it was Roope who had suddenly materialized in the Syndicate building at a very, very crucial time – 4.30 p.m. or thereabouts (according to Noakes) on the previous Friday; and it was Roope who had looked into the rooms of each of the graduate staff in turn. What exactly had he been doing there? And what had he done after Noakes had gone upstairs for tea ... ? Fourth, there was the strange animosity that existed between Roope and Bartlett, and it appeared to Morse that the explanation for such animosity probably lay deeper, far deeper, than any temporary clash of views over the appointment of Quinn. Yes ... It was interesting that the clash had been over *Quinn*. And that fitted well with the fifth fact, which Morse had patiently unearthed earlier that morning in the University Registry : the fact that Roope had been educated at a public school in Bradford, the city where Quinn had lived almost all his short life, first as a pupil and then as a teacher. Had the two men known each other before Quinn was appointed to the Syndicate? And why had Roope been so obviously anxious to get Quinn appointed? (Morse found himself dismissing the Dean's charitable view of his colleague's social conscience.) Why, then? Now, Quinn had been thirty-one and Roope was thirty, and if they had been friends ... Yet where was the logic in that? One didn't go around murdering one's friends. Unless, that is—

A trio of laughing, long-haired, bearded undergraduates came into the bar, T-shirted and bejeaned, and Morse pondered on the changing times. He had worn a scarf and a tie himself – and sometimes a blazer. But that seemed a long time ago. He drained his glass and looked at his watch.

'Chief Inspector Morse?' It was one of the bearded trio and Morse realized that he was a good deal further out of touch than he had imagined.

'Mr Roope?'

The young man nodded. 'Can I get you a refill?

'I'll get them—'

'No, no. My pleasure. What are you drinking?'

Over their beer a somewhat bemused Morse explained as much of the situation as he deemed prudent, and stressed the importance of trying to fix the exact time of Quinn's death. And when he came to ask about the visit to the Syndicate on the previous Friday, Morse was pleasantly impressed to find how carefully and indeed (if Noakes could be believed) how accurately Roope retraced his steps from the moment he had entered the building. All in all, Roope and Noakes appeared to corroborate each other's evidence neatly at almost every juncture. Yet there were several points on which Roope's memory seemed somewhat less than clear, and on which Morse immediately pressed him further.

'You say there was a note on Quinn's desk?'

'Yes. I'm sure the caretaker must have seen it too. We both—'

'But you don't remember exactly what it said?'

Roope was silent for a few seconds. 'Not really. Something about – oh, I don't know – being "back soon", I think.'

'And Quinn's anorak was on one of the chairs?'

'That's right. Over the back of the chair behind his desk.'

'You didn't notice if it was wet?'

Roope shook his head.

'And the cabinets were open, you say?'

'One of them was, I'm sure of that. The caretaker pushed it to and locked it.'

'Bit unusual for a cabinet to be left open – with Bartlett around, I mean?' Morse watched the chemist closely, but discerned no reaction.

'Yes.' And then Roope grinned disarmingly. 'Bit of a sod, you know, old Bartlett. Keeps 'em all on their toes.' He lit himself a cigarette and put the spent match carefully back into the box with his left hand.

'How do *you* get on with him, sir?'

'Me?' Roope laughed aloud. 'We don't see eye to eye, I'm afraid. I suppose you've heard—?'

'I gathered you weren't exactly bosom pals.'

'Oh, I wouldn't put it like that. You mustn't believe everything you hear.'

Morse let it ride. 'Mr Ogleby wasn't in his room, you say?'

'Not while I was there.'

Morse nodded, and believed him. 'How long *were* you there, sir?'

'Quarter of an hour, I suppose. Must have been. If Ogleby or any of the others were there – well, I just didn't see them, that's all. And I'm pretty sure I would have done if they *had* been there.'

Morse nodded again. 'I think you're right, sir. I don't think anyone was there.' His mind drifted off, and for a brief second one of the silhouettes on the cavern wall focused in full profile – a profile that Morse thought he could recognize without much difficulty ...

Roope interrupted his thoughts. 'Anything else I can tell you?'

Morse drained his beer and said there was. He asked Roope to account for his activities during the whole of the previous Friday, and Roope gladly obliged: he had caught the 8.05 to London; arrived at Paddington at 9.10; caught the Inner Circle tube to Mansion House; conferred with his publishers about the final proofs of a forthcoming opus on Industrial Chemistry; left about 10.45; had a chicken salad in the Strand somewhere; spent an hour or so in the National Portrait Gallery in Trafalgar Square; and then returned to Paddington, where he'd caught the 3.05 for Oxford.

Morse himself couldn't have specified the reason, but suddenly he became convinced that somehow, somewhere, Roope was lying. It was all too pat, too slick. A good deal of it must be true (the bit about the publishers, for instance). Mm. He'd obviously gone to London all right; but exactly when had he returned? Roope said he'd left his publishers at about 10.45 a.m. A taxi to Paddington, perhaps? Easy! *Roope could have been back in Oxford before lunchtime.* 'Just as a matter of interest, sir' (he asked it very mildly) 'do you think you could prove all that?'

Roope looked at him sharply. 'I don't suppose I could, no.' The eyes were steady and steely.

'You didn't meet anyone you knew in London?'

'I told you. I went to see—'

'Of course. But I meant later.'

'No, I didn't.' The words were slow and evenly spaced, and Morse sensed that in spite of his slim build and his rather mannered trendiness, Roope was probably considerably tougher, both physically and mentally, than he appeared to be. One thing was sure: he wasn't very happy when his word was questioned. Was that perhaps why he and Bartlett ... ?

'Well, never mind that now, sir. Tell me something else, if you will. Did you know Quinn before he came to Oxford?'

'No.'

'You came from that part of the country though, don't you?'

'You mean I haven't got an Oxford accent?'

'I'd put you down as a Yorkshireman.'

'You've done your homework, I see.'

'That's what they pay me for, sir.'

'I'm from Bradford, and so was Quinn. But let me spell it out. I'd never set eyes on him before he came before the interviewing committee. Do you believe that?'

'I believe everything you tell me, sir. Why shouldn't I?'

'You'd be a fool to believe everything some people told you.' There was little pretence now at masking the hostility in his voice, and Morse was beginning to enjoy himself.

'I think you ought to know,' said Morse quietly, 'that whatever else I am, I'm not a fool, sir.'

Roope made no reply and Morse resumed his questioning. 'Have you got a car?'

'No. I used to have, but I only live just up the Woodstock Road—'

'That's the bachelor flats, isn't it?'

Roope suddenly relaxed and smiled ingenuously. 'Look, Inspector, why don't you ask me something you *don't* know?'

Morse shrugged his shoulders. 'All right. Tell me this. Was it raining when you came back from London?'

'Raining like hell, yes. I—' Suddenly the light dawned in his eyes. 'Yes. I got a *taxi* from the station – straight to the Syndicate! There'll be a record of that somewhere, surely?'

'Do you remember the driver?'

'No. But I think I remember the cab firm.'

Roope was right, of course. It shouldn't be all that difficult. 'We could try to—'

'Why not?' Roope got to his feet and picked up a pile of books. 'No time like the present, they say.'

As they walked up to Carfax and then left into Queen Street, Morse felt that he had gone wrong somewhere, and he said nothing until they reached the railway station, where a line of taxis was parked alongside the pavement. 'You'd better leave it to me, sir. I've got a bit of experience—'

'I'd rather do it myself, if you don't mind, Inspector.'

So Morse left him to get on with it; and stood there waiting under the 'Buffet' sign, feeling (he told himself) like the proverbial spare part at a prostitute's wedding.

Five minutes later a crestfallen Roope rejoined him: it wasn't going to be so easy as he'd thought, though he'd still like to do it himself, if Morse didn't mind, that was. But why should Morse mind? If the young fellow was as anxious as all that to justify himself … 'Like another beer?'

They walked through the ticket area and came to the barrier. 'We only want a beer,' explained Morse.

'' 'Fraid you'll need platform tickets, sir.'

'Ah, bugger that,' said Morse. He turned to Roope: 'Let's walk down to the Royal Oxford.'

'Just a minute!' said Roope quietly. His eyes were shining again, and he retraced his steps and tapped the ticket collector on the shoulder. 'Do you remember me?'

'Don't think so, mate.'

'Were you here on duty last Friday afternoon?'

'No.' Dismissive.

'Do you know who was?'

'You'd have to ask in the office.'

'Where's that?'

The man pointed vaguely. 'Not much good now, though. Lunchtime, isn't it?'

Clearly it wasn't Roope's day, and Morse put a sympathetic hand on his shoulder, and turned to the ticket collector. 'Give us two of your platform tickets.'

*

Half an hour later, after Roope had left him, Morse sat deep in thought and, to the teenaged couple who came to sit opposite him at the narrow buffet table, his face seemed quite impassive. Yet had they looked more carefully at him, and rather less eagerly towards each other, they might just have spotted the mildest hint of a satisfied smile trying to hide itself around the corners of his mouth. He sat quite still, his grey eyes staring unblinkingly into some great blue beyond, as the unresting birds of thought winged round and round his brain ... until the London train came lumbering massively alongside the platform and finally broke the spell.

The young couple got up, kissed briefly but passionately, and said their fond farewells.

'I won't come on the platform,' he said. 'Always makes me miserable.'

'Yeah. You ge' off now. See you Sat'day.'

'You bet!'

The girl walked off in her high-heeled boots towards the door leading to Platform 1, and the boy watched her as she went, and fished for his platform ticket.

'Don't forge'. *I'll* bring the drinks this time.' She almost mouthed the words, but the boy understood and nodded. Then she was gone; and Morse felt the icy fingers running down from the top of his spine. *That* was the memory that had been eluding him. Yes! It all came back in a rushing stream of recollection. He'd been an undergraduate then and he'd invited the flighty little nurse back to his digs in Iffley Road and she'd insisted on bringing a bottle because her father kept a pub and she'd asked him what his favourite drink was and he'd said Scotch and she'd said it was hers too not so much because she enjoyed the taste but because it made her feel all sexy and ... Christ, yes!

Morse shut off the distant, magic memories. The main silhouette was growing blurred again; but others now appeared upon the wall of the darkened cave, and together they fell into a more logical grouping. Much more logical. And as Morse handed in his platform ticket and walked out into the bright afternoon, he was more firmly convinced than ever that *someone else* had been in Studio 2 that Friday afternoon. He looked at his watch: 1.45 p.m. Tempting. By Jove, yes! The cinema was only three or four minutes' walk away, and Inga would be showing 'em all a few tricks. Ah well.

He signalled for a taxi: 'Foreign Examinations Syndicate, please.'

# fifteen

'I don't care what you ask her,' snapped Morse. 'When I've fetched her in here, just keep her talking for ten minutes, that's all I ask.' Lewis, who half an hour previously had been summoned to the Syndicate building once more, looked inordinately uncomfortable. 'What do you want me to find out, though?'

'Anything you like. Ask her what her measurements are.'

'I wish you'd try to be serious, sir.'

'Well, ask her whether gin goes straight to her tits, or something.'

Lewis decided he would get nowhere with Morse in such a mood. What had happened to him? Something, surely; for suddenly he seemed as chirpy as a disc jockey.

Morse himself crossed the corridor, knocked on Monica's door, and went in. 'Can you spare a minute, Miss Height? Won't take long.' He escorted her politely to Quinn's office, showed her to the chair that faced Lewis, her reluctant interlocutor, and himself stood idly aside.

The phone went a few minutes later and Lewis answered it. 'For you, sir.'

'Morse here.'

'Ah, Inspector. Can I see you for a minute? It's er rather important. Can you come along straight away?'

'I'm on my way.'

Both Lewis and Monica had heard the voice plainly, and Morse excused himself without further explanation.

Once inside Monica's office, he worked swiftly. First, the bulky sheepskin jacket hanging up in the wall cupboard. Nothing much in either pocket – nothing much of interest, anyway. Next, the handbag. It would surely be here, if anywhere. Make-up, cheque book, diary, Paper-mate pen, comb, small bottle of perfume, pair of ear-rings, programme for a forthcoming performance of *The Messiah*, packet of Dunhill cigarettes, matches – and a purse. His hands trembled slightly as he opened the catch and poked his fingers amidst the small change and the keys and the stamps and – *there it was*. Ye gods. He'd been right! He was breathing nervously and noisily as he closed the handbag, placed it carefully back in its former position, left the room, closed the door quietly behind him, and stood alone in the corridor. He saw the implications – the extraordinarily grave implications – of the discovery he had just made. Certainly he'd been fairly sure that with a bit of luck he might find something. Yet now he'd found it, he knew there was something wrong, something that rang untrue, something that had not occurred to him before. Still, there was a quick way of finding out.

He hadn't been away for more than two or three minutes, and Lewis was relieved to see him back so soon. He sat on the corner of the table and looked at her. There were times (not very frequent, he admitted) when he seemed to lose all interest in the female sex, and this was one of them. She might as well have been a statue cast in frigid marble for all the effect she was having on him now. It happened to all men – or, at least, so Morse had heard. The womenopause, they called it. He took a deep breath. 'Why did you lie to me about last Friday afternoon?'

Monica's cheeks flushed a deep crimson, but she was not, it appeared, excessively surprised. 'It was Sally, wasn't it? I realized, of course, what your man was up to.'

'Well?'

'I don't know. I suppose it sounded less – less sordid, somehow, saying we went to my place.'

'Less sordid than what?'

'You know – motoring around, stopping in lay-bys and hoping no one else would pull in.'

'And that's what you did?'

'Yes.'

'Would Mr Martin back you up?'

'Yes. If you explained to him why—'

'You mean *you* haven't done that already?' The tone of Morse's voice was becoming increasingly harsh, and Monica coloured deeply again.

'Don't you think we ought to ask him?'

'No I don't! You've got him round your little finger, woman! Anyone can see that. I'm not interested in your web of lies. I want the truth! We're investigating a murder – not a bloody parking offence!'

'Look, Inspector. I can't do much more than tell you—'

'Of course you can! You can tell me the *truth*.'

'You seem terribly sure of—'

'And so I am, woman! What the hell do you think *that* is?' He banged his right hand furiously on the top of the desk, and revealed the torn-off half of a cinema ticket. Across the top were the letters 10, and almost immediately after them the number 2; beneath were the words 'Rear Lounge', and along the right-hand edge, running downwards, were the numbers 93556.

Monica looked down at the ticket as if mesmerized.

'Well?'

'I suppose it was *you* who arranged the little charade on the phone with Dr Bartlett?'

'I've done worse in my time,' said Morse. And suddenly, and quite inexplicably, he felt a surge of sympathy and warmth towards her, and his tone softened as he looked into her eyes: 'It'll come out in the end – you know that. Please let me have the truth.'

Monica sighed deeply. 'Do you mind getting me a cigarette, Inspector? As I think you know, mine are in my handbag.'

Yes (she said) Morse had been right. With Sally back from school that afternoon, there was no chance of going home, and she wasn't that keen, in any case. The whole thing was her fault quite as much as Donald's, of course; but recently she had been increasingly anxious to end the futile and dangerous affair. It was Donald who suggested they should go to the cinema and she had finally agreed. It would be an unnecessary risk to be seen going in together, and so it was arranged that he should go in at twenty past one, and she a few minutes later. They would each buy a ticket separately, and he would sit on the back row of the rear lounge in Studio 2 and watch out for her. And that's what they'd done. Everything had gone as planned, and they had left the cinema at about half-past three. They'd each taken their car, and hers had been parked in Cranham Terrace, at the side of the cinema. She herself had gone straight home afterwards, and so, for all she knew, had Donald. Naturally they'd both been worried when they heard that the police wanted to know their whereabouts on Friday afternoon, and so they'd foolishly – well, Morse knew what they'd done. It wasn't all that far from the truth, though, was it? But, yes, they'd lied about that Friday afternoon. Of course, they had.

'Do you mind if we get your boyfriend in?' asked Morse.

'I think it would be better if you did.' She looked a little happier now, in spite of the jibe – certainly happier than Morse.

Pathetically Martin himself began to repeat the unauthorized version, but Monica stopped him. 'Tell them the truth, Donald. I just have. They know exactly where we both were on Friday afternoon.'

'Oh. Oh, I see.'

Morse felt his morale sagging ever lower as Martin stumbled his way through the same cheap little story. No discrepancy anywhere. He, like Monica it seemed, had gone straight home afterwards. And that was that.

'One more question.' Morse got up from the edge of the table and leaned against the nearest cabinet. It was a vital question – *the* vital question, and he wanted to witness their immediate reactions. 'Let me ask you both once again – did either of you see Mr Quinn on Friday afternoon? Please think very, very carefully before you answer.'

But it seemed that neither of them had any wish to think unduly carefully. Their faces registered blank. They shook their heads, and with apparent simplicity and earnestness they said that they hadn't.

Morse took another deep breath. He might as well tell them, he thought – that is, if they didn't know already. 'Would it surprise you both if I told you that ...' (Morse hesitated – dramatically, he hoped) 'that there was another of your colleagues in Studio 2 last Friday afternoon?'

Martin turned deathly pale, and Monica opened her mouth

like a chronic asthmatic fighting for breath. Morse (as he later realized) would have been wiser if he had allowed his little speech to take its full effect. But he didn't. 'You may well look surprised. You see, we know exactly where Mr Quinn was on Friday afternoon. He was sitting along with the pair of you – in the rear lounge of Studio 2!'

Martin and Monica Height stared at him in stupefied astonishment.

After they had gone, Morse turned to Lewis: 'That'll give 'em something to think about.'

But Lewis was feeling far from happy, and he said so. 'I hope you'll forgive me, sir, but—'

'C'mon, Lewis. Out with it!'

'Well. I don't think you handled it very well.' He sat back and waited for the explosion.

'Nor do I,' said Morse quietly. 'Go on.'

'You see, sir, I had the impression that when you said one of the others was in the cinema – well, they didn't seem *surprised* at all. It was almost as if—'

'I know what you mean. It was almost as if they expected me to say someone else, wasn't it?'

Lewis nodded vigorously. 'But they really *were* surprised when you said it was Quinn.'

'Ye-es. You're right. And there's only one other person it could have been, isn't there? Bartlett was in Banbury that afternoon.'

'We haven't checked on that.'

'I don't think we shall have much trouble in finding a few headmasters to back up his alibi. No. I don't think there's much doubt where Bartlett was that afternoon.'

'That leaves Ogleby, then, sir.'

Morse nodded.

'Shall I go and fetch him, sir?'

'What do you think?' His customary confidence had deserted him, and Lewis got up and walked to the door. 'No, Lewis. Leave it a while, please. I want to think things through a bit more carefully.'

Lewis shrugged his shoulders with some impatience and sat

down again. Morse didn't seem quite the man he had been, one way or another; but Lewis knew from previous experience that it wouldn't be long before something happened. Something was always happening when Morse was around.

And even as Lewis righteously reviewed the perfectly valid points he had just been making, Morse himself was conscious of an even greater failure in his own powers of logical analysis. Clown of a clown! Martin and Monica Height! Why had they ever told that abject lie in the first place? There was every risk (with Sally home so often) that even a moderately competent detective would pretty soon ferret out the truth about that. Why, then? And suddenly the answer presented itself, pellucidly clear: *there was an even greater risk about telling the truth.* If they had gone to the cinema together, why not say so? It seemed an infinitely less reprehensible piece of behaviour than the sordid liaison to which they had both been prepared to admit. People *did* go to the pictures together. It would cause a bit of talk – of course it would – if someone saw them. But ... The silhouetted figures once again reformed, and they were all now grouping around one man. Arnold Philip Ogleby.

'You're right, you know, Lewis. Go and fetch him straight away.'

After they had left Quinn's office, Donald and Monica had stood silent for a few seconds in the polished corridor. 'Come in a second,' whispered Monica. She closed her own office door behind her, and looked at him fiercely. She spoke clearly and quietly, and with a force that was impressive. 'We don't say a word about it. Is that clear? *Not a single word!*'


## sixteen

Ogleby looked tired, and Morse decided he might as well be short and sharp. He knew he was taking a risk, but he'd played longer shots before – *and* won.

'You say, sir, that you came back to the office after lunch last Friday afternoon?'

'We've been over that before.'

Morse ignored him and continued. 'But you lied to me. You were seen outside this office last Friday afternoon. To be precise, you were seen going into Studio 2 in Walton Street.'

Ogleby sat placidly in his chair. He seemed in no way surprised indeed, if anyone were surprised it was Morse, who expected almost anything except the answer he received. 'Who saw me?'

'You don't deny it?'

'I asked you who it was that saw me.'

'I'm afraid I can't tell you that, sir. I'm sure you understand why.'

Ogleby nodded disinterestedly. 'As you wish.'

'We also have evidence, sir, that Mr Quinn was in Studio 2 that afternoon.'

'Really? Did somebody see him, too?'

Morse felt progressively less at ease with the man. It was one of the troubles with lies – his own lies; but he solved the problem by ignoring it. 'What time did you go to the cinema, sir?'

'Don't you know?' (There it was again!)

'I'd like your own statement.'

For a few seconds Ogleby appeared to be weighing the pros and cons of coming clean. 'Look, Inspector. In a way I suppose I lied to you a little.' (Lewis was scribbling as fast as he could.) 'We finish here, officially that is, at five. I try to put in my time as honestly as I can, and I think anyone you speak to here will confirm that. I'm never late, and I often work well after the rest have gone. On Friday, I agree, I left a bit early. I should think about a quarter to five, or so.'

'And you went to Studio 2.'

'I live in Walton Street, you know. It's not far away.'

'You went there?'

Ogleby shook his head. 'No.'

'Will you tell me why you went?'

'I didn't.'

'Have you ever been?'

'Yes.'

'Why?'

'I'm a lecherous old man.'

Morse switched his line of attack. 'Were you still here when Mr Roope came into the building?'

'Yes. I heard him talking to the caretaker.'

Again it was the answer that Morse had least expected, and he felt increasingly bewildered. 'But you weren't in your room. Your car—'

'I didn't come in a car on Friday.'

'You didn't see Quinn – in the cinema, I mean?'

'I wasn't in the cinema.'

'Did you see Miss Height and Mr Martin there?'

Surprise certainly registered now. 'Were *they* there?' Morse could have sworn that Ogleby had not known of *that*, at any rate, and in a blindingly perverse sort of way, he felt very tempted to believe the man. 'Did you enjoy the film, sir?'

'I didn't see it.'

'You enjoy pornographic films, though?'

'I've sometimes thought that if I were a film producer I'd make something *really* erotic, Inspector. I think I've got the right sort of imagination.'

'You didn't keep your ticket?'

'I didn't have a ticket.'

'Will you look for it, sir?'

'Not much point, is there?'

Whew!

Morse decided that he might as well go the whole hog now. Few secrets could be kept for long in a place like the Syndicate, and he realized that he would be losing nothing – might, in fact, be gaining – by coming out into the open.

With Ogleby gone, he invited Bartlett along to Quinn's office, and told him what he had learned that afternoon: told him of the deserted office he had left behind him when he'd gone to Banbury; told him of the mammary magnetism of Miss Inga Nielsson; told him of his difficulties in establishing the where-abouts of everyone on that Friday afternoon; told him, indeed, most of what he knew, or suspected, to be true. It wasn't really giving much away for most of it would have to come out in the wash fairly soon anyway. Finally, he told Bartlett that he would be grateful of a more accurate timetable of *his* movements; and all in all Bartlett hadn't taken things too badly. He could (he said) so very easily establish his own whereabouts; and there and then he rang the Head of Banbury Polytechnic and put him straight on to Morse. Yes, Bartlett had addressed a meeting of Heads; had arrived about five to three; together they had taken a glass of sherry; and the meeting was over about twenty, twenty-five past four. That was that, it seemed.

Bartlett asked if he was allowed to make his own observations on what he'd been told, and it was quite obvious that he was a far shrewder judge of his fellows than Morse had given him credit for. 'I'm not *all* that surprised, Inspector, about Miss Height and Martin. She's a very attractive girl: she's attractive to me, and I'm getting an old man; and Martin hasn't had the happiest of marriages, so I'm led to believe. There have been the occasional rumours, of course; but I've said nothing. I hoped it was just one of those brief infatuations – we've all had them in our time, and I thought it best to let it blow itself out. But – but, I must be honest, I'm very surprised by what you told me about Ogleby. It just doesn't seem to fit in. I've known him many years now, and he's – well, he's not like that.'

'We've all got our little weaknesses, sir.'

'No, you misunderstand me. I didn't mean whether he'd want to go to a sexy film or not. I've often . . . Well, never mind about that. No. It was about him saying he was *here*. You see, he's just not the sort of man who lies about things, and yet you say he insists that he was here when Roope came.'

'That's what he says.'

'And Roope says he wasn't in his own office, or anywhere around?'

'The caretaker backs him up.'

'He might have been upstairs.'

'I don't think so. Mr Ogleby himself says he heard Roope come in.'

Bartlett shook his head slowly and frowned. 'What do the girls say?'

'What girls?'

'The girls who collect the out-trays.'

Morse mentally kicked himself. 'What time are the trays collected?'

'Four o'clock every afternoon. The Post Office van is usually here about four-fifteen, and we like to have everything ready before then.'

I bet you do, thought Morse.

Bartlett rang through to the Registry and almost immediately a young, fair-haired girl came in and tried to keep her head as Morse questioned her. She had collected the trays on Friday afternoon. Yes, at four o'clock. And no one was there. Neither Ogleby, nor Miss Height, nor Martin, nor Quinn. No, she was *quite* sure. She'd mentioned to the other girls how odd it seemed.

Bartlett watched her distastefully as she left. He was wondering exactly how much work the 'other girls' had been doing when his back was turned.

Morse, as he walked slowly up the corridor with Bartlett, realized how very little he knew about the tangled complexity of relationships within the office. 'I'd like to have a long chat with you sometime, sir – about the office, I mean. There are so many things—'

'Why not come out and have a meal with us? My wife's a jolly good cook, you'll find. What about it?'

'That's very kind of you, sir. When do you suggest?'

'Well. Any time, really. Tonight, if you like.'

'Your wife—'

'Oh, don't worry about that. Leave it to me.' He disappeared into his office, and returned a couple of minutes later. 'Do you like steak, Inspector?'

As they walked to the car, both Lewis and Morse were deep in thought. The case was throwing up enough clues to solve a jumbo crossword, but somehow they wouldn't quite fit into the diagram.

'Nice fellow, Bartlett,' ventured Lewis, as they drove along the Woodstock Road towards the ring-road perimeter.

Morse did not reply. Bit too nice, perhaps, he was thinking. Far too nice, really. Like one of those suspects in a detective story who like as not turns out to be the crook. Was it possible! Was there any way in which the sturdy, shrewd, efficient little

Secretary could have contrived the murder of Nicholas Quinn? As Lewis picked up speed down the long hill towards Kidlington, Morse began to see that there *was* a way. It would have been fiendishly clever; but then for all Morse knew ... Oxford was full of clever people, wasn't it? And all at once it occurred to Morse that he was in very real danger of underestimating *all* of those he'd interviewed so far. Why, even now, perhaps, they were all sitting there quietly laughing at him.

# seventeen

Morse sat alone in his office. It was over two and a half hours before he was due at the Bartletts' and he welcomed the solitude and the chance to think.

The groceries which Quinn had purchased and the list of the provisions found in his kitchen proved more interesting than Morse had expected. Two pieces of steak and a bag of mushrooms, for instance. Bit extravagant, for one person? Might it have been for *two*? Two lovers? Morse pictured again the girl at the buffet door that led to Platform 1, and she merged into the figure of Monica Height. Could it have worked? Monica now admitted going to the cinema – with Martin, though. Could he forget Martin? Spineless creature. And so besotted with Monica that he'd say anything – if she told him to, or bribed him to. Think on, Morse! Monica and Quinn, then. Back row of the rear lounge; awkward unfastenings and frenetic fondlings, with the promise of still more glorious things in store – later. Later, yes. But where? Not at her place : impossible with Sally around. Why not at *his*? He could get some food in (steak? mushrooms?), and she would cook it for him. She'd love to. 'And don't forget, Nick, *I'll* bring the drinks this time. Sherry, isn't it? Dry sherry? I like that, too. And I'll bring a bottle of Scotch, as well. It always does things to me ...' Possible. A starting point anyway.

Morse looked at the two lists again, and noticed a fact he'd missed before. Quinn already had two half-pound packs of butter in his fridge, yet for some reason he'd bought another. Different brand, too. Very odd. Like a few other facts. He took a piece of paper and wrote them down:

(a) Position of Quinn's coffee table indicated that he'd probably been sitting in the draught. (Steady, Sherlock!)
(b) No spent matches found in either kitchen or living room; no matches found in Quinn's pockets. (Remember: Mrs E had already cleaned; she'd only returned for the ironing and had *not* cleared the wastepaper basket again.)
(c) More butter bought, when plenty in stock. (Forget it?)
(d) Note left by Quinn for Mrs E: vague enough to fit virtually any occasion? (Not *all* that vague though.)

Morse sat back and looked at his handiwork. Individually each point seemed pretty thin; but collectively – did they add up to something? Something like assuming that *Quinn did not return from work at all that Friday evening*? Had it been somebody else who lit the fire, and bought the groceries, and wrote a note for Mrs Evans? Think on, Morse! Think on, my boy! It was possible. Another starting point. Could the mysterious somebody have been Monica? (His mind kept coming back to her.) But she must have done home to Sally sometime. (Job for Lewis – check.) Martin? He must have gone home to his wife some time. When? (Job for Lewis – check.) And anyway, neither of them knew enough about cyanide, did they? Poisoning was a highly specialized job. (A woman's weapon, though.) Now, Roope was a chemist. And Ogleby knew enough ... Roope or Ogleby – a much likelier pair to choose from. But Roope was out of Oxford until about 4.15 p.m. (Or so he said.) And Ogleby went home a bit early. (Or so he said.) Mm. And what about Bartlett? Kidlington was on the main road from Banbury, and the main road passed no more than thirty yards from Pinewood Close. If he'd left Banbury at 4.25 p.m. and really pushed it, 70 mph say, he could have been in Kidlington by, well, ten to five? Opportunity enough for any of them really. For if Quinn had discovered that one of the four ...

Morse knew he wasn't getting very far. It was the *method* he couldn't fathom. But one thing was becoming an ever firmer conviction in his mind: whoever had come to Pinewood Close that Friday evening, *it hadn't been Nicholas Quinn*. Leave it there for the minute, Morse. Think of something else. Always the best way, and there was one thing he could check on straightaway.

He called in Peters, the handwriting pundit, showed him the note written to Mrs Evans, and gave him one of the sheets of Quinn's writing taken from Pinewood Close.

'What do you think?'

Peters hesitated. 'I'd need to study—'

'What's stopping you?'

Nothing had ever been known to hurry or ruffle Peters, an ex-Home Office pathologist, who in his younger days had made a considerable name and a considerable income for himself by disobeying the two cardinal rules for success – of thinking quickly and of acting decisively. For Peters thought at the speed of an arthritic tortoise and acted with the decisiveness of a soporific sloth. And Morse knew him better than to do anything but sit quietly and wait. If Peters said it was, it was. If Peters said that Quinn had definitely written the note, Quinn had definitely written the note. If he said he wasn't sure, he wasn't sure: and no one else in the world would be sure.

'How long will you be, Peters?'

'Ten, twelve minutes.'

Morse therefore knew that in about eleven minutes he would have his answer, and he sat quietly and waited. The phone went a few minutes later.

'Morse. Can I help you?'

It was the switchboard. 'It's a Mrs Greenaway, sir. From the John Radcliffe. Says she wants to talk to the man in charge of the Quinn murder.'

'That's me,' said Morse, without much enthusiasm. Mrs Greenaway, eh? The woman above Quinn. Well, well.

She had read the report in the *Oxford Mail* (she said) and felt that she ought to ring the police. Her husband wouldn't be very happy but— (Come on, girl, come on!) Well, she wasn't to have the baby until December, but she'd known – about four o'clock on Friday. The contractions— (Come on, girl!) Well, she'd rung up the works where Frank ('my husband, Inspector'), where Frank worked, and tried to get a message to him. But something must have gone wrong. She'd sat there by the window, watching and waiting, but no one came; and then she'd rung the works again about a quarter to five. She wasn't really worried, but she'd feel happier if Frank ... Anyway she could always ring the hospital herself. They would send an ambulance straightaway; and she wasn't *absolutely* sure. It could have been just— (Come *on*!) Anyway, she saw Quinn come in, in his car, just after five.

'You *saw* him?'

'Yes. About five past five, it must have been. He drove in and put his car in the garage.'

'Was anybody with him?'

'No.'

'Go on, Mrs Greenaway.'

'Well, there's nothing else, really.'

'Did he go out again?'

'I didn't see him.'

'*Would* you have seen him?'

'Oh yes. As I say, I was looking out of the window all the time.'

'We think he went out to the shops, Mrs Greenaway. But you say—'

'Well, he could have gone out the back way, I suppose. You can get through the fence and on to the path, but—'

'But you don't think he did?'

'Well, I didn't hear him, and he wouldn't have gone over the back. It's ever so muddy.'

'I see.'

'Well, I hope—'

'Mrs Greenaway, are you absolutely sure you *saw* Mr Quinn?'

'Well, perhaps I didn't actually ... I *heard* him on the phone, though.'

'You *what*?'

'Yes. We've got a shared line, and it was just after he came in. I was really getting worried, and I thought I'd try the works again; but I couldn't get through, because Mr Quinn was using the phone.'

'Did you listen to what he was saying?'

'No, I'm sorry, I didn't. I'm not nosy like that.' (Of course not!) 'You see I just wanted him to get off the line, that's all.'

'Was he talking for long?'

'Quite a while. I picked up the phone two or three times and they were still—'

'You don't remember a name, *any* name, that Mr Quinn used? Christian name? Surname? Anything at all that could help us?'

Joyce Greenaway was silent for a minute. There *was* a very vague recollection, but it slipped away from her. 'I—No, I can't remember.'

'Not a woman, was it?'

'Oh no. It was a man all right. Sounded an educated sort of man – well, you know what I mean, it wasn't a common sort of voice.'

'Were they having a row?'

'No. I don't think so. But I didn't listen in. I didn't *really*. I was just getting impatient, that's all.'

'Why didn't you go down and tell Mr Quinn what the situation was?'

Joyce Greenaway hesitated a little, and Morse wondered exactly why. 'Well, we weren't, you know, as friendly as all *that*.'

'Look, Mrs Greenaway. Please think very hard. It's vitally important – do you understand? If you could remember – even the slightest thing.'

But nothing would come, although the outline of that name still lurked subliminally. If only—

Morse did it for her. 'Ogleby? Mr Ogleby? Does that ring any bells?'

'No-o.'

'Roope? Mr Roope? Bartlett? Dr Bartlett? Mar—'

Joyce's scalp tingled. She'd been fishing for a verbal shape like 'Bartlett'. Could it have been? She wasn't really listening to Morse now. 'I can't be sure, Inspector, but it might have been Bartlett.'

Whew! What a turn-up for the books! Morse said somebody would be in to see her, but it would have to be the next day; and Joyce Greenaway, feeling a strange mixture of relief and trepidation, walked slowly back to the maternity ward.

Peters had been sitting quite motionless for the past two or three minutes, openly listening to the conversation, but he made no comment. 'Well?' said Morse.

'Quinn wrote it.'

Morse opened his mouth, but closed it again. Any protestation was futile. Peters said it was; so it *was*.

Why not go with the evidence, Morse and fling your flimsy fancies aside? Quinn got back home about five; he wrote a note for Mrs Evans; and he rang somebody up – a well-spoken somebody, whose name may have been Bartlett.

# eighteen

Mrs Bartlett was something of a surprise. She was three or four inches taller than her husband, and she ordered him around as if he were a naughty but lovable little schoolboy. There was another surprise, too. No one had mentioned to Morse that the Bartletts had a son, and the rather slovenly dressed, sullen-looking, bearded young man who was introduced as Richard seemed not particularly anxious to make an immediately favourable impression. But whilst the four of them sat rather awkwardly drinking their sherry, it became apparent that under his skin young Richard had a pleasant and attractive personality. As the ice thawed, he spoke with an easy humour and a total lack of self-consciousness; and as he and Morse discussed the respective merits of the Solti and Furtwängler recordings of *The Ring*, Mrs Bartlett slipped away to push a cautious fork into the Brussels sprouts, and summoned her husband to open the wine. The table was immaculately set for the four of them, the silver cutlery winking and sparkling on the white tablecloth in the dimly lit room. The vegetables were almost ready.

Bartlett himself refilled Morse's glass. 'Nice little sherry, isn't it?'

'Indeed,' said Morse. He noticed that the label was different from that on the sherry bottle found in Quinn's rooms.

'Any more for you, Richard?'

'No.' It sounded oddly abrupt, as though there lurked some dark and hidden enmity within the Bartlett clan.

The soup was ready now, and Morse tossed back the last of his sherry, got to his feet, and walked across the wide room rubbing his hands together.

'Come on then, Richard.' His mother said it pleasantly, but Morse could hear the underlying note of tension.

'Don't worry about me. I'm not hungry.'

'But you *must*, Richard. I've—'

The young man stood up, and a strange light momentarily blazed in his eyes. 'I've just told you, mother, I'm not hungry.'

'But I've got it all ready for you. Just have a—'

'I don't want any bloody food. How many times do you want telling, you stupid woman?' The words were cruel and harsh, the tone one of scarcely repressed fury. He stalked out of the room, and almost immediately the front door slammed with a thudded finality.

'I'm awfully sorry, Inspector.'

'Don't worry about me, Mrs Bartlett. Some of the youngsters these days, you know—'

'It's not that, Inspector. You see ... you see, Richard suffers from schizophrenia. He can be absolutely charming, and then – well, he gets like you saw him just now.' She was very near to tears and Morse tried hard to say the right things; but inevitably the incident had cast its shadow deep across the evening, and for a while they ate in awkward silence.

'Can it be treated?'

Mrs Bartlett smiled sadly. 'Good question, Inspector. We've spent literally thousands, haven't we, Tom? He's a voluntary patient at Littlemore at the moment. Sometimes he comes home at the weekends, and just occasionally, like tonight, he'll drop in and sit around or have something to eat.' Her voice was wavering and her husband patted her affectionately on the shoulder.

'Don't worry about it, my dear. We didn't ask the Inspector along to talk about *our* problems. He's got enough of his own, I should think.'

Only when Mrs Bartlett was washing the pots were the two

men able to talk, and Morse's earlier impression that the Secretary knew exactly what was going on in his own office was cumulatively confirmed: if anyone had any ideas about who had been prepared to prostitute the integrity of the Syndicate, Morse felt it would be Bartlett. But he didn't, it seemed. With every subtlety he knew, Morse tried to draw out any suspicion of secret doubts; but the Secretary was deeply loyal to his staff, and Morse knew that he was tiptoeing too delicately. He decided the time had come.

'What did Mr Quinn want when he rang you up?'

Bartlett blinked behind the window frames; and then looked down at his coffee, and was silent for a while. Morse knew perfectly well that if Bartlett denied that Quinn had spoken to him, that would be the end of it, for there was no hard evidence on the point. Yet the longer Bartlett hesitated (surely Bartlett must realize it?), the more obvious it became.

'You know that he did ring me, then?'

'Yes, sir.' He might as well push his luck a little.

'Do you mind telling me how you know?'

It was Morse's turn to hesitate, but he decided to come reasonably clean. 'Quinn's telephone is on a shared line. Someone overheard you.'

Did Morse catch a sudden flash of alarm behind the friendly lenses? If he did, it was gone as quickly as it had appeared.

'You want me to tell you what the conversation was about?'

'I think you should have told me before, sir. It would have saved a great deal of trouble.'

'Would it?' Bartlett looked the Inspector in the eye, and Morse suspected that he was still a long, long way from reaching to the bedrock of the mystery.

'The truth's going to come out some time, sir. I honestly think you'd be sensible to tell me all about it.'

'Haven't you got that information, though? You say someone was listening in? Despicable attitude of mind, isn't it? Eavesdropping on other people—'

'Perhaps it is, sir; but, you see, the er person wasn't really listening in at all – just trying to get a very important call through, that's all. There was no question of deliberately—'

'So you *don't* know what we were talking about?'

Morse breathed deeply. 'No, sir.'

'Well, I'm er I'm not going to tell you. It was a very personal matter, between Quinn and myself—'

'Perhaps it was a personal matter that led to him being murdered, sir.'

'Yes, I realize that.'

'But you're not going to tell me?'

'No.'

Morse slowly drained his coffee. 'I don't think you realize exactly how important this is, sir. You see, unless we can find out where Quinn was and what he was doing that Friday evening—'

Bartlett looked at him sharply. 'You said nothing about Friday before.'

'You mean—?'

'I mean that Quinn rang me up one evening last week, yes. But it wasn't Friday.'

Clever little bugger! Morse had let the cat out of the bag – about not really knowing what the conversation had been about – and now the cat had jumped away over the fence. Bartlett was right, of course. He *hadn't* actually mentioned Friday, but—

Mrs Bartlett came through with the coffee pot and refilled the cups. She appeared quite unaware of breaking the conversation at a vital point, sat down, and innocently asked Morse how he was getting on with his inquiries into the terrible terrible business of poor poor Mr Quinn.

And Morse was game for anything now. 'We were just talking about telephone calls, Mrs Bartlett. The curse of the times, isn't it? I should think you must get almost as many as I do.'

'How right you are, Inspector. I was only saying last week – when was it, Tom? Do you remember? Oh yes. It was the day you went to Banbury. The phone kept ringing all the afternoon, and I said to Tom when he came in that we ought to get an ex-directory number and – do you know what? – just as I said it, the wretched thing rang again! And you had to go out again, do you remember, Tom?

The little Secretary nodded and smiled ruefully. Sometimes life could be very unfair. Very unfair indeed.

*

Just after 8.15 p.m. that same evening a man was taking the lid off the highly polished bronze coal scuttle when he heard the knock, and he got slowly to his feet and opened the door.

'Well, well! Come on in. I shan't be a minute. Take a seat.' He knelt down again by the fire and extracted a lump of shiny black coal with the tongs.

In his own head it sounded as if he had taken an enormous bite from a large, crisp apple. His jaws seemed to clamp together, and for a weird and terrifying second he sought frantically to rediscover some remembrance of himself along the empty, echoing corridors of his brain. His right hand still held the tongs, and his whole body willed itself to pull the coal towards the bright fire. For some inexplicable reason he found himself thinking of the lava from Mount Vesuvius pouring in an all-engulfing flood towards the streets of old Pompeii; and even as his left hand began slowly and instinctively to raise itself towards the shattered skull, he knew that life was ended. The light snapped suddenly out, as if someone had switched on the darkness. He was dead.

# nineteen

Mrs Bartlett got up to answer the phone at a quarter to eleven and Morse realized that it would be as good an opportunity as he would get of taking a reasonably early leave of his hosts.

'It's probably Richard,' said Bartlett. 'He often feels a bit sorry later on, and tries to apologize. I shouldn't be surprised if—'

Mrs Bartlett came back into the room. 'It's for you, Inspector.'

Lewis told him as quickly and as clearly as he could what had happened. The Oxford City Police had been called in about nine o'clock – Chief Inspector Bell was in charge. It was only later that they realized how it might all tie in, and they'd tried to get Morse, and had finally got Lewis. The man had been killed instantly by a savage blow with a poker across the back of the skull. No prints or anything like that. The drawers had been ransacked, but not in any methodical way, it seemed. Probably the murderer had been interrupted.

'I'll see you there as soon as I can manage it, Lewis.'

As Morse came back into the room his face was pale with shock and he tried to keep his voice steady as he told the Bartletts the tragic news. 'It's Ogleby. He's been murdered.'

Mrs Bartlett buried her head in her hands and wept, whilst the Secretary himself, as he showed Morse to the front door, had difficulty in putting his words together coherently. He suddenly seemed an old man, shattered and uncomprehending. 'You asked about Quinn – when he rang – when he rang me – you asked about it – I said—'

Morse put his hand gently on the little man's shoulders. 'Yes. You tell me.'

'He said that – he said that he'd found out something I ought to know – he said that – that someone from the office was deliberately leaking question papers.'

'Did he say who it was?' asked Morse quietly.

'Oh yes, Inspector. *He said it was me.*'


When Morse arrived at the neat little terraced house in Walton Street, Lewis was engaged in low conversation with Bell. It was an ugly sight, and Morse turned his head away, closed his eyes, and felt the nausea rising in his gorge. 'Look, Lewis. I want you to get on to one or two things straight away. Phone, if you like, or go around to see 'em – but I want to know exactly where Roope was tonight, where Martin was, where Miss Height was, where—'

Bell interrupted him. 'I've just been telling the Sergeant. We know where Miss Height was. She was here. She was the one who found him.'

It was not what Morse had expected, and the news appeared to confound whatever provisional procedure he had planned. 'Where is she now?'

'She's in a pretty bad way, I'm afraid. She rang through on a 999 call and then fainted, it seems. Somebody found her slumped by the public telephone box just up the road. She's been seen by the doc and they've taken her to the Radcliffe for the night.'

'She's got a young daughter.'

Bell put his hand on Morse's shoulder. 'Relax, old boy. We've seen to all that. Give us a *bit* of credit.'

Morse sat down in an armchair and wondered about himself. He seemed to be losing his grip. He closed his eyes again, and breathed deeply several times. 'Do as I tell you, anyway, Lewis. Get on to Roope and Martin straight away. And there's something else. You'd better go up to the Littlemore hospital sometime, and find out what you can about Richard Bartlett – got that? Richard Bartlett. He's a voluntary patient there. Find out what time he got in tonight – *if* he got in, that is.'

Morse forced himself to look once more at the liquid squelch of brains and blood commingled on the carpet, beyond which the fire was now no more than an ashen glow. 'And try to find out if any of them changed their clothes, tonight. What do you think, Bell? Blood must have spurted all over the place, mustn't it?'

Bell shrugged his shoulders. 'The girl had blood on her hands and sleeves.'

'I'd better see her,' said Morse.

'Not tonight, old boy, I'm afraid. Doc says she's to see nobody. She's in a state of deep shock.'

'Why did she come here? Did she say.'

'Said she wanted to talk to him about something important.'

'Was the door unlocked?'

'No. She says it was locked.'

'How the hell did she get in then?'

'She's got a key.'

Morse let it sink in. 'Has she now! She certainly spreads the joys around, doesn't she?'

'Pardon?' said Bell.

It was in the early hours of Saturday morning that Morse found what he was looking for and he whispered incredulously. Only he and Lewis remained, apart from the two Oxford City constables standing guard outside.

'Come here, Lewis. Look at this.' It was the diary found in Ogleby's hip pocket. Bell had earlier flipped cursorily through it, but had found no entries whatsoever, and had put it down again. It was a blue University diary with a small flap at the back which could be used for railway tickets and the like. And as Morse had prised open the flap, he could hardly believe his eyes. It was a ticket, torn roughly in half, with IO 2 printed across the top, 'Rear Lounge' beneath it, and along the right edge, running down, the numbers 93592.

'What do you make of it?'

'He *was* there after all, then, sir.'

'*Four* of them. Just think of it. Four out of the five!'

Lewis himself picked up the diary and looked with his usual thorough care at every page in turn. It was clear that Ogleby had never used the diary during the year. But on a page headed 'Notes' at the back of the diary, Lewis saw something that made his eyeballs bulge. 'Sir!' He said it very quietly, as though the slightest noise might frighten it away. 'Look at this.'

Morse looked at the diary, and felt the familiar constriction of the temples as an electric charge seemed to flash across his head. There, drawn with accuracy and neatness, was a small diagram:

'My God!' said Morse. '*It's the same number as the ticket we found on Quinn.*'

Half an hour later, as the two policemen left the house in Walton Street, Morse found himself recalling the words of Dr Hans Gross, one-time Professor of Criminology at the University of Prague. He had them by heart: 'No human action happens by pure chance unconnected with other happenings. None is incapable of explanation.' It was a belief that Morse had always cherished. Yet as he stepped out into the silent street, he began to wonder if it were really true.

No more than fifty or sixty yards down the street he saw the building which housed both Studio 1 and Studio 2. The neon lighting still illuminated the white boards above the foyer, the red and royal-blue lettering garish and bright in the almost eerie stillness: *The Nymphomaniac* X (Strictly Adults Only). Was she trying to tell him something? He walked down to the cinema with Lewis and stood looking at the stills outside. She was certainly a big and bouncy girl, although a series of five-pointed stars had been superimposed by some incomparable idiot over the incomparable Inga's nipples.

# twenty

Morse was in his office at 7.30 a.m. the next morning, tired and unshaven. He had tried to catch a few hours' sleep, but his mind would give him no rest, and he had finally given up the unequal struggle. He knew that he would be infinitely better able to cope with his problems if he had a complete change. But while there was no chance of that, at least he could sharpen his brain on the crossword; and he folded over the back page of *The Times*, looked at his watch, wrote the time in the left-hand margin, and began. It took him twelve and a half minutes. Not his best, this week; but not bad. And barring that one clue, he would have been within ten minutes: *In which are the Islets of Langerhans* (8). –A–C–E–S had been staring him in the face for well over two minutes before he'd seen the answer. He'd finally remembered it from a quiz programme on the radio: one contestant had suggested the South China Sea, another the Baltic, and a third the Mediterranean; and what a laugh from the studio audience when the question master had told them the answer!

During the morning the seemingly endless flood of news poured in. Lewis had managed to see Martin who (so he said) had felt restless and worried the previous evening, gone out about 7.30 p.m., and got back home at about a quarter to eleven. He had taken his car, called at several pubs near Radcliffe Square, and on his return had been banished by his wife to the doghouse. Roope (so he said) had been at home working all evening. No callers – seldom did have any callers. He was preparing a series of lectures on some aspect of Inorganic Chemistry which Lewis had been unable to understand at the time, and was unable to remember now. 'So far as I can see, sir, they're both very strongly in the running. The trouble is we seem to be running out of suspects. Unless you think Miss Height—'

'It's a possibility, I suppose.'

Lewis grudgingly conceded the point. 'That's still only three, though.'

'Aren't you forgetting Ogleby?'

Lewis stared at him. 'I don't follow you, sir.'

'He's still on my list, Lewis, and I see no earthly or heavenly reason why I should cross him off. Do you?'

Lewis opened his mouth but shut it again. And the phone went.

It was the Dean of the Examinations Syndicate, phoning from Lonsdale. Bartlett had rung him up the previous evening. What a terrible business it all was! Frightening. He just wanted to mention a little thing that had occurred to him. Did Morse remember asking about relationships within the Syndicate? Well, somehow the murders of Quinn and Ogleby had brought it all back. It had been just a *little* odd, he'd thought. It was the night when they'd had the big do at the Sheridan, with the Al-jamara lot. Some of them had stayed very late, long after the others had gone off to bed. Quinn was one of them, and Ogleby another; and the Dean had felt at the time (he could be *totally* wrong, of course) that Ogleby had been waiting for Quinn to go; had been watching him in a rather curious way. And when Quinn had left, Ogleby had followed him out almost immediately. It was only a *very* small thing, and actually putting it into words made it seem even smaller. But there it was. The Dean had now unburdened himself, and he hoped he hadn't wasted the Inspector's time.

Morse thanked him and put the phone down. As the Dean said, it didn't seem to add up to much.

In mid-morning Bell rang from Oxford. The medical evidence suggested that Ogleby had died only minutes before he was found. There were no prints other than Ogleby's on the poker or on the desk where the papers had been strewn around; Morse could re-examine whatever he wanted at any time, of course, but there seemed (in Bell's view) little that was going to help him very much. The blow that had crushed Ogleby's thin skull must have been struck with considerable ferocity, but may have required only minimal strength. It had probably been delivered by a right-handed person, and the central point of impact was roughly five centimetres above the occipital bone, and roughly two centimetres to the right of the parietal foramen. The result of the blow—'

'Skip it,' said Morse.

'I know what you mean.'

'Is Miss Height still—?'

'You can't see her till lunchtime. Doc's orders.'

'Still in the Radcliffe?'

'Yep. And you'll be the second person to see her, I promise.'


A young nurse put her head round the screens curtaining the bed on the women's accident ward. 'You've got another visitor.'

Monica appeared drawn and nervous as Morse looked down at her, sitting up against the pillow, her ample hospital nightie softening the contours of her lovely body. 'Tell me about it,' said Morse simply.

Her voice was quiet but firm: 'There's not much to tell, really. I called to see him about half-past eight. He was just lying '

'You had a key?'

She nodded. 'Yes.' Her eyes seemed suddenly very sad, and Morse pressed the point no further. Whether Philip Ogleby had been to see *The Nymphomaniac* was a question still in doubt; but it was perfectly clear that the nymphomaniac had been to see *him* – at fairly regular intervals.

'He was lying there—?'

She nodded. 'I thought he must have had a heart attack or something. I wasn't frightened, or anything like that. I knelt down and touched his shoulder – and his – his head was – was almost in the fireplace, and I saw the blood—' She shook her head, as though to rid herself of that horrific sight. 'And I got blood and – and stuff, over my hands – and I didn't know what to do. I just couldn't stay in that terrible room. I knew there was a phone there but – but I went out into the street and rang the police from the phone box. I don't remember any more. I must have stepped out of the box and just – fainted. The next thing I remember was being in the ambulance.'

'Why did you go to see him?' (He had to ask it.)

'I – I hadn't really had any chance to talk to him about – about Nick and—' (Lying again!)

'You think he knew something about Quinn's murder?'

She smiled sadly and wearily. 'He was a very clever man, Inspector.'

'You didn't see anyone else?'

She shook her head.

'Could there have been anyone else – in the house?'

'I don't know. I just don't know.'

Should he believe her? She'd told so many lies already. But there must have been *some* cause for the lies; and Morse was convinced that if only he could discover that cause he would make the biggest leap forward in the case so far ... It was the Studio 2 business that worried him most. Why, he repeated to himself, *why* had Monica and Donald Martin lied so clumsily about it? And as he wrestled with the problem once again, he began to convince himself that all four of them – Monica, Martin, Ogleby, and Quinn – must have had some collective reason for being in Studio 2 that Friday afternoon, for he just could not bring himself to believe that their several paths had converged for purely fortuitous reasons. Even Morse, who accepted the majority of improbable coincidences with a curiously credulous gullibility, was not prepared to swallow that! Something – *something* must have happened at Studio 2 that afternoon. What? Think of anything, Morse, anything – it wouldn't matter. Quinn had got there early, just after the doors opened. Then Martin had come in, sneaking into the back row and waiting and looking nervously around. Had he seen Quinn? Had Quinn seen *him*? The lights must have been dim; but not so dim as all that, especially as the eyes slowly accustomed themselves to the gloom. *Then*, what? Monica had come in, and Martin saw her, and they sat there together, and Martin told her that he had seen *Quinn*. What would they do? They'd leave. Pronto! Go on, Morse. If Martin had seen Quinn – and Quinn had not seen him – he would have left the cinema immediately, waited outside for Monica, told her that they couldn't stay there, and suggested somewhere else ... Yes. But where had Ogleby fitted in? The number on his ticket, some forty-odd numbers after Quinn's, suggested (if the manageress had done her sums right) that Ogleby had not appeared in Studio 2 until about four or five o'clock. How did *that* fit into the pattern, though? Augh! It didn't fit. Try again, Morse. Something must have frightened *Monica* off, perhaps. Yes. That was a slightly more promising hypothesis. Had she seen something? Someone? The cause of all the lies? After learning that Quinn had been in Studio 2, she had told another lie, and ... Oh Christ! What a muddle his mind was in! The pictures flickered fitfully upon the wall, the faces fading and changing, and fading again ...

'You've been a long way away, Inspector.'

'Mm? Oh, sorry. Just daydreaming.'

'About me?'

'Among others.'

On the table beside the bed was a copy of *The Times*, folded at the crossword page; but only three or four words were written into the diagram, and Morse found himself wondering and wandering off again. Wondering if Monica knew where the Islets of Langerhans were situated ... Well, if she didn't, the nurse could soon— *Just a minute!* His thinning hair seemed to be standing on end, and his scalp suddenly tingled with a thousand tiny prickles. Oh yes! It was a beautiful idea, and the old questions flooded his brain. In what sea are the Islets of Langerhans? When was George Washington assassinated? Who was Kansas-Nebraska Bill? In what year did R. A. Butler become prime minister? Who composed the Trout Quartet? By what name was the Black Prince known when he became king? *The questions were all non-questions.* Georgie W. wasn't assassinated, and K.-N. Bill wasn't *anybody*; he was a Bill before the Senate. The same with all of them. They were questions which couldn't be answered, because they were questions which couldn't be asked. Morse had become besotted with trying to find out who had been at Studio 2, when they had been there, why they had been there. But what if they were all non-questions? What if *no one* had been in Studio 2? Everything in the case had been designed to mislead him into thinking that they had been there. Some of them – all of them, perhaps –

*wanted* him to think so. And he had blindly stumbled along the gangway down the darkened cinema, groping his way like a blind man, and trying to see (O fool of a fool!) who was sitting there. But perhaps there was no one, Morse. No one!

'Who did you see going into Studio 2, Miss Height?'

'Why don't you call me "Monica"?'

The nurse put her head through the curtains, and told Morse that he really ought to leave now; he'd already gone way over his time. He stood up and looked down at her once more, and kissed the top of her head gently.

'You didn't see anyone going in to Studio 2, did you, Monica?'

For a second there was hesitation in her eyes, and then she looked at him earnestly. 'No. I didn't. You must believe that.'

She took Morse's hand and squeezed it gently against her soft breast. 'Come again, won't you? And try to look after me.' Her eyes sought his and he realized once more how desperately desirable she would always be to lonely men – to men like him. But there was something else in her eyes: the look of the hunted fleeing from the hunter; the haunted look of fear. 'I'm frightened, Inspector. I'm so very frightened.'

Morse was thoughtful as he walked the long corridors before finally emerging through the flappy celluloid doors into the entrance road by the side of the Radcliffe, where the Lancia stood parked on an 'Ambulance Only' plot. He started up the engine and was slowly steering through the twisting alleys that led down into Walton Street when he saw a familiar figure striding up towards the hospital. He stopped the car and wound down the window.

'I'm glad to see you, Mr Martin. In fact I was just coming along to see you. Jump in.'

'Sorry. Not now. I'm going to see—'

'You're not.'

'Who says?'

'No one's going in to see her until I say so.'

'But when—?'

'Jump in.'

'Do I have to?'

Morse shrugged his shoulders. 'Not really, no. You please

yourself. At least, you please yourself until I decide to take you in.'

'What's that supposed to mean?'

'What it says, sir. Until I decide to take you in and charge you—'

'*Charge* me? What with?'

'Oh, I could think up something pretty quickly, sir.'

The dull eyes stared at Morse in anxious bewilderment. 'You must be joking.'

'Of course I am, sir.' He leaned across and opened the Lancia's nearside door, and Donald Martin sullenly eased his long body into the passenger seat.

The traffic was heavy as they drove up the narrow street, and Morse decided to turn right and cut straight across to Woodstock Road. As he stopped at yet another Pelican crossing, he realized just how close the Syndicate building was to Studio 2. And as the lights turned to flashing amber, he held the car on half-clutch as a late pedestrian galloped his way across: a bearded young man. He was in too much of a rush to recognize Morse; but Morse recognized *him*, and the last words that Monica had spoken re-echoed in his mind. In his rear mirror he could see that the man was walking briskly down the right-hand side of Woodstock Road towards the Radcliffe Infirmary, and he swung the Lancia sharp left at the next turning, furiously cursing the crawling stream of cars. He parked on the double yellow lines at the back of the Radcliffe, told Martin to stay where he was, and ran like a crippled stag to the accident ward. She was still there: still sitting up prettily amid the pillows as he peeped behind the screens. Phew! He rang up HQ from the Sister's office, told Dickson he was to get there immediately, and stood there breathing heavily.

'You all right, Inspector?'

'Just about, thank you, Sister. But listen. I don't want anyone to talk to Miss Height or to get anywhere near her. All right? And if anyone *does* try to visit her, I want to know who it is. One of my men will be here in ten minutes.'

He paced impatiently up and down the corridor waiting for Dickson's arrival. Like Pilgrim he seemed to be making but sluggish progress – up the hill of difficulty and down into the slough of despond. But there was no sign whatsoever of Richard Bartlett. Perhaps Morse was imagining things.

# twenty-one

Three-quarters of an hour later, with the office clock showing half-past two, Morse's irritation with the young philanderer was mounting towards open animosity. What a flabby character Donald Martin was! He admitted most things, albeit with some reluctance. His relationship with Monica had sputtered into sporadic passion, followed by the usual remorse and the futile promises that the affair had got to finish. Certainly it was he who had always tried to force the pace; yet when they were actually making love together (Morse drew the blinds across his imagination) he knew that she was *glad*. She could surrender herself so completely to physical love; it was wonderful, and he had known nothing like it before. But when the passion was spent, she would always retreat into indifference – callousness, almost. Never had she made any pretence about her reasons for letting him take her: it was purely physical. Never had she spoken of love, or even of deep affection ... His wife (he was sure of it) had no suspicions of his unfaithfulness, although she must have sensed (of course she must!) that the careless rapture of their early married days had gone – perhaps for ever.

How despicable the man was! His dark, lank hair, his horn-rimmed glasses, his long, almost effeminate fingers. Ugh! Nor was Morse's dark displeasure dissipated as Martin repeated what he had already told Lewis about his whereabouts the previous evening. He'd been lucky to find a parking space in the Broad, and he'd gone to the King's Arms first, where he thought the barmaid would probably remember him. Then to the White Horse, where he didn't know anyone. Another pint. Then down to the Turl Bar. Another pint. No he didn't often go out for a binge: very rarely in fact. But the last few days had been a nightmarish time. He'd found he couldn't sleep at all well, and beer had helped a bit; it usually did. But why did Morse keep on and on at him about it? He'd gone nowhere near Ogleby's! Why should he? What, for heaven's sake, could he have had to do with Ogleby's murder? He'd not even known him very well. He doubted if anybody in the office knew him very well.

Morse said nothing to enlighten him. 'Let's come back to last Friday afternoon.'

'Not again, surely! I've told you what happened. All right, I lied for a start, but—'

'You're lying now! And if you're not careful you'll be down in the cells until you *do* tell me the truth.'

'But I'm *not* lying.' He shook his head miserably. 'Why can't you believe me?'

'Why did you say you spent the afternoon at Miss Height's house?'

'I don't know, really. Monica thought ...' His voice trailed off.

'Yes. She's told me.'

'Has she?' His eyes seemed suddenly relieved.

'Yes,' lied Morse. 'But if you don't want to tell me yourself, we can always wait, sir. I'm in no great rush myself.'

Martin looked down at the carpet. 'I don't know why she didn't want to say we'd been to the pictures. I don't – honestly! But I didn't think it mattered all that much, so I agreed to what she said.'

'It's a bit odd to say you'd been to bed when all you'd done was sit together in the cinema!'

Martin seemed to recognize the obvious truth of the assertion, and he nodded. 'But it's the truth, Inspector. It's the honest truth! We stayed in the cinema till about a quarter to four. You've got to believe that! I had nothing at all – nothing! – to do with Nick's death. Nor did Monica. *We were together* – all the afternoon.'

'Tell me something about the film.'

So Martin told him, and Morse knew that he could hardly be fabricating such entirely gratuitous obscenities. Martin *had* seen the film; seen it some time, anyway. Not necessarily that Friday, not necessarily with Monica, but ...

Martin was convincing him, he knew that. Assume he *was* there that Friday afternoon. With Monica? Yes, assume that too. Sit them down there on the back row of the rear lounge, Morse. Martin had been waiting for her, and she'd come in. Yes, keep going! She'd come in and ... and they had stayed after all! Who, if anyone, had they seen? No. Go back a bit. Who had Martin seen going in? No. Who had Monica seen? Going in? Or ... ? Yes. Yes!

Think of it the other way for a minute. Ogleby had gone into the cinema at about quarter to five, say. But he must have known all about Quinn's ticket, mustn't he? In fact he must have *seen* it. When? Where? Why had he made a careful freehand drawing of that ticket? Ogleby must have known, or at least suspected,. that the ticket was vitally important. All right. Agree that Monica and Martin had seen the film together. But had *Quinn* gone? Or had someone just wished to make everyone else *think* that he'd gone? Who? Who knew of the ticket? Who had drawn it? Where had he found it, Morse? My God, yes! What a stupid blind fool he'd been!

Martin had stopped talking minutes before, and was looking curiously at the man in the black leather chair, sitting there smiling serenely to himself. It had all happened, as it always seemed to do with Morse, in the twinkling of an eye. Yes, as he sat there, oblivious to everything about him, *Morse felt he knew when Nicholas Quinn had met his death.*

# HOW?

# twenty-two

Early on Saturday evening Mr Nigel Denniston decided to begin. He found that the majority of his O-level English Language scripts had been delivered, and he began his usual preliminary task of putting the large buff-coloured envelopes into alphabetical order, and of checking them against his allocated schedule. The examiners' meeting was to be held in two days' time, and before then he had to look at about twenty or so scripts, mark them provisionally in pencil, and present them for scrutiny to the senior examiner, who would be interviewing each of his panel after the main meeting. Al-jamara was the first school on his list, and he slit open the carefully sealed envelope and took out the contents. The attendance sheet was placed on top of the scripts, and Denniston's eyes travelled automatically and hopefully down to the 'Absentee' column. It was always a cause of enormous joy to him if one or two of his candidates had been smitten with some oriental malady; but Al-jamara was a disappointment. According to the attendance sheet there were five candidates entered, and all five were duly registered as 'present' by the distant invigilator. Never mind. There was always the chance of finding one or two of those delightful children who knew nothing and who wrote nothing; children for whom the wells of inspiration ran dry after only a couple of laboured sentences. But no. No luck there, either. None of the five candidates had prematurely given up the ghost. Instead, it was the usual business: page after page of ill-written, unidiomatic, irrelevant twaddle, which it was his assignment to plough through (and almost certainly to plough), marking in red ink the myriad errors of grammar, syntax, construction, spelling and punctuation. It was a tedious chore, and he didn't really know why year after year he took it on. Yet he did know. It was a bit of extra cash; and if he didn't mark, he would only be sitting in front of the TV, forever arguing with the family about which of the channels they should watch ... He flicked through the first few sheets. Oh dear! These foreigners might be all right at Mathematics or Economics or that sort of thing. But they couldn't write *English* – that was a fact. Still, it wasn't really surprising. English was their second language, poor kids; and he felt a little less jaundiced as he took out his pencil and started.

An hour later he had finished the first four scripts. The candidates had tried – of course they had. But he felt quite unjustified in awarding the sort of marks that could bring them anywhere near the pass range. Tentatively he had written his own provisional percentages at the top right-hand corner of each script: 27%, 34%, 35%, 19%. He decided to finish off the last one before supper.

This was a better script. My goodness, it was! And as he read on he realized that it was very good indeed. He put aside his pencil and read through the essay with genuine interest, bordering on delight. Whoever the boy was, he'd written beautifully. There were a few awkward sentences, and a sprinkling of minor errors; but Denniston doubted whether he himself could have written a better essay under examination conditions. He had known the same sort of thing before, though. Sometimes a candidate would memorize a whole essay and trot it out: beautiful stuff, lifted lock, stock and paragraph from one of the great English prose stylists; but almost invariably in such cases, the subject matter was so wildly divorced from the strict terms of the question set as to be completely irrelevant. But not here. Either the lad was quite exceptionally able, or else he had been extraordinarily fortunate. That wasn't for Denniston to decide, though; his job was to reward what was on the script. He pencilled in 90%; and then wondered why he hadn't given it 95%, or even 98%. But like almost all examiners, he was always frightened of using the full range of marks. The lad would fly through, anyway. Wonderful lad! Perfunctorily Denniston looked at the name: Dubal. It meant nothing to him at all.

In Al-jamara itself, the last of the autumn examinations, crowded into just the one week, had finished the previous afternoon, and George Bland relaxed with an iced gin and tonic in his air-conditioned flat. It had taken him only a few weeks to regret his move. Better paid, certainly; but only away from Oxford had he begun fully to appreciate the advantages of his strike-ridden, bankrupt, beautiful homeland. He missed, above all, the feeling of belonging somewhere which, however loosely, he could think of as his home: the pub at night; the Cotswold villages with their greens and ancient churches; the concerts, the plays, the lectures, and the general air of learning; the oddities forever padding their faddish, feckless paths around the groves of the Muses. He'd never imagined how much it all meant to him ... The climate of Al-jamara was overwhelming, intolerable, endlessly enervating; the people alien – ostensibly hospitable, but secretly watchful and suspicious ... How he regretted the move now!

The news had worried him; would have worried anyone. It was for information only, really – no more; and it had been thoughtful of the Syndicate to keep him informed. The International Telegram had arrived on Wednesday morning: TRAGIC NEWS STOP QUINN DEAD STOP MURDER SUSPECTED STOP WILL WRITE STOP BARTLETT. But there had been another telegram, received only that morning; and this time it was unsigned. He had burned it immediately, although he realized that no one could have suspected the true import of the brief, bleak lines. Yet it had always been a possibility, and he was prepared. He walked over to his desk and took out his passport once more. All was in order; and tucked safely inside was his ticket on the scheduled flight to Cairo, due to leave at noon the following day.

# twenty-three

There was a car outside No 1 Pinewood Close as Frank Greenaway pulled into the crescent; but he didn't recognize it and gave it no second thought. He could fully understand Joyce's point of view, of course. He wasn't too keen to go back there himself, and it wasn't right to expect her to be there on her own while he was out at work. She'd have the baby to keep her company, but— No. He agreed with her. They would find somewhere else, and in the meantime his parents were being very kind. Not that he wanted to stay with them *too* long. Like somebody said, fish and visitors began to smell after three days ... They could leave most of their possessions at Pinewood Close for a week or two, but he had to pick up a few things for Joyce (who would be leaving the John Radcliffe the next morning), and the police had said it would be all right.

As he got out of his car, he noticed that the street lamp had been repaired, and the house where he and Joyce had lived, and wherein Quinn had been found murdered, seemed almost ordinary again. The front gate stood open, and he walked up to the front door, selecting the correct key from his ring. The garage doors stood open, propped back by a couple of house bricks. Frank opened the front door very quietly. He was not a nervous man, but he felt a slight involuntary shudder as he stepped into the darkened hallway, the two doors on his right, the stairs almost directly in front of him. He would hurry it up a bit; he didn't much fancy staying there too long on his own. As he put his hand on the banister he noticed the slim line of light under the kitchen door: the police must have forgotten ... But then he heard it, quite distinctly. Someone was in the kitchen. Someone was quietly moving around in there ... The demon fear laid its electrifying hand upon his shoulder, and without conscious volition he found himself a few seconds later scurrying hurriedly along the concrete drive towards his car.

Morse heard the click of the front door, and looked out into the passageway. But no one. He was imagining things again. He returned to the kitchen, and bent down once more beside the back door. Yes, he *had* been right. There was no mud on the carpets in the other downstairs rooms, and they had been hoovered only an hour or so before Quinn was due to return. But beside the back door there *were* signs of mud, and Morse knew that someone had taken off his shoes, or her shoes, and left them beside the doormat. And even as he had stood there his own shoes crunched upon the gritty, dried mud with the noise of someone trampling on corn flakes.

He left the house and got into the Lancia. But then he got out again, walked back, closed the garage doors, and finally the garden gate behind him.

Ten minutes later he drew up outside the darkened house in Walton Street, where a City constable stood guard before the door.

'No one's tried to get in, Constable?'

'No, sir. Few sightseers always hanging around, but no one's been in.'

'Good. I'll only be ten minutes.'

Ogleby's bedroom seemed lonely and bleak. No pictures on the walls, no books on the bedside table, no ornaments on the dressing table, no visible signs of heating. The large double bed monopolized the confined space, and Morse turned back the coverlet. Two head pillows lay there, side by side, and a pair of pale yellow pyjamas were tucked just beneath the top sheet. Morse picked up the nearer pillow, and there he found a neatly folded négligé – black, flimsy, almost transparent, with a label proclaiming 'St Michael'.

No one had yet bothered to clean up the other room, and the fire which had blazed merrily the night before was nothing now but cold, fine ash into which some of the detectives had thrown the tipped butts of their cigarettes. It looked almost obscene. Morse turned his attention to the books which lined the high shelves on each side of the fireplace. The vast majority of them were technical treatises on Ogleby's specialisms, and Morse was interested in only one: *Medical Jurisprudence and Toxicology*, by Glaister and Rentoul. It was an old friend. A folded sheet of paper protruded from the top, and Morse opened the book at that point: page 566. In heavy type, a quarter of the way down the page, stood the heading 'Hydrocyanic Acid'.

At the Summertown Health Clinic, Morse was shown immediately into Dr Parker's consulting room.

'Yes, Inspector, I'd looked after Mr Ogleby for – oh, seven or eight years now. Very sad really. Something may have turned up, but I very much doubt it. Extremely rare blood disease – nobody knows much about it.'

'You gave him about a year, you say?'

'Eighteen months, perhaps. No longer.'

'He knew this?'

'Oh yes. He insisted on knowing everything. Anyway, it would have been useless trying to keep it from him. Medically speaking, he was a very well-informed man. Knew more about his illness than I did. Or the specialists at the Radcliffe, come to that.'

'Do you think he told anybody?'

'I doubt it. Might have told one or two close friends, I suppose. But I knew nothing about his private life. For all I know, he didn't have any close friends.'

'Why do you say that?'

'I don't know. He was a – a bit of a loner, I think. Bit un-communicative.'

'Did he have much pain?'

'I don't think so. He never said so, anyway.'

'He wasn't the suicidal sort, was he?'

'I don't think so. Seemed a pretty balanced sort of chap. If he *were* going to kill himself, he would have done it simply and quickly, I should have thought. He would certainly have been in his right mind.'

'What would you say is the simplest and quickest way?'

Parker shrugged his shoulders. 'I think I'd have a quick swig of cyanide, myself.'

Morse walked thoughtfully to the car: he felt a sadder, if not a much wiser man. Anyway, one more call to make. He just hoped Margaret Freeman hadn't gone off to a Saturday night hop.


Although earlier in the evening Lewis had been quite unable to fathom the Inspector's purposes, he had quite looked forward to the duties assigned to him.

Joyce Greenaway was pleasantly co-operative, and she tried her best to answer the Sergeant's strange questions. As she had told Inspector Morse, she couldn't be certain that the name *was* Bartlett, and she could see no point whatsoever in trying (although she did try) to remember whether he'd been addressed as Bartlett or Dr Bartlett. She was quite sure, too, that she could never hope to recognize the voice again: her hearing wasn't all that good at the best of times and – well, you couldn't recognize a voice again just like that, could you. What were they talking about? Well, as a matter of fact, she did just have the feeling that they were arranging to meet somewhere. But further than that – when, where, why – no. No ideas at all.

Lewis got it all down in his notebook; and when he'd finished he made the appropriate noises to the little bundle of life that lay beside the bed.

'Have you got any family, Sergeant?'

'Two daughters.'

'We had a name all ready if it had been a girl.'

'There's a lot of nice boys' names.'

'Yeah, I suppose so. But somehow— What's your Christian name, Sergeant?'

Lewis told her. He'd never liked it much.

'What about the Inspector? What's his Christian name?'

Lewis frowned for a few seconds. Funny, really. He'd never thought of Morse as having one. 'I don't know. I've never heard anyone call him by his Christian name.'

From the John Radcliffe Lewis drove down to the railway station. There were four taxi firms, and Lewis received conflicting pieces of advice about the best way to tackle his assignment. It really should have been a comparatively easy job to find out who (if anyone) had taken Roope from the station to the Syndicate building at about 4.20 p.m. on the 21st November. But it wasn't. And when Lewis had finally completed his rounds he doubted whether the answer he'd come up with was the one that Morse had expected or hoped for.

It was after half-past eight before Lewis reached Littlemore Hospital.

Dr Addison, who was on night duty, had not himself had a great deal to do with Richard Bartlett's case, although he knew *of* it, of course. He fetched the file, but refused to let Lewis look through it himself. 'There are some very *personal* entries, you know, Officer, and I think that I can give you the information you want without—'

'I don't really want any details about Mr Bartlett's mental troubles. Just a list of the institutions that he's stayed in over the past five years, the clinics he's been to, the specialists he's seen – and the dates, of course.'

Addison looked annoyed. 'You want all that? Well, I suppose, if it's really necessary ...' The file contained a wadge of papers two inches thick, and Lewis patiently made his notes. It took them almost an hour.

'Well, many thanks, sir. I'm sorry to have taken up so much of your time.'

Addison said nothing.

As Lewis finally got up to leave he asked one last question, although it wasn't on Morse's list.

'What's the trouble with Mr Bartlett, sir?'

'Schizophrenia.'

'Oh.' Lewis thanked him once again, and left.


Morse was not in his office when Lewis arrived back. They'd arranged to meet again at about ten if each could manage it. Had Morse finished his own inquiries yet? Like as not he had, and gone out for a pint. Lewis looked at his watch: it was just after ten past ten, and he might as well wait. Morse must have been looking up something for his crossword, for the *Chambers* lay on the cluttered desk. Lewis opened it. 'Ski-'? No. 'Sci-'? No. He'd never been much of a hand at spelling. 'Sck-'? Ah! There it was: '*ski-zo-freni-a*, or *skid-zo*, n., dementia praecox or kindred form of insanity, marked by introversion and loss of connexion between thoughts, feeling and actions.'

Lewis had moved on to 'dementia' when Morse came in, and it was quite clear that for once in a lifetime he had *not* been drinking. He listened with great care to what Lewis had to tell him, but seemed neither surprised nor excited in any way.

It was at a quarter to eleven that he dropped his bombshell. 'Well, Lewis, my old friend. I've got a surprise for you. We're going to make an arrest on Monday morning.'

'That's when the inquest is.'

'And that's when we're going to arrest him.'

'Can you do that sort of thing at an inquest, sir? Is it legal?'

'Legal? I know nothing about the law. But perhaps you're

right. We'll make it just *after* the inquest, just as he's—'

'What if he's not there?'

'I think he'll be there all right,' said Morse quietly.

'You're not going to tell me who he is?'

'What? And spoil my little surprise? Now, what do you say we have a pint or two? To celebrate, sort of thing.'

'The pubs'll be shut, sir.'

'Really?' Morse feigned surprise, walked over to a wall cupboard, and fetched out half a dozen pint bottles of beer, two glasses, and an opener.

'You've got to plan for all contingencies in our sort of job, Lewis.'

Margaret Freeman had been tossing and turning since she went to bed at eleven, and she finally got up at 1.30 a.m. She tiptoed past her parents' room, made her way silently to the kitchen, and put the kettle on. It was no longer a matter of being frightened, as it had been earlier in the week, when she had blessed the fact that she didn't live on her own like some of the girls did; it was more a matter of being puzzled now: puzzled about what Morse had asked her. The other girls thought that the Inspector was a bit dishy; but she didn't. Too old – and too vain. Combing his hair when he'd come in, and trying to cover up that balding patch at the back! Men! But she'd liked Mr Quinn – liked him rather more than she should have done ... She poured herself a cup of tea and sat down at the kitchen table. Why had Morse asked her that question? It made it seem as if she held the secret to something important; it *was* important, he'd said. But why did he want to know? She had lain awake thinking and thinking, and asking herself just why he should have asked her *that*. Why was it so important for him to know if Mr Quinn had put her own initials on the little notes he left? Of course he had! She was the one who most needed to know, wasn't she? After all, she *was* his confidential secretary. Had been, rather ... She poured herself a second cup of tea, took it back to her room, and turned on the bedside reading lamp. Menacing shadows seemed to loom against the far wall as she settled herself into bed. She tried to sit very still, and suddenly felt very frightened again.

# twenty-four

On Monday morning Lewis was waiting outside as the door of Superintendent Strange's office opened, and he caught the tail-end of the conversation.

'... cock-eyed, but—'

'Have I ever let you down, sir?'

'Frequently.'

Morse winked at Lewis and closed the door behind him. It was 10.30 a.m. and the inquest was due to start at eleven. Dickson was waiting outside with the car, and together the three policemen drove down into Oxford.

The inquest was to be held in the courtroom behind the main Oxford City Police HQ in St Aldates, and a small knot of people was standing outside, waiting for the preceding hearing to finish. Lewis looked at them. He had written (as Morse had carefully briefed him) to all those concerned in any way with Quinn's murder: some would have to take the stand anyway; others ('but your presence will be appreciated') would not. The Dean of the Syndicate stood there, his hands in his expensive dark overcoat, academically impatient; the Secretary, looking duly grave; Monica Height looking palely attractive; Martin prowling around the paved yard like a nervous hyaena; Roope, smoking a cigarette and staring thoughtfully at the ground; Mr Quinn senior, lonely, apart, staring into the pit of despair; and Mrs Evans and Mrs Jardine, leagues apart in the social hierachy, yet managing to chat away quite merrily about the tragic events which had brought them together.

It was ten minutes past eleven before they all filed into the court, where the coroner's sergeant, acting as chief usher, quietly but firmly organized the seating to his liking, before disappearing through a door at the back of the court, and almost immediately reappearing with the coroner himself. All rose to their feet as the sergeant intoned the judicial ritual. The proceedings had begun.

First the identification of the deceased was established by Mr Quinn senior; then Mrs Jardine took the box; then Martin;

then Bartlett; then Sergeant Lewis; then Constable Dickson. Nothing was added to, nothing subtracted from, the statements the coroner had before him. Next the thin humpbacked surgeon gave evidence of the autopsy, reading from a prepared script at such a breakneck speed and with such a wealth of physiological detail that he might just as well have been reciting the Russian creed to a class of the educationally subnormal. When he had reached the last full stop, he handed the document perfunctorily to the coroner, stepped carefully down, and walked briskly out of the courtroom and out of the case. Lewis wondered idly what his fee would be ...

'Chief Inspector Morse, please.'

Morse walked to the witness box and took the oath in a mumbled gabble.

'You are in charge of the investigation into the death of Mr Nicholas Quinn.'

Morse nodded. 'Yes, sir.'

Before the coroner could proceed, however, there was a slight commotion at the entrance door; and a series of whispered exchanges, which resulted in a bearded young man being admitted and taking his place next to Constable Dickson on one of the low benches. Lewis was glad to see him: he had begun to wonder if his letter to Mr Richard Bartlett had gone astray.

The coroner resumed: 'Are you prepared to indicate to the court the present state of your investigations into this matter?'

'Not yet, sir. And with your honour's permission, I wish to make formal application for the inquest to be adjourned for a fortnight.'

'Am I to understand, Chief Inspector, that your inquiries are likely to be completed within that time?'

'Yes, sir. Quite shortly, I hope.'

'I see. Am I right in saying that you have as yet made no arrest in this case?'

'An arrest is imminent.'

'Indeed?'

Morse took a warrant from his inside pocket and held it up before the court. 'It may be somewhat unusual to introduce such a note of melodrama into your court, your honour; but immediately after the adjournment of this inquest – should, of course, your honour allow the adjournment – it will be my duty to make an arrest.' Morse turned his head slightly and ran his eyes along the front bench: Dickson, Richard Bartlett, Mrs Evans, Mrs Jardine, Martin, Dr Bartlett, Monica Height, Roope, and Lewis. Yes, they were all there, with the murderer seated right amongst them! Things were going according to plan.

The coroner formally adjourned the inquest for two weeks and the court stood as the august personage reluctantly departed. Now there was a hush over the assembly; no one seemed to breathe or to blink as Morse slowly stepped down from the witness box, and stood momentarily before Richard Bartlett, and then walked on; past Mrs Evans; past Mrs Jardine; past Martin; past Bartlett; past Monica Height; and then stood in front of Roope. And stayed there.

'Christopher Algernon Roope, I have here a warrant for your arrest in connection with the murder of Nicholas Quinn.' The words echoed vaguely around the hushed court, and still nobody seemed to breath. 'It is my duty to tell you—'

Roope stared at Morse in disbelief. 'What the *hell* are you talking about?' His eyes darted first to the left and then to the right, as if calculating his chances of making a quick dash for it. But to his right stood the bulky figure of Constable Dickson; and immediately to his left Lewis laid a heavy hand upon his shoulder.

'I hope you'll be sensible and come quietly, sir.'

Roope spoke in a harsh whisper. 'I hope you realize what a dreadful mistake you're making. I just don't know—'

'Leave it for later,' snapped Morse.

All eyes were on Roope as he walked out, Dickson on his right and Lewis on his left; but still no one said a word. It was if they had all been struck dumb, or just witnessed a miracle, or stared into the face of the Gorgon.

Bartlett was the first to move. He looked utterly dumbfounded and walked like an automaton towards his son. Monica's eyes crossed the gap that Bartlett had left, and found Donald Martin's looking directly into her own. It was the merest imperceptibility, perhaps; but it was there. The slightest shaking of her head; the profound, dead stillness of her eyes: 'Shut up, you fool!' they seemed to say. 'Shut up, you stupid fool!'

# twenty-five

'You had mixed luck in this wicked business, Roope. You had a bit of good luck, I know; and you made the most of it. But you also had some bad luck: things happened that no one, not even you, could have foreseen. And although you tried to cope as best you could – in fact, you almost succeeded in turning it to your own advantage – you had to be just that little bit *too* clever. I realized that I was up against an exceptionally cunning and resourceful murderer, but in the end it was your very cleverness that gave you away.'

The three of them, Morse, Lewis, Roope, sat together in Interview Room No 1. Lewis (who had been firmly cautioned by Morse to keep his mouth shut, whatever the provocation) was seated by the door, whilst Morse and Roope sat opposite each other at the small table. Morse, the hunter, seemed supremely confident as he sat back on the wooden chair, his voice calm, almost pleasant. 'Shall I go on?'

'If you must. I've already told you what a fool you're making of yourself, but you seem determined to listen to no one.'

Morse nodded. 'All right. We'll start in the middle, I think. We'll start at the point where you walked into the Syndicate building at about 4.25 p.m. a week last Friday. The first person you saw was the caretaker, Noakes, mending a broken light-tube in the corridor. But it was soon clear to you that there was no one else in the downstairs offices at all. No one! You concocted some appropriate tale about having to leave some papers with Dr Bartlett, and since he was out you had the best reason in the world for trying to find one of the others and for looking into their offices. You looked into Quinn's, of course, and everything was just as you'd known it would be – as you'd *planned* it would be. Everything was cleverly arranged to give the clear impression to anyone going into his room that Quinn was *there* – in the office; or, at least, would be there again very soon. It was raining heavily all day Friday – a piece of good luck! – and there, on the back of Quinn's chair, was his green anorak. Who would leave the office on a day like that without taking his coat? And the cabinets were left *open*. Now cabinets contain question papers, and the Secretary would have been down like a hawk on any of his colleagues who showed the slightest carelessness over security. But what are we asked to believe in Quinn's case? Quinn? Recently appointed; briefed, doubtless *ad nauseam*, about the need for the strictest security at every second of every day. And what does he do, Roope? He goes out and leaves his cabinets open! Yet, at the very same time, we find evidence of Quinn's punctilious adherence to the Secretary's instructions. Since he took up his job a few months previously, he has been told, very pointedly told, that it doesn't matter in the slightest if he takes time off during the day. *But* – if he does go out, he's to leave a note informing anyone who might want him exactly where he is or what he's doing. In other words, what Bartlett says is all the law and the commandments. Now, I find the combination of these two sets of circumstances extremely suggestive, Roope. Some of us are idle and careless, and some of us are fussy and conscientious. But very few of us manage to be both at the same time. Wouldn't you agree?'

Roope was staring through the window on to the concrete yard. He was watchful and tensed, but he said nothing.

'The caretaker told you that he was going off for tea, and before long you were alone – *or so you thought* – on the ground floor of the Syndicate building. It was still only about half past four, and although I suspect you'd originally planned to wait until the whole office was empty, this was too good a chance to miss. Noakes, quite unwittingly, had given you some very interesting information, though you could very easily have found it out for yourself. The only car left in the rear car park was *Quinn's*. Well, what happened then was this, or something very like it. You went into Quinn's room once more. You took his anorak, and you put it on. You kept your gloves on, of course, and you folded up the plastic mac you'd been wearing. Then you saw that note once more, and you decided that you might as well pocket it. Certainly Quinn wouldn't have left it on the desk if he'd returned, and from this point on you had to think and act exactly as Quinn would have done. You walked out of the back door and found – as you knew you would – that Quinn's car keys were in his anorak pocket. No one was around, of course: the weather was still foul – though ideal for you. You got into the car and you drove away from the building. Noakes in fact saw you leave as he sat upstairs having a cup of tea. But he thought – why shouldn't he? – that it was Quinn. After all, he could only see the top of the car. So? That was that. The luck was on your side at this stage, and you made the most of it. The first part of the great deception was over, and you'd come through it with flying colours!'

Roope shuffled uneasily on his hard wooden chair, and his eyes looked dangerous; but again he said nothing.

'You drove the car to Kidlington and you parked it safely in Quinn's own garage in Pinewood Close, and here again you had a curious combination of good and bad luck. First the good luck. The rain was still pouring down and no one was likely to look too carefully at the man who got out of Quinn's car to unlock his own garage doors. It was dark, too, and the corner of Pinewood Close was even darker than usual because someone – *someone*, Roope, had seen to it that the street lamp outside the house had been recently and conveniently smashed. I make no specific charges on that point, but you must allow me to harbour my little suspicions. So, even if anyone *did* see you, hunched up in Quinn's green anorak, head down in the rain, I doubt whether any suspicions would have been aroused. You were very much the same build as Quinn, and like him you had a beard. But in another way the luck was very much against you. It so happened, and you couldn't help noticing the fact, that a woman was standing at the upstairs front window. She'd been waiting a long time, frightened that her baby was going to be born prematurely; she had rung her husband at Cowley several times, and she was impatiently expecting him at any minute. Now, as I say, this was not in itself a fatal occurrence. She'd seen you, of course, but it never occurred to her for a second that the person she saw was anyone but Quinn; and you yourself must have totted up the odds and worked on exactly that assumption. Nevertheless, she'd seen you go *into the house*, where you immediately discovered that Mrs Evans – you must have had a complete dossier on all the domestic arrangements – as I say, Mrs Evans, by a sheer fluke, had not finished the cleaning. What's more, she'd left a note to say she would be coming back! That was bad luck, all right, and yet you suddenly saw the chance of turning the tables completely. You read the note from Mrs Evans, and you screwed it up and threw it into the wastepaper basket. You lit the gas fire, putting the match you used carefully back into your matchbox. You shouldn't have done that, Roope! But we all make mistakes, don't we? And then – the masterstroke! You had a note in your pocket – a note written by Quinn himself, a note which not only looked genuine; it *was* genuine. Any handwriting expert was going to confirm, almost at a glance, that the writing was Quinn's. Of course he'd confirm it. The writing *was* Quinn's. You were hellishly lucky, though, weren't you? The note was addressed to Margaret Freeman, Quinn's confidential secretary. But not by name. By initials. MF. You found a black thin-point biro in Quinn's anorak, and very carefully you changed the initials. Not too difficult, was it? A bit of a squiggle for "rs" after the M, and an additional bar at the bottom of the F, converting it into an E. The message was good enough – vague enough, anyway – to cover the deception. How you must have smiled as you placed the note carefully on the top of the cupboard. Yes, indeed! And then you went out again. You didn't want to take any risks, though; so you went via the back door, out into the back garden, through the gap in the fence and over the path across the field to the Quality supermarket. You had to get out of the house anyway, so why not carry through with the bluff? You bought some provisions, and even as you walked round the shelves your brain was working non-stop. Buy something that made it look as though Quinn was having someone in for a meal that evening! Why not? Another clever touch. Two steaks and all the rest of it. But you shouldn't have bought the butter, Roope! You got the wrong brand, and he had plenty in the fridge, anyway. As I say, it was clever. But you were getting a bit *too* clever.'

'Like you are, Inspector.' Roope bestirred himself at last. He took out a cigarette and lit it, putting the match carefully into the ashtray. 'I can't honestly think that you expect me to believe such convoluted nonsense.' He spoke carefully and rationally, and appeared much more at ease with himself. 'If you've nothing better to talk about than such boy-scout fancy-dress twaddle, I suggest you release me immediately. But if you want to persist with it, I shall have to call in my lawyer. I refused to do this when you told me of my rights earlier – I knew my rights, anyway, Inspector – but I thought I'd rather have my own innocence at my side than any pettifogging lawyer. But you're driving me a bit too far, you know. You've not the slightest shred of evidence for any of these fantastic allegations you've made against me. Not the slightest! And if you can't do any better than this I suggest that it may be in your own interests, not just mine, to pack in this ridiculous charade immediately.'

'You deny the charges then?'

'Charges? *What* charges? I'm not aware that you've made any charges.'

'You deny that the sequence of events—'

'Of *course*, I deny it! Why the hell should anyone go to all that trouble—?'

'Whoever murdered Quinn had to try to establish an alibi. And he did. A very clever alibi. You see all the indications in this case seemed to point to Quinn being alive on Friday evening, certainly until the early evening, and it was vital—'

'You mean Quinn *wasn't* alive on Friday evening?'

'Oh no,' said Morse slowly. '*Quinn had been dead for several hours.*'

There was a long silence in the small room, broken finally by Roope. 'Several hours, you say?'

Morse nodded. 'But I'm not *quite* sure exactly when Quinn was murdered. I rather hoped you might be able to tell me.'

Roope laughed aloud, and shook his head in bewilderment. 'And you think *I* killed Quinn?'

'That's why you're here, and that's why you're going to stay here – until you decide to tell me the truth.'

Roope's voice suddenly became high-pitched and exasperated. 'But – but I was in London that Friday. I *told* you that. I got back to Oxford at four-fifteen. Four-fifteen! Can't you believe that?'

'No, I can't,' said Morse flatly.

'Well, look, Inspector. Let's just get one thing straight. I don't suppose I could account for my movements – at least not to your satisfaction – from, let's say, five o'clock to about eight o'clock that night. And you wouldn't believe me, anyway. But if you're determined to keep me in this miserable place much longer, at least charge me with something I *could* have done. All right! I drove Quinn's car and did his shopping and God knows what else. Let's accept all that bloody nonsense, if it'll please you. *But charge me with murdering Quinn as well.* At twenty past four – whenever you like, I don't care! Five o'clock. Six o'clock. Seven o'clock. Take your pick. But for Christ's sake show *some* sense. *I was in London until three o'clock or so, and I was on the train until it reached Oxford.* Don't you understand that? Make something up, if you like. But please, *please* tell me when and how I'm supposed to have murdered the man. That's all I ask.'

As Lewis looked at him, Morse seemed to be growing a little less confident. He picked up the papers in front of him and shuffled them around meaninglessly. Something seemed to have misfired somewhere – that was for sure.

'I've only got your word, Mr Roope' (it was *Mr* Roope now) 'that you caught that particular train from London. You were at your publishers', I know that. We've checked. But you could—'

'May I use your phone, Inspector?'

Morse shrugged and looked vaguely disconsolate. 'It's a bit unusual, I suppose, but—'

Roope looked through the directory, rang a number, and spoke rapidly for a few minutes before handing the receiver to Morse. It was the Cabriolet Taxis Services, and Morse listened and nodded and asked no questions. 'I see. Thank you.' He put down the phone and looked across at Roope. 'You had more success than we did, Mr Roope. Did you find the ticket collector, too?'

'No. He's had flu, but he'll be back at work this week sometime.'

'You've been very busy.'

'I was worried – who wouldn't be? You kept asking me where I was, and I thought you'd got it in for me, and I knew it would be sensible to try to check. We've all got an instinct for self-preservation, you know.'

'Ye-es.' Morse ran the index finger of his left hand along his nose – many, many times; and finally came to a decision. He dialled a number and asked for the editor of the *Oxford Mail*. 'I see. We're too late then. Page one, you say? Oh dear. Well, it can't be helped. What about Stop Press? Could we get anything in there? ... Good. Let's say er "Murder Suspect Released. Mr C. A. Roope (see page 1), arrested earlier today in connection with the murder of Nicholas Quinn, was released this afternoon. Chief Inspector—" What? No more room? I see. Well, it'll be better than nothing. Sorry to muck you about ... Yes, I'm afraid these things do happen sometimes. Cheers.'

Morse cradled the phone and turned towards Roope. 'Look, sir. As I say, things like this do—'

Roope got to his feet. 'Forget it! You've said enough for one day. Can I assume I'm free to go now?' There was a sharp edge on his voice.

'Yes, sir. And, as I say ...' Roope looked at him with deep contempt as the feeble sentence whimpered away. 'Have you a car here, sir?'

'No. I don't have a car.'

'Oh no, I remember. If you like, Sergeant Lewis here will—'

'No, he won't! I've had quite enough of your sickening hospitality for one day. I'll bus it, thank you very much!'

Before Morse could say more, he had left the room and was walking briskly across the courtyard in the bright and chilly afternoon.

During the last ten minutes of the interview Lewis had felt himself becoming progressively more perplexed, and at one stage he had stared at Morse like a street-idler gaping at the village idiot. What *did* Morse think he was doing? He looked again at him now, his head down over the sheets of paper on the table. But even as Lewis looked, Morse lifted his head, and a strangely self-satisfied smile was spreading over his face. He saw that Lewis was watching him, and he winked happily.

# twenty-six

The man inside the house is anxious, but reasonably calm. The phone rings stridently, imperiously, several times during the late afternoon and early evening. But he does not answer it, for he has seen the post-office van repairing (repairing!) the telephone wires just along the road. Clumsy and obvious. They must think him stupid. Yet all the time he knows that *they* are not stupid, either, and the knowledge nags away in his mind. Over and over again he tells himself that they cannot *know*; can only guess; can never prove. The maze would defeat an indefatigable Ariadne, and the ball of thread leads only to blind and bricked-up alleyways. Infernal phone! He waits until the importunate caller has exhausted a seemingly limitless patience, and takes the receiver off its stand. But it purrs – intolerably. He turns on the transistor radio at ten minutes to six and listens, yet with only a fraction of his conscious faculties, to the BBC's City correspondent discussing the fluctuations in the *Financial Times* index, and the fortunes of the floating pound. He himself has no worries about money. No worries at all.

The man outside the house continues to watch. Already he has been watching for over three and a half hours, and his feet are damp and cold. He looks at his luminous watch: 5.40 p.m. Only another twenty minutes before his relief arrives. Still no movement, save for the shadow that repeatedly passes back and forth across the curtained window.

*

If sleep be defined as the relaxation of consciousness, the man inside the house does not sleep that night. He is dressed again at 6 a.m. and he waits. At 6.45 a.m. he hears the clatter of milk-bottles in the darkened road outside. But still he waits. It is not until 7.45 a.m. that the paper boy arrives with *The Times*. It is still dark, and the little business is speedily transacted. Uncomplicated; unobserved.

The man outside the house has almost given up hope when at 1.15 p.m. the door opens and a man emerges and walks unhurriedly down towards Oxford. The man outside switches to 'transmission' and speaks into his mobile radio. Then he switches to 'reception', and the message is brief and curt: 'Follow him, Dickson! And don't let him see you!'

The man who had been inside the house walks to the railway station, where he looks around him and then walks into the buffet, orders a cup of coffee, sits by the window, and looks out onto the car park. At 1.35 a car drives slowly past – a familiar car, which turns down the incline into the car park. The automatic arm is raised and the car makes for the furthest corner of the area. The car park is almost full. The man in the buffet puts down his half-finished coffee, lights a cigarette, puts the spent match neatly back into the box, and walks out.

At 2.00 p.m. the young girl in the maroon dress can stand it no longer. The customers, too, though they are only few, have been looking at him queerly. She walks from behind the counter and taps him on the shoulder. He is not much above medium height. 'Excuse me, sir. Bu' have you come in for a coffee, or somethin'?'

'No. I'll have a cup o' tea, please.' He speaks pleasantly, and as he puts down his powerful binoculars she sees that his eyes are a palish shade of grey.

It is just after five when Lewis gets home. He is tired and his feet are like ice.

'Are you home for the night?'

'Yes, luv, thank goodness! I'm freezing cold.'

'Is that bloody man, Morse, tryin' to give you pneumornia, or somethin'?'

Lewis hears his wife all right, but he is thinking of something else. 'He's a clever bugger, Morse is. Christ, he's clever! Though whether he's *right* or not . . .' But his wife is no longer listening, and Lewis hears the thrice-blessed clatter of the chip pan in the kitchen.

# twenty-seven

In the Syndicate building on Wednesday morning, Morse told Bartlett frankly about the virtual certainty of some criminal malpractice in the administration of the examinations. He mentioned specifically his suspicions about the leakage of question papers to Al-jamara, and passed exhibit No 1 across the table.

3rd March

Dear George,
Greetings to all at Oxford. Many thanks for your
letter and for the summer examination package.
All Entry Forms and Fees Forms should be ready
for final dispatch to the Syndicate by Friday
20th or at the very latest, I'm told, by the 21st.
Admin has improved here, though there's room
for improvement still; just give us all two or three
more years and we'll really show you! Please
don't let these wretched 16+ proposals destroy
your basic O- and A-pattern. Certainly this
sort of change, if implemented immediately,
would bring chaos.
Sincerely yours,

Bartlett frowned deeply as he read the letter, then opened his desk diary and consulted a few entries. 'This is er a load of nonsense — you realize that, don't you? All entry forms had to be in by the first of March this year. We've installed a mini-computer and anything arriving after—'

Morse interrupted him. 'You mean the entry forms from Al-jamara were already in when that letter was written?'

'Oh yes. Otherwise we couldn't have examined their candidates.'

'And you did examine them?'

'Certainly. Then there's this business of the summer examination package. They couldn't possibly have received that before early April. Half the question papers weren't printed until then. And there's something else wrong, isn't there, Inspector? The 20th March isn't a Friday. Not in my diary, anyway. No, no. I don't think I'd build too much on this letter. I'm sure it can't be from one of our—'

'You don't recognize the signature?'

'Would anybody? It looks more like a coil of barbed wire—'

'Just read down the right-hand side of the letter, sir. The last word on each line, if you see what I mean.'

In a flat voice the Secretary read the words aloud: 'your – package – ready – Friday – 21st – room – three – Please – destroy – this – immediately.' He nodded slowly to himself. 'I see what you mean, Inspector, though I must say I'd never have spotted it myself ... You mean you think that George Bland was—'

'– was on the fiddle, yes. I'm convinced that this letter told him exactly where and when he could collect the latest instalment of his money.'

Bartlett took a deep breath and consulted his diary once more. 'You may just be onto something, I suppose. He wasn't in the office on Friday 21st.'

'Do you know where he was?'

Bartlett shook his head and passed over the diary, where among the dozen or so brief, neatly written entries under 21st March Morse read the laconic reminder: 'GB not in office.'

'Can you get in touch with him, sir?'

'Of course. I sent him a telegram only last Wednesday – about Quinn. They'd met when—'

'Did he reply?'

'Hasn't done yet.'

Morse took the plunge. 'Naturally I can't tell you everything, sir, but I think you ought to know that in my view the deaths of both Quinn and Ogleby are directly linked with Bland. I think that Bland was corrupt enough to compromise the integrity of this Syndicate at every point – if there was money in it for him. But I think there's someone *here*, too, not necessarily on the staff, but someone very closely associated with the work of the Syndicate, who's in collaboration with Bland. And I've little doubt that Quinn found out who it was, and got himself murdered for his trouble.'

Bartlett had been listening intently to Morse's words, but he evinced little surprise. 'I thought you might be going to say something like that, Inspector, and I suppose you think that Ogleby found out as well, and was murdered for the same reason.'

'Could be, sir. Though you may be making a false assumption. You see, it may be that the murderer of Nicholas Quinn has already been punished for his crime.'

The little Secretary was genuinely shocked now. His eyebrows shot up an inch, and his frameless lenses settled even lower on his nose, as Morse slowly continued.

'I'm afraid you must face the real possibility, sir, that Quinn's murderer worked here under your very nose; the possibility that he was in fact your own deputy-secretary – *Philip Ogleby*.'

Lewis came in ten minutes later as Morse and Bartlett were arranging the meeting. Bartlett was to phone or write to all the Syndicate members and ask them to attend an extraordinary general meeting on Friday morning at 10 a.m.; he was to insist that it was of the utmost importance that they should cancel all other commitments and attend; after all, two members of the Syndicate had been murdered, hadn't they?

In the corridor outside Lewis whispered briefly to Morse. 'You were right, sir. It rang for two minutes. Noakes confirms it.'

'Excellent. I think it's time to make a move then, Lewis. Car outside?'

'Yes, sir. Do you want me with you?'

'No. You get to the car; we'll be along in a minute.' He walked along the corridor, knocked quietly on the door, and entered. She was sitting at her desk signing letters, but promptly took off her reading glasses, stood up, and smiled sweetly. 'Bit early to take me for a drink, isn't it?'

'No chance, I'm afraid. The car's outside – I think you'd better get your coat.'

The man inside does not go out this same Wednesday morning. The paper boy lingers for a few seconds as he puts *The Times* through the letter box, but no lucrative errand is commissioned this morning; the milkman delivers one pint of milk; the postman brings no letters; there are no visitors. The phone has gone several times earlier, and at twelve o'clock it goes again. Four rings; then, almost immediately it resumes, and mechanically the man counts the number of rings again – twenty-eight, twenty-nine, thirty. The phone stops, and the man smiles to himself. It is a clever system. They have used it several times before.

The man outside is still waiting; but expectantly now, for he thinks that the time of reckoning may be drawing near. At 4.20 p.m. he is conscious of some activity at the back of the house, and a minute later the man inside emerges with a bicycle, rides quickly away up a side turning, and in less than five seconds has completely disappeared. It has been too quick, too unexpected. Constable Dickson swears softly to himself and calls up HQ, where Sergeant Lewis is distinctly unamused.

The car park is again very full today, and Morse is standing by the window in the buffet bar. He wonders what would happen if a heavy snowshower were to smother each of the cars in a thick white blanket; then each of the baffled motorists would need to remember exactly where he had left his car, and go straight to that spot – and find it. Just as Morse finds the spot again through his binoculars. But he can see nothing, and half an hour later, at 5.15 p.m., he can still see nothing. He gives it up, talks to the ticket collector, and learns beyond all reasonable doubt that Roope was not lying when he said he'd passed through the ticket barrier, as if from the 3.05 train from Paddington, on Friday, 21st November.

As he steps out of his front door at 9.30 a.m. the next day, Thursday, 4th December, the man who has been inside is arrested by Sergeant Lewis and Constable Dickson of the Thames Valley Constabulary, CID Branch. He is charged with complicity in the murders of Nicholas Quinn and Philip Ogleby.

# twenty-eight

The case was over now, or virtually so, and Morse had his feet up on his desk, feeling slightly over-beered and more than slightly self-satisfied, when Lewis came in at 2.30 on Thursday afternoon. 'I found him, sir. Had to drag him out of a class at Cherwell School – but I found him. It was just what you said.'

'Well that's the final nail in the coffin and—' He suddenly broke off. 'You don't look too happy, Lewis. What's the trouble?'

'I still don't understand what's happening.'

'Lewis! You don't want to ruin my little party-piece in the morning, do you?'

Lewis shrugged a reluctant consent, but he felt like an examinee who has just emerged from the examination room, conscious that he should have done very much better. 'I suppose you think I'm not very bright, sir.'

'Nothing of the sort! It was a very clever crime, Lewis. I was just a bit lucky here and there, that's all.'

'I suppose I missed the obvious clues – as usual.'

'But they *weren't* obvious, my dear old friend. Well, perhaps ...' He put his feet down and lit a cigarette. 'Let me tell you what put me on to the track, shall I? Let's see now. First of all, I think, the single most important fact in the whole case was Quinn's deafness. You see Quinn was not only hard of hearing; he was very very deaf. But we learned that he was quite exceptionally proficient in the art of lip-reading; and I'm quite sure that because he could lip-read so brilliantly Quinn discovered the staggering fact that one of his colleagues was crooked. You see the real sin against the Holy Ghost for anyone in charge of public examinations is to divulge the contents of question papers beforehand; and Quinn discovered that one of his colleagues was doing precisely that. *But*, Lewis, I failed to take into account a much more obvious and a much more important implication of Quinn's being deaf. It sounds almost childishly simple when you think of it – in fact an idiot would have spotted it before I did. It's this. Quinn was a marvel at reading from the lips of others – agreed? He might just as well have had ears, really. But he could only, let's say, *hear* what others were saying when he could *see* them. Lip-reading's absolutely useless when you can't see the person who's talking; when someone stands behind you, say, or when someone in the corridor outside shouts that there's a bomb in the building. Do you see what I mean, Lewis? If someone knocked on Quinn's office door, he couldn't hear anything. But as soon as someone opened the door and *said* something – he was fine. All right? Remember this, then: *Quinn couldn't hear what he didn't see.*'

'Am I supposed to see why all that's important, sir?'

'Oh yes. And you *will* do, Lewis, if only you think back to the Friday when Quinn was murdered.'

'He was definitely murdered on the Friday, then?'

'I think if you pushed me I could tell you to within sixty seconds!' He looked very smug about the whole thing, and Lewis felt torn between the wish to satisfy his own curiosity and a reluctance to gratify the chief's inflated ego even further. Yet he thought he caught a glimpse of the truth at last ... Yes, of course. Noakes had said ... He nodded several times, and his curiosity won.

'What about all this business at the cinema, though? Was that all a red herring?'

'Certainly not. It was *meant* to be a red herring, but as things turned out – not too luckily from the murderer's point of view – it presented a series of vital clues. Just think a minute. Everything we began to learn about Quinn's death seemed to take it further and further forward in time: he rang up a school in Bradford at about 12.20; he went to Studio 2 at about half-past one, after leaving a note in his office for his secretary; he came back to the office about a quarter to five, and drove home; he left a note for his cleaning woman and got some shopping in; he's heard on the phone about ten past five; certainly no one except Mrs Evans comes to see him before six-thirty or so, because Mrs Greenaway is keeping an eagle eye on the drive. So? So Quinn must have been murdered later that evening, or even on the following morning. The medical report didn't help us much either way, and we had little option but to follow our noses – which we did. But when you come to add all the evidence up, no one actually *saw* Quinn after midday on Friday. Take the phone call to Bradford. If you're a schoolmaster – and all of the staff at the Syndicate had taught at one point – you know that 12.20 is just about the worst time in the whole day to try to get a member of staff. School lessons may finish earlier in a few schools but the vast majority don't. In other words that call was made with not the least expectation that its purpose would be successful. That is, unless the purpose was to mislead *me* – in which case I'm afraid it was highly successful. Now, take the note Quinn left. We know that Bartlett is a bit of a tartar about most aspects of office routine; and one of his rules is that his assistant secretaries must leave a note when they go out. Now, Quinn had been with the Syndicate for three months, and being a keen young fellow and anxious to please his boss, he must have left dozens of little notes during that time; and anyone, if he or she was so minded, could have taken one, especially if that someone needed one of the notes to further an alibi. And someone did. Then there's the phone call Mrs Greenaway heard. But note once again that she didn't actually *see* him making it. She's nervous and anxious: she thinks the baby's due, and the very last thing she wants to indulge in is a bit of eavesdropping. All she wants is the line to be free! When she hears voices she doesn't want to listen to them – she wants them to *finish*. And if the other person – the one she thinks Quinn is ringing – is doing most of the talking at that point ... You see what I was getting at with Roope, Lewis? If *Roope* were talking

– putting in just the occasional "yes" and "no" and so on –
Mrs Greenaway, who says she doesn't hear too well anyway,
would automatically assume it was *Quinn*. Both Quinn and
Roope came from Bradford, and both spoke with a pretty broad
northern accent, and all Mrs Greenaway remembers clearly is
that *one* of the voices was a bit cultured and donnish. Now,
that doesn't take us much further, I agree. At the most it tells
us that the telephone conversation wasn't between Quinn and
Roope. But I knew that, Lewis, because I knew that Quinn
must have been dead for several hours when someone spoke
from Quinn's front room.'

'It was a bit of luck for him that Mrs Greenaway didn't—'

Morse was nodding. 'Yes. But the luck wasn't all on his side.
Remember that Mrs Evans—'

'You've explained how that could have happened, sir. It's
just this Studio 2 business I can't follow.'

'I'm not surprised. We had everybody telling us lies about it.
But let me give you one or two clues. Martin and Monica
Height had decided to go to the pictures on Friday afternoon,
and yet they stupidly tried to change their alibi – change a good
alibi for a lousy alibi. Just ask yourself *why*, Lewis. The only
sensible answer that I could think of was that they had *seen*
something – or one of them had seen something – which they
weren't prepared to talk about. Now, I think that Monica, at
least on this point, was prepared to tell me the truth –the literal
truth. I asked her whether she had seen someone else going *in*;
and she said no.' Morse smiled slowly: 'Do you see what I
mean now?'

'No, sir.'

'Keep at it, Lewis! You see, whatever happened in the early
afternoon of that Friday, *Martin and Monica stayed to see the
film*. Do you understand that? Whatever upset them – or, as I
say, upset one of them – it didn't result in their leaving the
cinema. Need I go on?'

Need he go on! Huh! Lewis was more lost than ever, but
his curiosity would give him no peace. 'What about Ogleby,
then?'

'Ah. Now we're coming to it. Ogleby lied to me, Lewis. He
told me one or two lies of the first water. *But the great majority*

*of the things Ogleby said were true.* You were there when I questioned him, Lewis, and if you want *some* of the truth, just look back to your notes. You'll find he said some very interesting things. You'll find, for example, that he said he was in the office that Friday afternoon.'

'And you think he was?'

'I know he was. He just *had* to be, you see.'

'Oh,' said Lewis, unseeing. 'And he went to Studio 2 as well, I suppose?'

Morse nodded. 'Later on, yes. And remember that he'd made a careful sketch of another ticket – the ticket that was found in Quinn's pocket. Now. There's a nice little poser for you, Lewis: when and why did Ogleby do that? Well?'

'I don't know, sir. I just get more confused the more I think about it.'

Morse got up and walked across the room. 'It's easy when you think about it, Lewis. Ask yourself just one question: Why didn't he just *take* the ticket? He must have seen it; must have had it in his hands. There's only one answer, isn't there?'

Lewis nodded hopefully and Morse (praise be!) continued. 'Yes. Ogleby wasn't meant to find the ticket. But he did; and he knew that it had been placed wherever it was for a vital purpose, Lewis, *and he knew that he had to leave it exactly where he'd found it.'*

The phone rang and Morse answered it, saying he'd be there straightaway. 'You'd better come along, Lewis. His lawyer's arrived.' As they walked together down to the cellblock, Morse asked Lewis if he had any idea where the Islets of Langerhans were.

'Sounds vaguely familiar, sir. Baltic Sea, is it?'

'No, it's not. It's in the pancreas – if you know where that is.'

'As a matter of fact, I do, sir. It's a large gland discharging into the duodenum.'

Morse raised his eyebrows in admiration. One up to Lewis.

# twenty-nine

As Morse looked at the Thursday evening class with their hearing aids, private or NHS, plugged into their ears, he reminded himself that during the previous weeks of the term Quinn had sat there amongst his fellow students, sharing the mysteries and the silent manifestations. There were eight of them, sitting in a single row in front of their teacher, and at the back of the room Morse felt that he was watching a TV screen with the sound turned off. The teacher was talking, for her lips moved and she made the natural gestures of speech. But no sound. When Morse had managed to rid himself of the suspicion that *he* had suddenly been struck deaf, he watched the teacher's lips more closely, and tried as hard as he could to read the words. Occasionally one or other of the class would raise a hand and voice a silent question, and then the teacher would write up a word on the blackboard. Frequently, it appeared, the difficult words – the words that the class were puzzled by – began with 'p', or 'b', or 'm'; and to a lesser extent with 't', 'd', or 'n'. Lip-reading was clearly a most sophisticated skill.

At the end of the class, Morse thanked the teacher for allowing him to observe, and spoke to her about Quinn. Here, too, he had been the star pupil, it seemed, and all the class had been deeply upset at the news of his death. Yes, he really had been very deaf indeed – but one wouldn't have guessed; unless, that is, one had experience of these things.

A bell sounded throughout the building. It was 9 p.m. and time for everyone to leave the premises.

'Would he have been able to hear that?' asked Morse.

But the teacher had temporarily turned away to mark the register. The bell was still ringing. 'Would Quinn have been able to hear that?' repeated Morse.

But she still didn't hear him and, belatedly, Morse guessed the truth. When finally she looked up again, he repeated his question once more. 'Could Quinn hear the bell?'

'Could Quinn hear them all, did you say? I'm sorry, I didn't quite catch—'

'H-ear th-e b-e-ll,' mouthed Morse, with ridiculous exaggeration.

'Oh, the *bell*. Is it ringing? I'm afraid that none of us could ever hear that.'

Thursday was guest night at Lonsdale College, but after a couple of post-prandial ports the Dean of the Syndicate decided he'd better get back to his rooms. He was decidedly displeased at having to rearrange his Friday morning programme, since one of the few duties he positively enjoyed was that of interviewing prospective entrants. As he walked along the quad he wondered morosely how long the Syndicate meeting would last, and why exactly Tom Bartlett had been so insistent. It was all getting out of hand, anyway. He was getting too old for the post, and he looked forward to his retirement in a year's time. One thing was certain: he just couldn't cope with events like those of the past fortnight.

He looked through the pile of UCCA forms on his desk and read the fulsome praises heaped upon the heads of their pupils by headmasters and headmistresses, so desperately anxious to lift their schools a few places up the table in the Oxbridge League. If only such heads would realize that all their blabber was, if anything, counter productive! On the first form he read some headmistress's report on a young girl anxious to take up one of the few places at Lonsdale reserved for women. The girl was (naturally!) the most brilliant scholar of her year and had won a whole cupboardful of prizes; and the Dean read the headmistress's comments in the 'Personality' column: 'Not unattractive and certainly a very vivacious girl, with a puckish sense of humour and a piquant wit.' The Dean smiled slowly. What a sentence! Over the years he had compiled his own little book of synonyms:

'not unattractive'  =  'hideous to behold'
'vivacious'          =  'usually drunk'
'puckish'            =  'batty'
'piquant'            =  'plain rude'

Ah well. Perhaps she wasn't such a bad prospect after all! But he wouldn't be interviewing her himself. Blast the Syndicate!

It would have been interesting to test his little theory once more. So often people tried to create the impression of being completely different from their true selves, and it wasn't all that difficult. A smiling face, and a heart as hard as a flintstone! The opposite, too: a face set as hard as a flint and ... A vague memory stirred in the Dean's mind. Chief Inspector Morse had mentioned something similar, hadn't he? But the Dean couldn't quite get hold of it. Never mind. It couldn't be very important.

Bartlett had received the call from Mrs Martin at eight o'clock. Did he know where Donald was? Had he got a meeting? She knew he had to work late some nights, but he had never been away as long as this. Bartlett tried to make the right noises; said not to worry; said he would ring her back; said there must be some easy explanation.

'Oh Christ!' he said, after putting the receiver down.

'What's the matter, Tom?' Mrs Bartlett had come through into the hall and was looking at him anxiously. He put his hand gently on hers, and smiled wearily. How many times have I told you? You mustn't listen in to my telephone calls. You've got enough—'

'I never do. You know that, Tom. But—'

'It's all right. It's not your problem; it's mine. That's what they pay me for, isn't it? I can't expect a fat salary for nothing, can I?'

Mrs Bartlett put her arm lovingly on his shoulder. 'I don't know what they pay you, and I don't want to know. If they paid you a million it wouldn't be too much! But—' She was worried, and the little Secretary knew it.

'I know. The world suddenly seems to have gone crazy, doesn't it? That was Martin's wife. He's not home yet.'

'Oh no!'

'Now, now. Don't start jumping to silly conclusions.'

'You don't think—?'

'You go and sit down and pour yourself a gin. And pour one for me. I shan't be a minute.' He found Monica's number and dialled. And like someone else the day before, he found himself mechanically counting the dialling tones. Ten, twenty, twenty-five. Sally must be out, too. He let it ring a few more times, and then slowly replaced the receiver. The Syndicate seemed to be on the verge of total collapse.

He thought back on the years during which he had worked so hard to build it all up. And somehow, at some point, the foundation had begun to shift and cracks to appear in the edifice above. He could almost put the exact time to it: the time when Roope had been elected on to the Board of the Syndics. Yes. That was when things had started crumbling. Roope! For a few minutes the little Secretary stood indecisively by the phone, and knew that he could willingly murder the man. Instead he rang Morse's number at the Thames Valley HQ, but Morse was out, too. Not that it mattered much. He'd mention it to him in the morning.

# thirty

Mrs Seth arrived at a quarter to ten and made her way upstairs to the Board Room. She was the first of the Syndics to arrive, and as she sat down her thoughts drifted back ... back to the last time she had sat there, when she had recalled her father ... when Roope had spoken ... when Quinn had been appointed ... The room was gradually filling up, and she acknowledged a few muted 'good mornings'; but the atmosphere was one of gloom, and the other Syndics sat down silently and let their own thoughts drift back, as she had done. Sometimes one or two of the graduate staff attended Syndics' meetings, but only by invitation; and none was there this morning except Bartlett, whose tired, drawn face did little more than reflect the communal mood. A man was sitting next to Bartlett, but she didn't know him. Must be from the police. Pleasant-looking man: about her own age – mid-, late-forties; going a bit thin on top; nice eyes, though they seemed to look at you and through you at the same time. There was another man, too – probably another policeman; but he was standing diffidently outside the magic circle, with a notebook in his hands.

At two minutes past ten, when all except one of the chairs were occupied, Bartlett stood up and in a sad and disillusioned little speech informed the assembly of the police suspicions – his own, too – that the integrity of their own foreign examinations had been irreparably impaired by the criminal behaviour of one or two people, people in whom the Syndicate had placed complete trust; that it was the view of Chief Inspector Morse ('on my right') that the deaths of Quinn and Ogleby were directly connected with this matter; that, after the clearing-up of the comparatively small autumn examination, the activities of the Syndicate would necessarily be in abeyance until a complete investigation had been made; that the implications of a possible shut-down were far-reaching, and that the full co-operation of each and every member of the Syndicate would be absolutely essential. But such matters would have to wait; the purpose of their meeting this morning was quite different, as they would see.

The Dean thanked the Secretary and proceeded to add his own lugubrious thoughts on the future of the Syndicate; and as he tediously ummed and ahed his way along, it became clear that the Syndics were getting rather restless. Words were whispered along the tables: 'One or *two*, didn't Bartlett say?' 'Who do you think?' 'Why have we got the police *here*?' 'They *are* the police, aren't they?'

The Dean finished at last, and the whispering finished, too. It was a strange reversal of the natural order, and Mrs Seth thought it had everything to do with the man seated on Bartlett's right, who thus far had sat impassively in his chair, occasionally running the index finger of his left hand along the side of his nose. She saw Bartlett turn towards Morse and look at him quizzically; and in turn she saw Morse nod slightly, before slowly rising to his feet.

'Ladies and gentlemen. I asked the Secretary to call this meeting because I thought it only proper that you should all know something of what we've discovered about the leakage of question papers from this office. Well, you've heard something about that and I think' (he looked vaguely at the Dean and then at Bartlett) 'I think that we may say that officially the meeting is over, and if any of you have commitments that can't wait, you should feel free to go.' He looked around the tables with cold, grey eyes, and the tension in the room perceptibly tautened. No one moved a muscle, and the stillness was profound. 'But perhaps it's proper, too,' resumed Morse, 'that you should know something about the police investigations into the deaths of Mr Quinn and Mr Ogleby, and I'm sure you will all be very glad to know that the case is now complete – or almost complete. Let's put it in the official jargon, ladies and gentlemen, and say that a man has been arrested and is being held for questioning in connection with the murders of Quinn and Ogleby.'

The silence of the room was broken only by the rustle of papers as Lewis turned over a page in his notebook: Morse held the ring and the assembled Syndics hung on his every word. 'You will know, or most of you will, that last Monday one of your own colleagues, Mr Christopher Roope, was detained in connection with Quinn's murder. You will know, too, I think, that he was released shortly afterwards. The evidence against him appeared to us insufficient to warrant further detention, and everything seemed to point to the fact that he had a perfectly valid alibi for the period of time on Friday, 21st November, when in the view of the police Quinn must have been murdered. Yet I must tell you all here and now that without a shadow of doubt Roope was the person responsible for selling the soul of the Syndicate – certainly in Al-jamara, and for all I know in several of your other oversea centres as well.' Some of the Syndics drew in their breaths, some opened their mouths slightly, but never for a second did their eyes leave Morse. '*And*, ladies and gentlemen, in all this his principal lieutenant was your former colleague, Mr George Bland.' Again the mingled surprise and shock around the table; but again the underlying hush and expectation. 'The whole thing was brought to light by the vigilance and integrity of one man – Nicholas Quinn. Now, precisely when Quinn made his discovery we shall perhaps never know for certain; but I should guess it may well have been at the reception given by the Al-jamara officials, when the drink was flowing freely, when some of the guilty were less than discreet, and when Quinn read things on the lips of others so clearly that they might just as well have been shouted through a megaphone. And it was, I believe, as a direct result of Quinn's deeply disturbing discovery that he was murdered – to stop him talking, and so ensure that those guilty of betraying public confidence should continue to draw their rewards – very considerable rewards, no doubt – from their partners in crime abroad. Furthermore, I think that in addition to telling the guilty party of what he knew, or at least of what he strongly suspected, Quinn told someone else: someone he firmly believed had absolutely nothing to do with the crooked practices that were going on. That someone was Philip Ogleby. There is evidence that Quinn had far too much to drink at the reception, and that Ogleby followed him out as he left. Again I am guessing. But I think it more than likely that Ogleby caught up with Quinn, and told him that he would be a fool to drive himself home in such a drunken condition. He may have offered to drive him home, I don't know. But what is almost certain is that Quinn told Ogleby what he knew. Now, if Ogleby were in the racket himself, many of the things which were so puzzling about Quinn's murder would begin to sort themselves out. Of all Quinn's colleagues, Ogleby was the one person who had no alibi for the key period of Friday afternoon. He went back to the office after lunch, and he was there – or so he said – the rest of the afternoon. Now whoever killed Quinn had to be in the office both in the latter part of the morning, and again between half-past four and five; and if any single person from the office was guilty of murdering Quinn, there was only one genuine suspect – *Ogleby*, the very man in whom Quinn had confided.'

There was a slight murmur around the table and one or two of the Syndics stirred uneasily in their chairs; but Morse resumed, and the effect was that of a conductor tapping his baton on the rostrum.

'Ogleby lied to me when I questioned him about his exact whereabouts that Friday afternoon. I've been able to look back on the evidence he gave, since my Sergeant here' – a few heads turned and Lewis sheepishly acknowledged his moment of glory – 'took full notes at the time, and I can now see where Ogleby lied – where he *had* to lie. For example, he insisted that he was in the office at about 4.30 p.m., when not only Mr Roope but also Mr Noakes, the caretaker, could swear quite categorically that he *wasn't*. Now, this I find very strange. Ogleby lied to me on the one point which seemed to prove his guilt. Why? Why did he say he was here all that afternoon? Why did he begin to tie the noose round his own neck? It's not an easy question to answer, I agree. But there *is* an answer; a very simple answer: *Ogleby was not lying*. On that point, at least, he was telling the truth. He *was* here, although neither Roope nor Noakes saw him. And when I looked back on his evidence, I began to ask myself whether one or two other things, which on the face of it seemed obvious lies, were in fact nothing of the sort. So it was that I gradually began to understand exactly what had happened that Friday afternoon, and to realize that Ogleby was entirely innocent of the murder of Nicholas Quinn. The fact of the matter is that precisely because Ogleby was in the office on the afternoon of Friday, 21st November, *he knew who had murdered Quinn*; and because of this knowledge, he was himself murdered. Why Ogleby didn't confide his virtually certain suspicions to me, I shall never really know. I think I can guess, but ... Anyway, we can only be grateful that the murderer has been arrested and is now in custody at Police Headquarters. He has made a full statement.' Morse pointed dramatically to the empty chair. 'That's where he usually sits, I believe. Yes, ladies and gentlemen, your own colleague, *Christopher Roope*.'

A babel of chatter now broke out in the room, and Mrs Seth was weeping silently. Yet even before the general hubbub had subsided there was a further moment of high drama. After several whispered conversations along the top table, the Vice-Dean requested permission to make a brief statement, and Morse sat down and began doodling aimlessly on the blotter in front of him.

'I hope the Chief Inspector will forgive me, but I wish to clear up one point, if I may. Did I understand him to say that who-ever killed Quinn had to be in the Syndicate building both in the morning and also at the end of the afternoon?'

Morse replied at once. 'You understood correctly, sir. I don't wish to go into all the details of the case now; but Quinn was murdered at about twelve noon on Friday — no, let me be more honest with you — at *precisely* twelve noon on Friday 21st, and his dead body was taken from this building, in the boot of his own car, at approximately 4.45 p.m. Does that satisfy you, sir?'

The Vice-Dean coughed awkwardly and managed to look extraordinarily uncomfortable. 'Er, no, Chief Inspector. I'm afraid it doesn't. You see I myself went to London that Friday morning and I caught the 3.05 back to Oxford, arriving here about a quarter, twenty past four; and the plain truth is that *Roope was on the same train.*'

In the stunned silence which greeted this new evidence, Morse spoke quietly and slowly. 'You travelled back with him, you mean?'

'Er no, not exactly. I er I was walking along the platform and I saw Roope getting into a first-class carriage. I didn't join him because I was travelling second.' The Vice-Dean was glad not to have to elaborate on the truth. Even if he'd had a first-class ticket he would rather have sat in a second-class carriage than share a journey with Roope. He'd always hated Roope. What an ironic twist of fortune that he, the Vice-Dean, should be instrumental in clearing him of murder!

'I wish,' said Morse, 'that you could have told me that earlier, sir – not, of course' (he held up a hand to forestall any misunderstanding) 'that you could have known. But what you say is no surprise, sir. You see, *I knew that Roope caught the 3.05 from Paddington.*'

Several of the Syndics looked at each other; and there was a general air of bewilderment in the room. It was Bartlett himself who tried to put their unspoken questions into words. 'But only a few minutes ago you said—'

'No, sir,' interrupted Morse. 'I know what you're going to say, and you'd be wrong. I said that no one could have murdered Quinn without being in this building at two key periods; and that fact is quite unchallengeable. I repeat, *no single person* could have carried out the devilish and ingenious plan which was put into operation.' He looked slowly round the room and the full implication of his words slowly sunk into the minds of the Syndics. To Mrs Seth his voice seemed very quiet and far away now; yet at the same time heightened and tense as if the final disclosure were imminent at last. She saw Morse nod across and over her head, and she turned slightly to see Sergeant

Lewis walk quietly to the door and leave the Board Room. What—? But Morse was talking again, in the same quiet, steely voice.

'As I say, we must accept the undoubted fact that one person, on his or her own, could not have carried through the murder of Quinn. And so, ladies and gentlemen, the inference is inevitable: *we are looking for two people.* Two people who must share the same motives; two people for whom the death of Quinn is a vital necessity; two people who have a strangely close relationship; two people who can work and plot together; two people who are well known to you – *very* well known ... And before Sergeant Lewis comes back, let me just emphasize one further point, because I don't think some of you listened very carefully to what I said. I said that Roope had been arrested and charged with murder. But I did not say *whose* murder. In fact I am absolutely convinced of one thing – *Christopher Roope did not murder Nicholas Quinn.*'

In Quinn's former office Monica Height and Donald Martin had not spoken to each other, although it was now more than half an hour since the two constables had fetched them. Monica felt herself moving through a barren, arid landscape, her thoughts, her emotions, even her fears, now squeezed dry – passionless and empty. During the first few minutes she had noticed one of the constables eyeing her figure; but, for once, she experienced complete indifference. What a fool she'd been to think that Morse wouldn't guess! Little or nothing seemed to escape that beautifully lucid mind ... Yes, he had guessed the truth, though quite how he had seen through her story she couldn't begin to understand. Funny, really. It hadn't been a big lie, at all. Not like the stupid, stupid lies that she and Donald had told at the beginning. Donald! What a non-man he now seemed, sitting there next to her: sullen, silent, contemptible; as hopeless as she, for there was little chance for him, either. The truth would have to come out – all of it. The courts, the newspapers ... For a moment she managed to feel a fraction of sympathy for him, for it was her fault really, not his. From the day of his appointment she had known, known instinctively, that she could do with him exactly as she wished ...

The door opened and Lewis came in. 'Will you please come with me, Miss Height?'

She got to her feet slowly and walked up the wooden stairs. The door of the Board Room was closed and she hesitated a few seconds as Lewis opened it and stood aside for her. The burden on her conscience had become intolerable. Yes, it would be relief at last.


Mrs Seth turned her head as the door behind her opened. The Inspector had just been talking about Studio 2 in Walton Street; but her mind was growing numb and she had hardly been able to follow him. She heard a man's voice say quietly, 'After you, Miss Height.' Monica Height! Dear God, no! It couldn't be. Monica Height and Martin! She'd heard rumours, of course. Everyone must have heard rumours but ... Monica was sitting in Roope's seat now. Roope's! Had Morse meant Roope and Monica? *Two* people, he'd said ... But Morse was speaking again.

'Miss Height. I interviewed you early on in the case, and you claimed you had spent the afternoon of Friday, 21st November, with Mr Martin. Is that correct?'

'Yes.' Her voice was almost inaudible.

'And you said that you had spent the afternoon at your own house?'

'Yes.'

'And subsequently you agreed that this was not the truth?'

'Yes.'

'You said that in fact you had spent the afternoon with Mr Martin at Studio 2 in Walton Street?'

'Yes.'

'When I originally questioned you about this, I asked whether, apart from Mr Martin, you had seen anyone you knew in the cinema. Do you remember?'

'Yes, I remember.'

'And your answer was that you had not?'

'Yes; I told you the truth.'

'I then asked you whether you had seen anyone you knew going into the cinema, did I not?'

'Yes.'

'And you said "no".'

'Yes.'

'And you still stick by what you said?'

'Yes.'

'You saw a film called *The Nymphomaniac*?'

'Yes.'

'And you stayed with Mr Martin until the film was finished?'

'We left just a few minutes before it was due to finish.'

'Am I right, Miss Height, in saying that I could have asked you a different question? A question which might have had a vital bearing on the murder of Nicholas Quinn?'

'Yes.'

'And that question would not have been "Who did you see going *into* the cinema?" but "Who did you see coming *out*?"'

'Yes.'

'And you did see somebody?'

'Yes.'

'Could you recognize the person you saw coming out of Studio 2 that day?'

'Yes.'

'And is that person someone known to you?'

'Yes.'

'Is that someone here, in this room, now?'

'Yes.'

'Will you please indicate to us who that person is?'

Monica Height lifted her arm and pointed. It seemed almost like a magnetic needle pointing to the pole, gradually settling on to its true bearing. At first Mrs Seth thought that the arm was pointing directly at Morse himself. But that couldn't be. And then she followed that accusing finger once more, and she couldn't believe what she saw. Again she traced the line. Again she found the same direction. Oh no. It *couldn't* be, surely? For Monica's finger was pointing directly at one man – *the Secretary of the Syndicate*.

# thirty-one

Lewis (*mirabile dictu*) had not been kept completely in the dark. It was Lewis who had taken his turn of guard-duty in watching Roope's house. It was Lewis who had seen Roope leave that house and walk slowly to the car park at the railway station. It was Lewis who had traced the paperboy and who had discovered the address of the person to whom Roope had written his brief and urgent note. It was Lewis who had summoned Morse to the station buffet, and who had shared with him the magnificent view of two men seated in the front of a dark brown Vanden Plas at the furthest reach of the railway car park. It was Lewis who had arrested Roope as he had ventured forth, for the last time, the previous morning.

But if Lewis had not been kept in the dark, neither had he exactly been thrown up on to the shores of light; and later the same afternoon he was glad of the oppotunity to get a few things clear.

'What really put you on to Bartlett, sir?'

Morse sat back expansively in the black leather chair and told him. 'We learned fairly early on in the case, Lewis, that there was some animosity between Bartlett and Roope; and I kept asking myself why. And very gradually the light dawned: I'd been asking myself the wrong question – a non-question, in fact. There was *no* antagonism between the two at all, although there had to *appear* to be. The two of them were hand in glove over the Al-jamara business, and whatever happened they were anxious for the outside world never to have the slightest suspicion of any collusion between them. It wasn't too difficult, either. Just a bit of feigned needle here and there; sometimes a bit of a row in front of the other Syndics; and above all they had their superb opportunity when the appointment of a successor to Bland cropped up. They had the whole thing planned. It didn't matter much to either of them *who* was appointed; what mattered was that they should disagree, and disagree publicly and vehemently, about the new appointment.

So when Bartlett went one way Roope went the other. It was as simple as that. If Bartlett had been pro-Quinn, Roope would have been anti-Quinn.' A slight frown furrowed Morse's forehead, but was gone almost immediately. 'And it worked beautifully. The rest of the Syndics were openly embarrassed about the hostility between their young colleague, Roope, and their respected Secretary, Bartlett. But that was just as it was meant to be. No one was going to believe that either of them had the slightest thing in common. No one. At first their carefully nurtured antagonism was merely meant to serve as a cover for the crooked arrangements they made with the emirate; but later on, when Quinn discovered the truth about them, the arrangement was ideal for the removal of Quinn. You see what I mean?'

'Yes, I do,' said Lewis slowly. 'But why on earth did Bartlett, of all people, agree to—'

'I know what you mean. I'm sure that in the normal course of events he would never have been tempted in the slightest to line his own pockets at the expense of the Syndicate. But he had an only child, Richard; a young man who had started off life with quite brilliant promise; who carried the high hopes of a proud mum and a proud dad. And suddenly the whole world collapses round the Bartlett's ears. Richard's been working too hard, expectations are too high, and everything goes wrong. He has a nervous breakdown, and goes into hospital. And when he comes out it is clear to the Bartletts that they've got a terrible problem on their hands. He's sent to specialist after specialist, consultant after consultant – and always the same answer: with a prolonged period of treatment he *might* get well again. You discovered yourself, Lewis, that within the past five years Richard Bartlett has spent some time in the most advanced and expensive psychiatric clinics in Europe: Geneva, Vienna, London, and God knows where else. And this isn't for *free*, remember. It must have cost Bartlett thousands of pounds, and I don't think he'd got that sort of money. His salary's more than adequate, but— Well, Roope must have known all about this and, however it came about, the two of them struck a pact. Originally it had been Bland and Roope, I should think. But Bland decided to go for even richer pickings, and Roope had to have someone *inside* the Syndicate if the goose was still to lay the golden eggs. I don't know exactly how they worked it between them, but—'

'Do you know exactly how Bartlett murdered Quinn, sir?'

'Well, not exactly. But I've a pretty good idea, because it was the *only* way the deception could have been worked. Just think a minute. You get your dose, a pretty hefty dose, of cyanide. Roope sees to that side of things. Now, from an indecently large dose of cyanide death follows almost immediately, so there's little problem about actually *killing* Quinn. I should think that Bartlett called him into his office and suggested a drink together. He knew that Quinn was very fond of sherry and told him to pour himself one – and probably one for Bartlett at the same time. He must have wiped the sherry bottle and the glasses beforehand so that—'

'But wouldn't Quinn have smelled the cyanide?'

'He might have done, in normal circumstances; but Bartlett had timed his actions almost to the second. Everything that morning had been geared with devilish ingenuity to the next few minutes.'

'The fire drill you mean.'

'Yes. Noakes had been instructed to set off the alarm at twelve noon precisely and he'd been told to wait for the word from the boss. So? What happens? As soon as Quinn is pouring the sherries, Bartlett picks up the phone, probably turning his back on Quinn, and says "OK Noakes". And a second or two later the alarm goes. But this is the point, Lewis. *Quinn can't hear the alarm.* The bell is just inside the entrance hall, and although everybody else can hear it perfectly clearly, Quinn can't; and it gives Bartlett just the little leeway he needs. As soon as Quinn has poured the sherries, and only when the time is *exactly* ripe, does he say something like: "The fire alarm! I'd forgotten about that. Toss that back quickly; we can talk afterwards." Quinn must have drained at least half the small glass at a gulp, and almost immediately he must have known that something was desperately wrong. His respiration becomes jerky and he suffers from violently convulsive seizures. In a minute, or at the outside a couple of minutes, he's dead.'

'Why didn't he shout for help, though. Surely—?'

'Ah! I see you still don't appreciate the infinite subtlety of Bartlett's plan. What's happening outside? A fire drill! As you yourself found out, Noakes had been instructed to let the alarm ring for two minutes. Two minutes! That's a long, long time, Lewis, and during it everybody is chattering and clattering down the stairs and along the corridors. Perhaps Bartlett made quite sure that Quinn didn't shout for help; but even if he had managed to shout, I doubt if anyone would have heard him. And remember! *No one is going into Bartlett's office.* The red light has been turned on outside, and none of the staff is going to disobey the golden rule. And even if *everything* had gone wrong, Lewis, even if someone had come in – though I expect Bartlett had locked the door anyway – Quinn's prints are on the bottle and on the glasses, and police inquiries are going to centre on the fundamental question of who had poisoned Bartlett's sherry – presumably with the intention of poisoning *Bartlett*, not Quinn. Anyway, Quinn is dead and *the building is now completely deserted.* Bartlett puts on a pair of gloves, pours his own sherry and whatever is left of Quinn's down the sink in his private little cloakroom – remember it, Lewis? – and locks away the sherry bottle and Quinn's glass in a briefcase. So far so good. Quinn was a fairly slight man and Bartlett may have carried him over his shoulder, or put him into one of the large plastic containers they use there for rubbish, and then dragged him along the polished floor. Probably he carried him, since no scratches or abrasions were found on Quinn's body. But whatever he did, it was only a few yards to the rear entrance, and Quinn's parking place was immediately outside the door. Bartlett, who has already taken Quinn's car key and house key from his pocket – or from his anorak – dumps the body and the briefcase in the boot, locks it, and the deed is done.'

'We should have examined the boot, I suppose, sir.'

'But I did. There were no traces of Quinn at all. That's why I think Bartlett may have used a container of some sort.'

'Then he goes out to join the rest of the staff—'

Morse nodded. 'Standing meekly outside in the cold, yes. He takes over the list, which by this time has been handed round the thirty or so permanent staff, ticks in himself and Quinn as present, and finally decides that all are accounted for.'

'And it was Bartlett who rang the school in Bradford?'

'Certainly. Doubtless he'd been looking out for anything that could be used to help mislead the inevitable investigation, and he must have seen that particular letter in Quinn's tray in the registry earlier that week. If you remember, it was postmarked Monday, 17th November.'

'Then he went home and had a hearty lunch.'

'I doubt it,' said Morse. 'Bartlett's a very clever man, but basically he's not as ruthless as someone like Roope. Anyway, he's still got a lot on his mind. Certainly the trickier half of the plan is over, but he hasn't finished yet. He must have left home at about ten past one, telling his wife – perfectly correctly – that he had to call in at the office before going off to his meeting in Banbury. But before he did that—'

'He called in at Studio 2.'

'Yes. Bartlett bought a ticket, had it torn through, asked the usherette where the "Gents" was, waited there a few minutes, and then nipped out when the girl in the ticket office was busy with one or two more clients. But after that things began to go awry. Not that Bartlett saw Monica Height – I'm pretty sure of that. But she saw him, coming *out* of Studio 2. Monica and Donald Martin, remember want to spend the afternoon together. They can't go to her place, because her daughter's home from school; they can't go to his, because his wife's there all the time; they can go somewhere in the car, but that's hardly a romantic proposition on a rainy November afternoon. So they decide to go to the pictures. But they mustn't be seen going in together; so Martin gets there fairly early, soon after the doors open, and buys a ticket for the rear lounge and sits there waiting. Monica's due to come a few minutes later, and he's straining his eyes and watching *everybody* who comes in. Now get this clear in your mind, Lewis. If Quinn had gone into Studio 2 that afternoon, Martin would certainly have seen him. He'd have seen Bartlett, too. And if he'd seen either of them, *he wouldn't have stayed*. He'd have left immediately, waited discreetly outside for Monica, and told her the bad news. But he did no such thing! Now, put yourself in Monica's shoes. When we questioned her – and Martin – one thing became quite clear:

*they'd seen the film*; and they certainly wouldn't have done that if any other member of the Syndicate had come *in*. There was only one explanation: Monica had seen something that, in the light of what she learned later, troubled her sorely. Yet whatever it was, it had not prevented her from joining Martin inside the cinema, all right? We can only draw one conclusion: she saw someone coming *out*. And that someone was Bartlett! He goes back to the Syndicate and he's got a ticket. But where is he to leave it? He could leave it in Quinn's room, because he's got to go in there anyway to leave the note for Margaret Freeman, and to open the cabinets. Bit careless of Bartlett that, when you come to think of it ...' Morse shook his head as if a fly had alighted on his balding patch. But whatever was troubling him, he let it go. 'Just remember that all this had to be planned meticulously in advance, and from this point onwards things had to be arranged to meet Roope's convenience, not Bartlett's. Roope has dutifully fixed himself up with a water tight alibi until late afternoon, but now he needs some plausible reason for visiting the Syndicate. He couldn't know – nor could Bartlett – that not one of the graduate staff would be there; so it's arranged that he will leave some papers in Bartlett's office. You see, if anyone else is around, he hasn't got much excuse poking around in *Quinn's* office. He'll have to go there later, of course, to get the anorak; but by then he'll have been able to see the lie of the land and he can play things by ear. So they've decided between them that the cinema ticket and Quinn's keys are to be left somewhere carefully concealed on Bartlett's desk or in one of his drawers. Well? What happened then? Roope knocks on Bartlett's door, gets no answer, goes in quickly, leaves his papers, and picks up the ticket and the keys. Easy. Originally the plan must have been for him to hang around somewhere, probably by the trees at the back, until the rest of the graduate staff went home. Then he would only have to nip in the back entrance, pick up the anorak from Quinn's office, and drive off in Quinn's car. But in fact it was easier than he could have hoped. Noakes, it's true, was an unforeseen problem, but as things turned out this helped him enormously. Noakes was able to confirm that *none of the graduate staff was in his office that afternoon.* And when he told Roope that he was off upstairs for a cup of tea, the coast was clear – half an hour or so earlier than he'd expected it to be.'

'And from then onwards it must have gone very much as you said before.'

'Except for one thing. I suggested to Roope when we first brought him in that he'd pocketed the note from Quinn's desk; but I don't think he could have done. Otherwise I can think of no earthly reason why he had to phone Bartlett when he discovered the shattering information that Mrs Evans was going to return. It was the worst moment of the lot, I should think, and Roope almost panicked. The rain was sluicing down outside, and he couldn't just dump the body and run for it. Mrs Greenaway – he must have seen her – was sitting in full view in the room upstairs with the curtains open, and there was only one way for Quinn's body to be carted out, and that was by the front door of the garage. There was nothing to do but to wait; but he couldn't wait *there.* He must have been feeling desperate when he rang up Bartlett; but Bartlett came up with the masterstroke – the note on Quinn's desk! It was a wonderful piece of luck but, my God!, they needed some luck at that stage. Bartlett had only just got back from Banbury, but he drove off again almost immediately, called in at the Syndicate for the note, and met Roope as arranged at the shopping area behind Pinewood Close, where Roope had already bought the groceries. I suppose it must have taken Bartlett at least twenty minutes, but time was still on their side – just. Roope got back to Quinn's, took off his muddy boots, left the note – and went out again. He must have got wet through; but imagine his immense relief, as he watched and waited, first to see Mrs Evans come and go, and then, almost miraculously, an ambulance draw up and take Mrs Greenaway off to the maternity hospital. The house was in darkness then; no one was about; the street lamp was broken; the curtain could go up on the last act. He carries Quinn's body to the back door and into the house, puts it on the carpet by the chair in the living-room, arranges the sherry bottle and the glass on the coffee table, lights the fire – and Bob's your uncle. He walks over the back field again, and catches a bus down to Oxford.'

Lewis reflected. Yes, that's how it must have happened all right, but one thing still puzzled him mightily: 'What about Ogleby? Where does he fit in?'

'As I've told you, Lewis, a good deal of what Ogleby told us was true, and I think he was virtually certain that Bartlett had killed Quinn long before I ever—'

'Why did he keep it all to himself, though?'

'I dunno. I suppose he must have been trying to prove something to himself before—'

'It doesn't sound very convincing, sir.'

'No, perhaps not.' Morse stared out onto the yard and once again wondered why on earth Ogleby ... Mm. There were still one or two loose ends that wouldn't quite tie in. Nothing vital, though – and Lewis interrupted his thoughts.

'Ogleby must have been a clever fellow, sir.'

'Oh, I don't know. Remember he had a couple of leagues' start on me.'

'How do you mean, sir?'

'How many times do I have to tell you? *He was in the office that afternoon.*'

'Must have been upstairs, then, because—'

'No. That's where you're wrong. He must have been *downstairs*. And what's more we know exactly where he was and when he was there. He must have realized when he finally got back from lunch that he was the only one of the graduates in the office, and that this was as good a chance as he was going to get to poke around in Bartlett's room. Whether Quinn had told him that he suspected Bartlett *and* Roope, or just Bartlett – we can't know for certain. But he's got cause to suspect Bartlett, and he decides to do a bit of investigation. No one is going to come in, because no one's there. At about 4.30 he hears voices outside – Roope's and Noake's – and he doesn't want to get caught. Where's the obvious place for him to hide, Lewis? In the small cloakroom just behind Bartlett's desk, where I went the first afternoon we went to the office. Ideal! He just stands inside and waits; and he doesn't have to wait long. But what does Ogleby find when he emerges from the cloakroom? He discovers that the cinema ticket and the keys which he'd found earlier have gone! His thoughts must have been in a complete whirl, and he daren't leave Bartlett's office. He hears Noakes in the corridor outside, and later he hears someone walking about, and a few doors opening and slamming to. And still he has to stay where he is. Anyway, he finally satisfies himself that it's safe to come out, and the first thing he notices is that Quinn's car has gone! Perhaps he looks into Quinn's room, I don't know. Has Quinn come in? And gone out again? I don't know how much of the truth he suspected at that point – not much, perhaps; but he knows that Roope has taken some keys and a mysterious cinema ticket, a ticket which he has carefully copied into his diary. It's his one piece of real evidence, and he does what I did. He rang Studio 2, and tried to find out—'

'But he couldn't. So he went along himself.'

Morse nodded. 'And found nothing, poor blighter, except one thing: that in all probability the ticket he'd found must have been bought *that very afternoon.*'

'Funny, isn't it, sir? They were *all* there that afternoon.'

'All except Quinn,' corrected Morse sombrely. 'Have you got your car here?'

'Where are we going, sir?'

'I think we'd better follow in Ogleby's footsteps, and have a look around in Bartlett's office.'

As Lewis drove him for the last time to the Syndicate building, Morse allowed his mind to come to tentative grips with the one or two slight inconsistencies (very slight, he told himself) that still remained. People did odd things on occasions; you could hardly expect a smoothly logical motive behind *every* action, could you? The machine was in good working order now, there was no doubt of that, the cogs fitting neatly and biting powerfully. Just a bit of grit in the works somewhere. Only a little bit, though . . .

In Cell No 2, the little Secretary sat on the bare bed, his mind, like Yeats's long-legged fly, floating on silence.

WHO ?

# thirty-two

The Syndicate building had been locked up, and all the staff informed to stay away until further notice. Only Noakes was performing his wonted duties, and was on hand to let the two policemen in.

Seated at Bartlett's desk, Morse amused himself by switching the red and green lights on and off. He seemed like a little lad with a new toy, and it was clear to Lewis that as usual he would have to do the donkey-work himself.

It was over half an hour later, after Lewis had methodically gone through the safe (and found nothing of interest) that Morse, who had hitherto been staring vacantly round the room, finally condescended to bestir himself. The top right-hand drawer of Bartlett's desk had little to offer but neatly stacked piles of office notepaper, and Morse idly abstracted a sheet and surveyed the decimated graduate team:

T. G. Bartlett, PhD, MA  Secretary
P. Ogleby, MA Deputy Secretary
G. Bland, MA
Miss M. M. Height, MA
D. J. Martin, BA

Mm. The typists had been instructed to strike through Bland's name, and print in Quinn's at the bottom. But that wouldn't be necessary any longer. Just strike through the top three; much quicker ... And then there were two ... Would Miss Height be asked to take over? Advertise for new personnel? Or would the Syndicate just fold up? God knew that Donald Martin wasn't going to make much of a Deputy if it were to carry on. What a wet he was! And God help the young men they might appoint if Monica twitched her bewitching backside at 'em! Morse took out his Parker pen and slowly crossed through the names: Dr Bartlett; Philip Ogleby; George Bland. Yes, just the two of them left – and now they could fornicate for a few months to their hearts' content. A few months! Huh! That's all Quinn had been there; not even long enough to get his name printed on the notepaper. Nicholas Quinn ... Morse thought back for a few moments to the lip-reading class he'd attended. Would Quinn have been able to cope at the office if his hearing had failed him completely? No, perhaps not. Lip-reading might be a wonderful thing, but even the teacher of the class had made a mistake, hadn't she? When he'd asked her ...

Morse froze where he sat, and the blood seemed to surge away from his arms and from his shoulders, leaving the top of his body numbed and tingling. Oh God – no! No! Surely not! Oh Christ, oh Blessed Virgin Mary, oh all the Saints and all the Angels – no! His hand was shaking as he wrote out the two names on the notepaper, and he found it impossible to keep his voice steady.

'Lewis! Drop whatever you're doing. Go and stand over by the door and take this notepaper with you.'

A puzzled Lewis did as he was told. 'What now, sir?'

'I want you to read those two names to me – just using your lips. Don't whisper them. Just mouth them, if you know what I mean.'

Lewis did his best.

'Again,' said Morse, and Lewis complied.

'And again ... and again ... and again ... and again.' Morse nodded and nodded and nodded and nodded, and there was a vibrant excitement in his voice as he spoke again. 'Get your coat, Lewis. We've finished here.'

She would say nothing at all for a start, but Morse was merciless. 'Did *you* clean the blood off?' (He'd asked the question a dozen times already.) 'My God, you must be blind if you can't see what's been happening. How many other women has he had? Who was he with last night? Don't you know? Have you never suspected? Did *you* clean the blood off? Did you? Or did he? Don't you understand? – I've got to know. Did *you* clean it off? *I've got to know.*'

Suddenly she broke down completely and burst into bitter, hysterical tears. 'He said – there'd been – an accident. And he – he said he'd – tried – tried to help – until – the ambulance came. It was – it was in – in the Broad – just opposite – opposite Blackwells – and—'

The door opened and a man came in. 'What the *hell*?' His voice had the lash of a whip, and his eyes shone with a primitive, blazing madness. 'What's that fucking man Roope been telling you, you snooping bastard?' He advanced on Morse, and lashed out wildly, whilst Mrs Martin rushed from the room with a piercing scream.

'You should get yourself into better shape, Morse. You're pretty flabby, you know.'

'It's the beer,' mumbled Morse. 'Ouch!'

'That's the last one. See me in a week's time, and we'll take 'em out. You're all right.'

'Bloody good job I had Lewis with me! Otherwise you'd have had another corpse.'

'Good, was he?'

Morse smiled crookedly and nodded. 'Christ, you should have seen him, doc!'

In Morse's office the next morning it was Lewis's turn to grin. 'Must be a bit tricky talking, sir – with all those stitches round your mouth.'

'Mm.'

'Well? Tell me, then.'

'What do you want to know?'

'What finally put you on to Martin?'

'Well, it's what I said before, though I didn't really have a clue what I was talking about. I told you the key to this case lay in the fact that Quinn was deaf. And so it was. But I kept on thinking what a marvel he must have become at lip-reading, and I overlooked the most obvious thing of all: that even the best lip-reader in the world is sometimes going to make a few mistakes; and Quinn did just that. He saw Roope talking to the sheik, and *he read a name wrongly on his lips*. I learned from the lip-reading class that the commonest difficulty for the deaf is between the consonants "p", "b" and "m", and if you mouth the words "Bartlett" and "Martin", there's very little difference on the lips. The "B" and the "M" are absolutely identical, and the second part of each of the names gets swallowed up in the mouth somewhere. But that's not all. It was *Doctor* Bartlett, and *Donald* Martin. Just try them again. *Very* little difference to see; and if you put the two names together, there's every excuse for a deaf person mixing them up. You see, Roope would never have called the Secretary "Tom", would he? He'd never been on Christian name terms with him, and he never would be. He'd have called him "Bartlett" or "*Doctor* Bartlett". And the sheik would almost certainly have given him his full title. But Martin — well, he was one of them; one of the boys. He was *Donald* Martin.'

'Bit of a jump in the dark, if you ask me.'

'No, it wasn't. Not really. There were one or two loose ends that somehow refused to tuck themselves away, and I had an uneasy feeling that I might have got it all wrong. As you yourself said, it was so much out of character. Bartlett's spent so much of his life building up the work of the Syndicate that it's very difficult to see him stooping to the sort of corruption we've got in this case — let alone murder. But I still couldn't see in what other direction the facts were pointing. Not, that is, until I suddenly saw the light as we sat in Bartlett's office, and then all the loose ends seemed to tidy themselves up automatically. Just think. Quinn discovered — or so he believed — that Bartlett was crooked, and he rang him up. Rang him up, Lewis! You can guess how Quinn dreaded ringing *anyone* up. The fact of the matter was that he couldn't face Bartlett with it any other way, because *he just couldn't believe that he was guilty.*'

'Did Quinn tell Bartlett that he suspected Roope as well?'

'I should think so. Quinn must have been a man remarkably free from any deception, and he probably told both Bartlett and Roope everything he suspected.'

'But why didn't Bartlett do something about it?'

'He must have thought that Quinn had got everything cock-eyed, mustn't he? Quinn was accusing him — the Secretary! — of swindling the Syndicate; and if Quinn was totally wrong about himself, why should he think that Quinn was right about Roope?'

Lewis shook his head slowly. 'All a bit thin, if you ask me, sir.'

'In itself, yes. But let's turn to Monica Height. How on earth are we to account for the bundle of lies she was prepared to tell?

It's fairly easy now to see why Martin must have been happy to agree to the lies they cooked up together after Monica told him she'd seen Bartlett coming out of the cinema. In fact I should think that he almost certainly instigated them himself, because it was going to suit his book very well not to have himself associated with Studio 2 in any way. And later, after Monica learned that Quinn himself might have been in Studio 2 that same afternoon she immediately realized that things would look pretty black for Bartlett if she said anything about seeing him there. And so she continued to conceal the truth. Why, Lewis? For the very same reason that Quinn couldn't face Bartlett: *because she just couldn't believe that he was guilty.*'

Lewis nodded. Perhaps it was all adding up slightly better now.

'And above all,' continued Morse, 'there was Ogleby. He worried me the most, Lewis, and you made the key point yourself: why didn't he tell me what he knew? I think there are two possible reasons. First, that Ogleby was quite prepared to go it alone – he was always a loner, it seems. He knew he hadn't long to live anyway, and it may have added that extra bit of mustard to his life to carry out a single-handed investigation into the quite extraordinary situation he'd stumbled across. It couldn't have mattered much to him that he might be living dangerously – he was living dangerously in any case. But that's as may be. I feel sure there was a second reason, and a much more compelling one. He'd discovered what looked like extremely damning evidence against Bartlett – a man he'd known and worked with for fourteen years – *and he just couldn't believe that he was guilty.* And he was determined to say nothing which could lead us to suspect him – not until he could prove it, anyway.'

'But he didn't get the chance—'

'No,' said Morse quietly. He leaned back in his chair and gently rubbed his swollen lip. 'Anything else while we're at it, my son?'

Lewis thought back over the whole complex case and realized that he hadn't quite got it straight in his mind, even now. 'It was Martin, then, who did all of the things you accused Bartlett of?'

'Indeed it was. And *more.* Martin killed Quinn at exactly

the same time and in almost exactly the same way. The deed was done in Martin's office, and Martin had exactly the same opportunity as Bartlett would have had. Admittedly, he was taking a slightly bigger risk, but he'd planned the whole thing – at least up to this point – with meticulous care. You see, the main plot must have been hatched up immediately after Bartlett had announced the fire drill for Friday. But the Syndicate staff only received that notice on the Monday, and there wasn't *all* that much time; and in the event they had to improvise a bit as the situation developed. On the whole I suppose they made the best of the opportunities that arose, but they tried to be a bit too clever – especially about the Studio 2 business, which landed them both in a hell of a lot of unnecessary trouble.'

'Don't get cross with me, sir, but can you just go over that again. I still—'

'I don't think Studio 2 figured in the original plan at all – though I may be wrong, of course. The original idea must have been to try to persuade any caller at Quinn's office that he was there or thereabouts during that Friday afternoon. It was all a bit clumsy, but just about passable – the note to his typist, the anorak, the filing cabinet, and so on. Now, I'd guess that Martin's nerves must have been pretty near breaking-point after he'd killed Quinn, and he must have breathed a huge sigh of relief when he managed to persuade Monica to spend the afternoon with him: the fewer people in the office that afternoon the better, and being with Monica gave him a reasonable alibi if things didn't go according to plan. As I say, I don't think that at this stage there was the remotest intention of planting the torn half of a cinema ticket on Quinn's body. But remember what happened. Martin and Monica decided to lie about going to the cinema; and Martin himself gradually began to take stock of the situation. He must have realized that the elaborate attempt to convince everyone that Quinn was alive and well at the Syndicate was pretty futile. No one's there to be convinced. Bartlett's not there – he knows that; he himself and Monica are not there, either; Quinn is dead; and Ogleby is out lunching with the OUP people and may not go back to the office at all. So. He gets his brainwave: he'll get Roope to put the cinema ticket in one of Quinn's pockets.'

'But when—?'

'Just a minute. After leaving the cinema – by the way, Martin lied to me there, and I ought to have noticed it earlier. He tried to stretch his alibi by saying he left at a quarter to four; but as we know from Monica they both left just before the film was due to end – at about a quarter past three. Obviously they'd want to get out before the general exodus – less risk of being seen. Anyway, after leaving the cinema, they went their separate ways : Monica went home; and so did Martin, except that on his way he called in at the Syndicate, at about 3.20, found no one about – not even Ogleby – and left his own cinema ticket in Bartlett's room for Roope to pick up.'

'But Roope wouldn't have known—?'

'Give me a chance, Lewis. Martin must have written a very brief note – "Stick this in his pocket", or something like that – and put it with the ticket and the keys. Then, about ten minutes later, Ogleby got back, found everyone else out, and decided that this was as good an opportunity as he'd get of poking around in Bartlett's room; and he was so puzzled by what he found there that he copied out the cinema ticket into his diary.'

'And then Martin went home, I suppose.'

Morse nodded. 'And made sure, I should think, that somebody saw him, especially during the vital period between 4.30 and five o'clock, when he knew that Roope was performing *his* part in the crime. He must have thought he could relax a bit; but then Roope rang him up from Quinn's house at just after five o'clock with the shattering news that Quinn's charlady— Well, you know the rest.'

Lewis let it all sink in, and he finally seemed to see the whole pattern clearly. Almost the whole pattern. 'What about the paperboy? Did Roope send him with a letter to Bartlett just—'

'– just to make things difficult for Bartlett, yes. Roope must have said he wanted to have an urgent talk with him about police suspicions – or something like that. Roope knew, of course, that we were watching him like a hawk, and so he walked slowly down to the railway station and let us follow him.'

'You haven't talked to Bartlett about that?'

'Not yet. After we'd let him go, I thought we ought to give

him a bit of a breather, poor fellow. He's had a rough time.'

Lewis hesitated. 'There *is* just one more thing, sir.'

'Yes?'

'Bartlett will have *something* to explain away, won't he? I mean he *did* go to Studio 2.'

Morse smiled as widely as his swollen mouth would allow him. 'I reckon I can answer that one for you. Bartlett's as human as the rest of us, and perhaps it's a long time since he's seen the likes of Inga Nielsson unbuttoning her blouse. The film started at 1.30, and since he didn't need to leave for Banbury until about 2.30, he decided to be a dirty old man for an hour or so. But don't blame him, Lewis! Do you hear me? Don't blame him. He must have gone in immediately the doors opened, sat there in the rear lounge, and then, as his eyes accustomed themselves to the darkness, *he saw Martin come in.* But Martin didn't see *him*; and Bartlett did what anyone in his position would do – he got out, quick.'

'And that's when Monica saw him?'

'That's it.'

'So he didn't see the film after all?'

Morse shook his head sadly. 'And if you've got any more questions, leave 'em till tomorrow. I've got a treat for you tonight.'

'But I promised the wife—'

Morse pushed the phone over. 'Tell her you'll be a bit late.'

They sat side by side in a fairly crowded gathering, with only the green 'Exit' lights shining up brightly in the gloom. Morse had bought the tickets himself – rear lounge: after all, it was something of a celebration.

'Christ, look at those!' whispered Morse, as the camera moved in on the buxom blonde beauty, her breasts almost toppling out over the low-cut closely-clinging gown.

'Take it off!' shouted a voice from somewhere near the front, and the predominantly male audience sniggered sympathetically, whilst Morse settled himself comfortably in his seat and prepared to gratify his baser instincts. And with only token reluctance, Lewis prepared to do the same.

# epilogue

The Syndicate was forced to close down as soon as the autumn examination results had been issued, and its oversea centres were parcelled out amongst the other GCE Boards. The building itself has been taken over by a department of HM Inspectorate of Taxes, and today female clerks clack up and down its polished corridors, and talk of girlish things in the rooms where once the little Secretary and his graduate staff administered their examinations.

From her considerable private income, Mrs Bartlett bought a farm in Hampshire, where Richard at last found a life which served to soothe his troubled mind, and where his father's eyes were occasionally seen to blink almost boyishly again behind the rimless spectacles.

Until Sally had completed her undistinguished school career, Miss Height stayed in Oxford, taking on some part-time teaching. Several times in the months that followed the conviction of the Syndicate murderers, she had found her way to the Horse and Trumpet – just for old time's sake, she told herself. How dearly she would have loved to see him again! She owed him a drink, anyway, and she wanted to square the account; to make up for things, as it were. But much as she had willed it, she had never found him there.

More than sufficient evidence was found to justify the immediate disqualification of Master Muhammad Dubal from all his autumn O-level examination; and six weeks later his father, the sheik, was listed among the 'missing' after a 'bloodless' coup within the emirate.

George Bland, though reported to have been seen in various eastern capitals, remains unpunished still; yet perhaps no criminal can live without some little share of justice.

No 1 Pinewood Close is tenanted again, both upstairs and down; and Mrs Jardine is thinking of buying herself a new outfit. As she'd expected, it had been no more than a few weeks before the notoriety had died down. Life was like that, as she had known.

Just after Christmas, at a christening in East Oxford, the minister dipped a delicate finger into the font, and in the name of the Holy Trinity enlisted his little charge in the myriad ranks of the great Church Militant. But the water was icy cold and Master Nicholas John Greenaway squawked stentoriously. In the end, the name had been Frank's choice: it had sort of grown on him, he said. But as Joyce took the baby in her arms and lovingly there-thered his raucous cries, her mind ranged back to the day when Nicholas, her son, was born, and when another man called Nicholas had died.

Colin Dexter
**The Dead of Jericho** £3.99

The shapely divorcee no better than she ought to be — hanged by
the neck; the seedy odd-job man murdered amongst his home library
of porn: both of them neighbours in the mean streets of Oxford's
Jericho, closer to the murky canal than the dreaming spires.
Inspector Morse might have taken a more coolly professional interest
if he'd not been on the point of accepting a lady's very open
invitation only minutes after the murder investigations began ... By
the acclaimed new master of the crime novel.